Fully
INVOLVED

Acclaim for *Sequestered Hearts*

"*Sequestered Hearts* tells of two very private women dealing with the magnetic attraction between them. It is the story of the difficult dance between them, and how each is able to resolve her individual issues and find happiness. Cori and Bennett are likeable, well developed characters and their story will keep the reader turning the pages to see how it all works out." – *Just About Write*

"*Sequestered Hearts* is packed with raw emotion, but filled with tender moments too. The author writes with sophistication that one would expect from a veteran author. She builds anticipation and demonstrates Ben's and Cori's obvious attraction at the beginning of the novel, but we also see the antagonism and frustration these two characters experience with each other. Ben leaves Cori after she gets the interview with every intention of walking away from this enigmatic woman, and that is what Cori wants, too, or so we are led to believe....A romance is about more than just plot and character development. It's about passion, physical intimacy, and connection between the characters. The reader should have a visceral reaction to what is going on within the pages for the novel to succeed. Dutton's words match perfectly with the emotion she has created. Every encounter oozes with Ben's and Cori's hunger for each other. *Sequestered Hearts* is one book that cannot be overlooked. It is romance at its finest." – *L-word Literature.com*

By the Author

Sequestered Hearts

Fully INVOLVED

by

Erin Dutton

2007

FULLY INVOLVED

ISBN 10: 1-933110-99-6
ISBN 13: 978-1-933110-99-8

This Trade Paperback Original Is Published By
Bold Strokes Books, Inc.,
New York, USA

First Edition: December 2007

Credits
Editors: Shelley Thrasher and Stacia Seaman
Production Design: Stacia Seaman
Cover Design By Sheri (GRAPHICARTIST2020@HOTMAIL.COM)

Acknowledgments

I first saw the cover for this book nearly a year ago, while I was still writing the first draft. It was breathtaking and it captured all of the emotions I hoped to bring to the story as well. Sheri, it's perfect. And I am honored to have it embracing these pages.

Special thanks to Radclyffe and Senior Editor Jennifer Knight for continuing to believe in my stories and allowing me to work with people who make both them and me better.

To my editors—Shelley Thrasher for your patient guidance and well-placed questions, and Stacia Seaman for seeing all the details.

Prologue

The late-summer sun fought through the leaves and dappled Reid Webb's bare legs. The fringed hem of her threadbare cut-offs tickled her thigh. She and her friend Jimmy Grant had been climbing trees all afternoon and her muscles were pleasantly sore, her body's way of reminding her that she'd pushed them nearly to the limit. They'd chosen the tallest tree in Jimmy's grandparents' backyard as their final conquest.

Midway up the oak, Reid had found the perfect limb and lay down, tucked into a crook that cradled her body. The press of rough bark against her back made her feel secure despite the fifteen feet that separated her from the ground. She folded her arms behind her head and closed her eyes, reveling in the laziness of the ideal day, which was probably one of the last before they started junior high.

"I wish we never had to go back to school," Jimmy said from his own perch two limbs above hers.

Reid smiled in agreement. Jimmy lay on his stomach, his arms and legs dangling. His royal blue nylon shorts set off his deeply tanned bare torso. They had spent the entire summer outdoors, and Reid both admired and envied his full tan. With his dark shaggy hair and indolent pose, he reminded Reid of a big cat, escaping the sun in the largest tree on the savannah.

Jimmy's grandparents had invited Reid, Jimmy, and Jimmy's little sister, Isabel, to spend the final week of their summer vacation at their home in Florida. They had arrived five days ago and stopped inside the house only long enough to drop their backpacks before dashing into the backyard. They'd spent most of the week outside playing ball, swimming, and climbing trees, despite the heat.

By the last day of their visit, Jimmy said he was tired of Isabel trailing them. She was two years younger and not as strong as they were. He complained that he'd spent most of his week helping her up trees or baiting her hook when they went fishing. That afternoon he'd talked Reid into sneaking off into the sprawling backyard.

Jimmy's parents would arrive later that evening, and the next morning they would all begin the drive back to Nashville. School resumed the following Monday, but Jimmy started junior varsity football practice the day after they got home, so Reid wouldn't see as much of him then.

"Do you think you'll get to play receiver this year?"

Jimmy shrugged. "I hope so. All their good wideouts from last year moved up to varsity."

"Jimmy, I wanna come up." Isabel's plaintive voice interrupted them.

Jimmy swore under his breath.

Reid rolled her head to the side to see Isabel standing at the base of the tree. Strands of red hair fell from what had been a neat ponytail earlier that morning. Dirt streaked her khaki shorts, and she had a purple Popsicle stain on her white tank top.

"Let's just help her up," Reid suggested. She didn't mind Isabel hanging around and was used to being a go-between for the siblings. When Jimmy tried to avoid Isabel, they sometimes spent more time ducking her than actually having fun.

"She's always following me. Why can't she get her own friends?" Jimmy swung off his branch and climbed down.

"I couldn't find you," Isabel said as he dropped to the ground beside her.

"Good," Jimmy snapped.

Reid scrambled down as he began to walk away. "Where are you going, Jimmy?"

"Back to the house."

"I want to climb the tree," Isabel said.

"We're all done climbing, Iz. You'll have to go up by yourself." Jimmy turned to Reid with an expectant look. "Are you coming?"

Reid glanced uncertainly at Isabel. She didn't think Jimmy's grandparents would want Isabel left down here alone. And she knew Isabel couldn't make it into the tree on her own. But Isabel was Jimmy's sister and it was really his job to look after her, wasn't it? Jimmy didn't wait for her to sort it out before he turned his back.

Still torn, Reid glanced at Isabel, who was already trying to climb the tree by herself. Isabel attempted to get a good foothold on a knob on the trunk a couple of times, but her foot kept slipping off. Deciding Isabel was safe since she couldn't get off the ground anyway, Reid followed Jimmy.

"Wait up."

When she finally caught up with him, they were almost back to the house and could see Jimmy's grandmother on the back porch in a rocking chair. Jimmy stuck his arm out to stop Reid.

"She'll ask us where Isabel is. Let's circle around so she can't see us." He walked quietly toward the edge of the yard where they would be hidden by a stand of trees.

"Maybe we shouldn't have left her there alone."

"She'll be fine," he said brusquely.

Reid grabbed his arm before he could turn away. "What if she gets up in the tree and can't get down?"

Jimmy stared at her for a moment, rebellion shining in his eyes. He shoved his thick bangs off his forehead and jerked his arm away. "Fine. We'll go back."

Reid could barely keep up with his long strides as he retraced their steps. As they approached, Reid scanned the height of the tree for Isabel but didn't see her.

"She's not—" Reid began, but she saw Isabel's still body lying beneath the tree and the words seemed trapped in her throat. She yelled, "Jimmy!"

He had already begun to run toward her. Reid sprinted across the grass and reached the base of the tree just seconds after Jimmy knelt beside Isabel. She lay on her side, and her left arm was twisted awkwardly beneath her.

"Iz." Jimmy gently shook her shoulder, then pushed it harder when he got no response. "Wake up, Iz." His voice shook.

Tears filled Reid's eyes and her stomach lurched violently.

"Go get Grandpa," Jimmy yelled over his shoulder. Reid stood frozen. "Reid, go!"

She stumbled backward, then ran toward the house as fast as her shaking legs would carry her. Panic screamed in her head like a fire alarm, and she felt like she was moving in slow motion, but she pumped her legs as hard as she could.

CHAPTER ONE

Sirens screamed as Nashville Fire Department's Engine 9 flew down Broadway en route to a hotel fire at the Hilton. From the backseat, Reid watched the engine's flashing red lights reflect in the windows of the downtown storefronts as they passed. The excitement of a big fire never failed to make Reid's heart pump. At just after four o'clock that October morning, too early for commuters, the streets were nearly deserted. Reid was glad, because they didn't have to compete with traffic for the right-of-way. Drivers sometimes panicked when they heard sirens and often didn't know how to get out of the way in heavy traffic.

The air brakes whined in protest as the large vehicle stopped abruptly in front of the hotel, and Captain Jimmy Grant barked into the radio, "Engine 9, we're first on scene of a multistory hotel. We've got heavy smoke and flames showing on the A side. We'll be pulling a line and passing command."

Jimmy gave the initial on-scene report, indicating to the dispatcher that smoke and flames were visible at the front of the building and that they would begin to assemble hose. He left the responsibility of being incident commander to the captain of the next crew to arrive, as his crew would be busy assessing the scene.

Reid, along with Jimmy and the two other members of their

crew, jumped out and went to work, relieved that they functioned as a team. Everyone knew their role so well that they didn't have to say much to each other.

She knew exactly what engineer Joey Moss would be doing when he moved to the panel located on the side of the engine. He would engage the pumps as soon as his crew mates established a water supply.

Reid grabbed the crosslay hoses from the bin under the pump panel. They would use those lines to attack the fire. Jimmy jumped on the back step and grabbed one end of the five-inch supply hose. The yellow hose was folded back and forth on top of itself in the bed of the engine so it wouldn't tangle when Jimmy pulled it out. He handed the brass coupling to the fourth and newest member of their crew, Nathan Brewer, who then hooked it to the fire hydrant directly in front of the hotel.

A crowd had already gathered in the horseshoe drive at the front of the hotel, and a flood of people continued to spill out of the building, pushing each other in their haste to get to safety. It wasn't uncommon for people to watch the action at a fire, even those unaffected by it. Reid noticed them only long enough to ensure that the police officers were able to keep the crowd back a safe distance, then returned her attention to the scene.

She craned her head back to stare up at the building and noticed with dread how the smoke billowed thick and black from the tips of flames that licked out of several windows on the right side. She estimated the fire was concentrated on the third and fourth floors, but it was spreading quickly. They would need the trucks with aerial hoses as soon as possible.

"There's not much time," Jimmy said from beside her, echoing her assessment. "If we don't get some serious water on it soon we'll lose the whole place."

He stopped a passing police officer. "Officer, don't let anyone back inside for any reason. It's going to be hard enough to account for all of the guests."

She nodded and moved toward the crowd, calling out to another officer along the way.

The dispatcher's voice came over the radio mic clipped to Jimmy's collar. "Dispatch to Engine 9."

"Go ahead."

"Be advised we're getting reports of people trapped inside."

"Copy."

Reid surged forward, thinking only about getting to the victims, but Jimmy grabbed the thick sleeve of her turnout coat and jerked her to a stop.

"We've got to go in there," she yelled.

"We'll go in as soon as the next crew gets here."

Reid wanted to argue; she'd always been more impulsive than Jimmy. But that was what made him a good leader—he remained calm in every situation. She knew he was right. Ideally, there should be a team outside for every team inside so the first responders wouldn't become victims themselves.

The police officer approached them. "Captain, there's a lady over there saying she can't find her kid."

She gestured over her shoulder where another officer was struggling to keep a hysterical-looking woman from dashing inside the burning building. The crying woman was probably begging the officer to let her go. He looked very uncomfortable with his arms wrapped forcibly around her.

Jimmy and Reid crossed to the woman in long, quick strides, and Jimmy grabbed her arm. "Ma'am, where was your child when the fire started?"

"She was in the room. We were out of towels and I couldn't get any answer at the front desk. I was down in the lobby when the fire alarm started going off. I was only gone for a few minutes," she stuttered between sobs.

Jimmy held her firmly and spoke in a clear, distinct voice. "What room were you staying in?"

"Four-fifteen."

"What's her name?"

"Sarah. She's eleven."

As Reid and Jimmy headed back to the engine, Reid felt a surge of excitement. "Now we go in?"

"Now we go in," he confirmed. "Nathan, you're with us. Joey, when the next crew gets here, charge that line and have them stand by."

The next responders on scene would man the hose Reid's team had already laid out, and Joey would operate the pumps for them.

While Jimmy radioed the update to the dispatcher and the responding district chief, Reid pulled her lightweight SCBA mask over her face and replaced her helmet. Nathan grabbed a couple of radios from the engine, and Reid shoved one in the breast pocket of her flame-resistant turnout coat. Finally, Jimmy grabbed a Halligan tool and strode toward the front door. Firefighters routinely used the three-foot metal bar with a claw at one end and an adze and pick at the other for prying doors, breaking locks, and punching through walls. Reid followed without hesitation, just as she had been doing since they were five years old.

They were halfway up the stairs when over the radio Reid heard their chief arrive and tell dispatch he would be the incident commander. The dispatcher acknowledged his transmission and informed him a crew was already inside. As IC, the chief would now coordinate all decisions regarding the incident.

As they reached the landing on the fourth floor, Reid heard the chief say, "Command to Engine 9, give me a status report."

Jimmy reached for his radio mic. "Chief, we're just getting to the fourth floor now." As he pushed open the door, Reid saw smoke immediately flood the stairwell and heard Jimmy say, "We should be at the room in a second."

They hurried carefully down the hallway. The radio continued to chatter as other companies arrived and got assignments from Command. The air thickened with smoke that hung around them like a curtain so heavy that the beams of their flashlights barely cut through it. Reid stayed within touching distance of Jimmy, her training keeping her calm despite the constrictive atmosphere.

When they reached room 415, Jimmy pressed a hand to the door before he forced it open. Reid filed in behind him and followed as they moved immediately to the right, methodically searching the room.

Suddenly, in the midst of the other routine transmissions, their chief's voice dominated. "Command to all units. We're going to a defensive operation. Anyone still inside the building, evacuate at this time. We'll be in a defensive operation."

Jimmy turned toward the door, and Reid knew she should follow him, but she grabbed his sleeve. "One more minute," she shouted, her muffled voice echoing back at her. For some odd reason the image of the eleven-year-old Isabel lying prone at the bottom of an oak tree blazed through her mind.

"We've got to go."

Jimmy's order wrenched her back from her memories and forced her to focus on their situation. "Jimmy, we just got in here. Can't we at least do a quick search?"

After a momentary pause he nodded and signaled Nathan to check the closet and Reid to check the bathroom while he hurried to the center of the room to look under the bed. They called out Sarah's name, but Reid wondered if she would hear them.

Reid touched the bathroom door and found no significant heat difference. But when she grabbed the door knob it wouldn't open. *Damn it.* She pushed harder, but it still didn't budge. Needing the Halligan, she glanced around for Jimmy, but he was still crouching to peer under the bed.

Frustrated, she slammed her shoulder against the door, which gave way with a satisfying crack. She instinctively jerked the shower curtain back and found the young red-haired girl huddled in the bathtub, unconscious. Relieved to find her and charged with adrenaline, she scooped the limp child up as if she were a doll and rushed back into the bedroom, where she carefully handed the girl to Nathan.

"Engine 9 to Command. We've got her and are on our way out."

Jimmy led them back into the hallway and pushed open the exit door at the end of the hallway. Right behind him, Reid was horrified to see black smoke billow up the inside of the stairwell and feel a wall of heat assault her even through her gear. Their nearest escape route was blocked.

"We'll have to try the west stairs," Jimmy shouted.

Nodding, Nathan started for the other end of the building with Reid close behind him and Jimmy at the rear. They had covered only about twenty feet when an explosion boomed from somewhere below them. Before Reid could react, a cracking sound tore through the building and the entire east end of the hallway collapsed, including the floor directly beneath Jimmy.

Reid instinctively leapt toward him, grabbed, and managed to catch a fistful of his collar just as he disappeared through the floor. She was pulled with him, falling prone. Her chest slammed against the edge of the now-gaping rift in the floor, and blinding pain shot through her ribs as Jimmy's body weight jerked his coat from her fingertips.

"Jimmy!" she screamed as he disappeared into the rubble below them. Reid felt a part of herself disappear with Jimmy, who was swallowed by the smoke- and dust-filled dark maw.

Nathan scrambled to her side, but he was too late.

"Command to Engine 9, what's your status?" the chief barked through the radio.

Frantic, Reid jumped to her feet and shouted into her radio. "Engine 9 to Command, man down. We've got a man down. He's on the third floor, B side."

"Engine 9, evacuate immediately. There's been an explosion and we have heavy fire on the first three floors."

Reid shook her head, though she knew the chief couldn't see her. "Chief, it's Jimmy. I'm going after him," she yelled. Her injured ribs protested with every panting breath. *Control your breathing. You'll need every minute of that air to get him out of here. I'm coming, Jimmy. Hold on, I'm coming to get you.*

She was running, headed toward the other end of the hallway, before the chief responded. "Negative. Engine 9, evacuate immediately."

She reached the door to the stairwell and rushed through it without checking to see if Nathan was with her. She *had* to get to Jimmy. To *save* him.

"I repeat, negative, Engine 9. Evacuate."

After she flew down the stairs and barely missed taking a header several times, Nathan caught up with her. He grabbed her arm and pulled her to a stop.

The chief's voice demanded, "Command to Engine 9, acknowledge."

"Take her out, Nathan. I'm going after Jimmy," Reid ordered as she gestured to the girl in his arms.

"I'm not leaving you here."

"Go!"

"Command to Engine 9. Webb, I said get out of there. Now!"

Nathan wouldn't let go of her arm. "Come on, they'll send in a team for him."

Something in his voice penetrated Reid's consciousness in spite of the adrenaline pumping through her veins. Nathan would never leave her in here alone. It went against everything they'd been taught, and they had to get the girl out. Reid could see the gentle rise and fall of her shallow breathing, but she was still unconscious. She looked utterly helpless and obviously needed medical attention as soon as possible. Torn between her concern for Jimmy and the ingrained need to rescue, she headed for the exit.

❖

As Reid stumbled through the door, two firefighters took her arms and pulled her away from the building. "Change my tank. I'm going back in," she gasped after she yanked off her helmet and mask. She waved off the paramedics who rushed to her side. "I'm fine," she insisted, despite the stabbing pain in her chest. "Change my tank."

"You're not going back," Chief Perez said. "I'm sending a fresh team, but we've got to get this fire knocked down some first."

"No! Jimmy's still in there. I need to go back in now." Reid shrugged out of her pack. "I'll change it myself."

"Reid!"

"Somebody give me a damn tank," she shouted. Blind with panic, she fumbled with the empty cylinder.

Perez grabbed the front of her jacket, demanding her attention. "Reid, he's one of my men. I'm doing everything I can."

Reid stared at him through eyes blurry with tears and relented when she saw the fear that lanced through her reflected in his eyes. They would find him. They would find him and he would be okay. Reid wouldn't allow herself to consider any other possibility.

Perez nodded. "I'm sending Banks's crew in. Tell him exactly where you were when you last saw Jimmy."

The minutes it took to reenter and locate Jimmy were the longest of Reid's life. In an effort to keep from picturing the scene inside, she tried to concentrate on the fact that Nathan had emerged from the burning building right behind her and handed off the child to the waiting paramedics. At least they'd saved her. Then she stared at the lines of charged hose that snaked across the asphalt and supplied water to crews on the ground. Streams from the aerial ladders attacked the fire from above.

When Jimmy was carried unconscious from the building, she fought to keep her knees from buckling. His body hung like an empty hammock between the four firefighters who held his arms and legs. Just outside the door he was placed on a waiting stretcher and rushed toward an ambulance.

"Thank God," Joey breathed from beside her. Joey had been a member of the crew when she had been assigned to Engine Company 9. He had been with the department for twenty-five years and had been a mentor, almost a father to Reid in her early years on the job.

The deep rumble of his voice comforted Reid.

"He had to be out of air," Nathan murmured.

"Shut up," Reid rasped. Lightning bolts of pain shot through her ribs whenever she drew more than a shallow breath.

"Ours were on empty when we came out. He's been in there too long," he said defensively.

"Nathan, shut up," Joey barked and drew himself up to his full height. At six-foot-four with broad shoulders and huge arms, he cut an imposing figure. The slight recession of his hairline and a softening around his middle were the only signs of aging.

Joey's dark glare silenced any further comment, and Reid watched numbly as the stretcher was loaded in the rig. She tried desperately to glimpse Jimmy's face, but the paramedics who were working feverishly on him obscured her view. She took several steps forward and nearly tripped over her own discarded air pack as the doors closed and they pulled away, siren wailing.

Dazed, she barely heard Chief Perez call out to the officer whom Jimmy had asked earlier to keep the crowd back.

"Yeah, Chief."

"Everything I've got is pretty much blocked in right now," he said. "Can you take three of my crew members to the hospital?"

"Sure."

Reid noticed the compassion in the officer's eyes as she said, "Come on," and led them toward her patrol car. But Reid didn't want compassion; she wanted to know that the dread forming an aching ball in her stomach didn't mean that she had lost Jimmy.

Juggling bags of food from the deli down the street and the mail she'd picked up downstairs, Isabel Grant pushed open the door to her one-bedroom apartment. She dropped everything on the kitchen counter.

I need a vacation, maybe just a weekend trip over to Gatlinburg to watch the leaves change. She'd forgotten how long it had been since she'd had even a day completely to herself. She had moved to Knoxville ten years before with big plans to spend weekends in the nearby Smoky Mountains, but had been too busy, first with college and then with work. Starting her own business had been harder than she'd anticipated. *Luckily I don't have a life outside of work.* Aside from the occasional visit back home, nothing disrupted the routine she'd developed in the past few years.

She paused by the couch, kicked off her spike heels, and slid her feet into her fleece-lined pink slippers. *Ah, the perks of working from home.* She freed her shoulder-length red hair from the twist she had fashioned that morning and shook it loose.

With a deep sigh she headed for the bedroom, feeling like she'd been working nonstop for weeks. She would love nothing more than to take a hot bath and slip into some sweats. Instead, she stayed in her black pencil skirt, tailored lavender cotton blouse, and pantyhose, hoping the less comfortable clothing would keep her in a work mindset. She did, however, allow herself to remove her black Kenneth Cole blazer, which she draped over the back of the desk chair.

The bedroom doubled as her office. Pressed for space, she'd squeezed her large glass-topped desk into one corner and her small double bed into the other. At least the large walk-in closet eliminated the need for a bureau of any kind. A small bookcase filled with an assortment of suspense novels and old college textbooks occupied the remaining wall space opposite the room's only window.

She had been planning for over a year to look for a bigger place. After all, she could afford it now that she was finally confident she would stay in the black. It had taken her some time to quit worrying that her new job as an independent investment counselor would fall apart on her. Truthfully, she didn't mind her small apartment. It was cozy, and she really didn't need any more space.

Isabel pulled a file from the stack that threatened to topple off the corner of the desk and flipped through the paperwork while she checked her e-mail. After she finished deleting all the junk messages, she was left with only a few. The most important was from her closest friend and colleague, Anna Hill, who wanted to remind her that her twelve-year-old twins were starring in their school play that weekend and she'd promised to attend. Isabel and Anna had met in college. When Isabel's parents passed away, she had leaned on Anna, and Anna had relied on her friendship when her marriage fell apart.

The vibration of the BlackBerry tucked against her hip demanded her attention.

"Isabel Grant," she said after she touched the Bluetooth earpiece to answer the call. She grimaced when she heard the familiar voice. Alan Warner called her at least once a week, concerned about this investment or that. He constantly wanted to sink large chunks of his money into the latest fad. More than once Isabel had saved him from losing a bundle, only to have him call her a week later about another get-rich-quick scam.

While Warner was in mid-ramble, her home phone rang from the kitchen. Her brother Jimmy was the only person who ever called her on that line, and when she had talked to him the day before, he mentioned he was working today. Realizing she couldn't possibly get off her cell right then, she resigned herself to letting her machine get it.

"I don't care what kind of advice you're getting from other people," she interrupted Warner, finally losing patience. "Don't worry about your money. That's what you pay me to do." She paced the length of the small room and gestured sharply into the air as she spoke.

Three quick strides took her back to her desk, where she shot a quick reply to Anna that she would indeed attend the girls' play. She didn't miss a beat in the conversation, though she almost wished she had.

Having listened to Warner rant for as long as she could stand, she interrupted again. "I'm your financial planner, Alan. Now, you need to decide who you're going to trust to advise you, *me* or your *gardener.*" She confidently twirled a pen between her first two fingers and thumb and waited for the expected response. "Good. Relax. I'll check out those stock options and give you a call back."

She hung up before he could argue. Making a mental to-do list for the afternoon, she returned to the kitchen to check her phone message. A voice she didn't recognize commanded her full attention when he announced himself as the chaplain with the Nashville Fire Department. By the end of his message her hands were shaking and her legs barely kept her upright.

The next fifteen minutes passed in a blur as she ran through the apartment flinging far too many clothes into a suitcase. She grabbed her keys and her cell phone on her way out the door, frantic to begin the three-hour drive to Nashville.

Chapter Two

"We have to leave in thirty minutes, dear."

Reid didn't respond as her mother called her through the closed bedroom door. She couldn't move from the edge of her bed, where she sat rigidly. A fine sheen of sweat coated her face, and behind her closed eyelids nightmarish images played on a loop—continuous and unrelenting. She forced her eyes open as the reel began again. Numbly, she stood and crossed the room to the closet.

She dressed in her Class A uniform, somewhat comforted by putting on the midnight blue wool-blend pants and starched white dress shirt. She added the four-button jacket with a silver band of braid three inches from each cuff. To calm her nerves she adjusted the already straight tie and checked her reflection in the mirror.

As she grasped the doorknob to head downstairs, she saw her hand around another knob, in front of another door. She was back in the smoky building, gripping the bathroom doorknob and pushing on it with all her strength. It didn't budge. She knew what came next, and if she didn't stop the sequence, her mind would replay it through to that horrible moment. She couldn't stand to see Jimmy fall through that floor one more time.

Stunned and breathing hard, she stumbled back several steps and dropped onto the bed. Slowly, the blurred edges receded and she returned to the present. She sat there for a moment longer, soaking in the familiarity of her surroundings. The antique Cape Cod–style furniture could probably use a fresh coat of white paint, and at the very least she should have replaced the cracked mirror on the dresser. But she always had something more important to do around the house.

Focusing on the details of her bedroom seemed to be doing the trick. Her heart rate was already returning to normal, and the cool perspiration that dotted her skin was evaporating. She rolled her shoulders and tried to relax the remaining stiffness in her chest. After she shook away the lingering nausea, she flung the door open and headed downstairs.

As Reid entered the living room and saw its lone occupant, she didn't even break her stride when she felt the familiar twinge in her stomach. She was totally used to it. The sight of Isabel had made her react the same way ever since she was old enough to realize she liked girls more than boys. But as Jimmy's kid sister, his *straight* kid sister, Isabel had always been off-limits. Afraid Isabel wouldn't be interested or, worse yet, might be offended if she expressed her attraction, Reid hadn't wanted to make Jimmy have to choose between his friend and his sister. Still, seeing her slim figure, hair the color of polished copper, and laughing gray eyes never failed to affect Reid.

Now, however, when Isabel turned at the sound of Reid's footsteps on the hardwood floor, her eyes were red-rimmed and filled with grief. Reid noticed the framed photograph in her hands, which had been taken right after Jimmy was promoted to captain. She didn't need to see the photo close up to envision the broad smile on Jimmy's face as they stood together in front of the engine. She remembered the way the sun had shone that early spring day and how the slight breeze had carried the scent of damp earth and new growth.

"Your mother went next door to help Chase get ready," Isabel said, glancing once more at the photo before she returned it to the mantel. Shortly after their wedding, Jimmy and his wife Amanda had purchased the house that neighbored Reid's, but they had been able to live in that house together only two years.

Reid nodded silently and thought about Jimmy's son, Chase. At seven years old, he had suffered too many losses in his young life. Jimmy had been working the day when Amanda, barely seven months pregnant, began to have severe abdominal pains. She'd called Jimmy's parents to drive her to the hospital, but on the way a terrible accident had occurred.

The police report said the semi came out of nowhere. Amanda and Jimmy's parents all were fatally injured, and the doctors had to struggle to try to save the baby. Born weighing only 3 pounds 12 ounces, Chase had spent several weeks in the hospital before Jimmy was allowed to take him home.

Isabel interrupted Reid's bitter memories. "I couldn't get Chase to put on a tie. I should have just brought him over. When he sees that you're wearing one, he'll want one, too."

Seeing Reid in her dress uniform, Isabel felt tears she thought she had exhausted in the past three days threaten again. She had often teased Jimmy that putting on the tie and dark jacket with its gleaming gold buttons transformed him. He displayed manners and a bearing she had never seen in him before. She joked that he even stood differently. Now she realized Reid stood the same way—stiffly, formally—even in her own living room.

Isabel had been barely holding herself together since the chaplain had called her in Knoxville four days before. It was the longest drive of her life. She had driven her Honda faster than was safe and still arrived at the hospital too late. The moment she rushed through the emergency-room doors, she realized he was already gone.

The waiting room had been full of firefighters, some still half dressed in turnout gear, others in navy blue T-shirts and BDU pants. The acrid smell of stale smoke hung heavily in the air. Isabel had noticed the distinctive odor before, clinging to Jimmy's clothes after his shifts, but in the congested room it seemed more pungent.

Isabel had searched the crowd for a familiar figure and finally found her sitting flanked by two silent men. She barely registered them as the other two members of Jimmy's crew. Her attention was focused on Reid, who sat bent over with her head cradled in her hands.

As if sensing Isabel's gaze, Reid looked up. Her short, dark hair was damp and plastered to her forehead. The pale, wet tracks of her tears stood out against the black soot that streaked her face. Isabel knew in that moment, as she saw the agony in Reid's expression, that her world had once more been turned upside down.

"No," Isabel rasped, feeling the blackness close in.

All she could see was Reid, who stood quickly. The crowd parted as she strode across the room and, without hesitation, took Isabel in her arms. The offered comfort pierced the grief already swamping Isabel's heart. What seemed like a lifetime of tension between them faded for an instant, eclipsed by shared pain.

Reid brushed a hand over the back of Isabel's head and cupped her neck. Isabel, her arms around Reid's chest, tightened her embrace and felt Reid flinch slightly. Though they were nearly the same height, Isabel tucked her head against Reid's shoulder. They held each other for several long moments, sealed together by their love for Jimmy.

"I'm so sorry," Reid whispered against Isabel's ear.

Isabel heard the guilt that saturated Reid's voice.

"One minute he was there and then—" Her voice broke. But before Isabel could respond, Reid eased back. "I—your shirt."

Isabel glanced down at the black smudges on her lavender blouse. She started to tell Reid not to worry about her clothes, but the firefighter was already pulling completely away from her. Reid straightened her shoulders and swiped at her eyes.

That day in the waiting room, Isabel had watched Reid change as her pride overtook her grief and made her back away. She guessed that same pride now kept Reid standing rigidly across the living room. *That damn uniform.* It and a misguided sense of duty had stolen her brother from his son and from her.

Isabel smoothed a hand over her hip and picked at invisible pieces of lint on her linen skirt simply to have something to do with her hands. The past three days had restored the distance between them. "Is your father meeting us at the church?"

"I haven't been able to get in touch with him." Reid shrugged, but her indifference seemed forced. Isabel wondered if she imagined the fleeting dejection that swept over Reid's expression. "I left a message."

"Reid!"

Reid barely had a chance to react as a small boy hurtled through the back door. She squatted down and braced for impact seconds before Chase threw himself into her arms. Reid's mother came in behind him wearing a defeated smile, a clip-on tie in her hand. Reid looked at her with sympathy. It was rare that her mother couldn't sweet-talk Chase.

Reid recalled how her mother, Meredith Webb, had become a surrogate grandmother to Chase. When she and Reid's father divorced ten years before, she had come to live with Reid, and after Jimmy lost his wife a few years later, she had been there next door to babysit Chase while Jimmy was at work. In the early years, when Jimmy had been consumed by grief and uncertain how to care for his infant son, Meredith had been his savior. In the seven years since, Jimmy and Chase had become part of the Webb family.

"What's up, buddy?" Reid searched Chase's face.

He remained silent. His lower lip poked out and he absently played with the shiny badge pinned to her chest. She watched his small fingers trace the black band stretched over the center of it.

Reid took the tie from her mother and fastened the top button of Chase's shirt. Though his eyes flashed defiantly, he stood still while she clipped on the tie and straightened his collar around it. He clenched his jaw and held himself as rigidly as Reid, whose heart shattered as a glimmer of Jimmy's stubborn pride flashed across his son's face.

❖

Isabel climbed the steps to the church, wishing she didn't have to go inside. The large stone edifice with its twin spires that reached endlessly into the azure sky depressed her. The sun shone brightly, as if the heavens were unaware of the shadow that hung over the day. *This isn't really happening*. She imagined she could go home, crawl into bed, and pretend the events of the past week had never happened. But the evidence of just how futile her wishes were milled about her in dark uniforms and with somber faces.

Amanda's mother, a stout woman with a take-charge attitude, approached Isabel. Though she initially irritated some people, those who really knew her forgave her tendency to try to boss them around because they knew she genuinely cared. She folded Isabel in a comforting embrace.

"Dear, you look like you need to get some rest. As soon as this is over, you and I can have a long talk. How are you holding up?"

"As well as can be expected. Thank you both for coming." Isabel included Amanda's father with an appreciative smile, and he squeezed her shoulder firmly.

Since Amanda's death, they had been Chase's only link to her side of the family, and Isabel was grateful that they kept in touch with him. Though they lived in Florida, they sent him presents on his birthday and at Christmas and on other holidays.

In addition to the several long weekends when they made the trip to Tennessee, Chase always spent two weeks in the summer with them. Isabel suddenly recalled the summer Reid had gone with her and Jimmy to visit their grandparents in Florida, but her sudden inexplicable pain made her focus outward on the words that Amanda's mother was murmuring.

"Of course, dear."

"Hi, Grandma," Chase said, climbing the steps with Reid.

Amanda's mother swept him up in a hug, tears filling her eyes. As if he knew it was what she needed, he allowed her to hold him.

Reid stepped forward and shook hands with Amanda's father.

"I'm so sorry," he said gruffly.

Reid could only nod in response, emotion bringing a lump to her throat. Seeing Amanda's mother cry brought to mind the day she had stood next to a stone-faced Jimmy as they'd grieved for Amanda and for Jimmy's parents. She had never dreamed that she'd be doing the same for Jimmy in just a few years.

"Let's go in and sit down," Amanda's mother said.

Her husband, obviously used to following her suggestions, pulled open one of the heavy oak doors and waited while they preceded him inside.

The beginning of the ceremony passed in a blur for Reid. Her mind refused to focus on the events around her; instead, it played a slideshow of memories. Jimmy had been beside her for almost her entire life. They'd become best friends from their first day in kindergarten when Reid had dared him to jump off the swing at the playground. They'd played on the same Little League team and taken swimming lessons together at the YMCA in the summer. And when Jimmy broke his arm while trying to learn a new skateboard trick, Reid had walked him home and promised not to tell anyone that he'd cried.

Most people had expected they would end up dating when they reached the appropriate age, but they didn't. Instead, they spent their time throwing a football, riding bikes, and later fixing up Jimmy's first truck, a 1976 Chevy.

And when Reid sat him down right before their senior year and told him she was gay, she had wondered if their friendship would end. But in his typical laid-back fashion, Jimmy had merely shrugged and said, "Just promise me one thing. Don't ever steal one of my girlfriends."

Contrasting Jimmy's vitality to the stillness of the body in the coffin in front of the church, Reid tried not to shift in the pew while the chaplain read the eulogy. She glanced across the aisle at Nathan, Joey, and the crew from Truck Company 9, who would serve as pallbearers, and was reminded that she needed to quit daydreaming. She had a duty to fulfill, and she felt torn between it and her responsibility to her family. Her mother had requested that she not join the other firefighters, arguing that Chase needed her with him. So she sat between Meredith and Chase, feeling out of place. She should be with her crew.

Chase fidgeted and tugged at his collar. Seated on his other side, Isabel glanced at him and draped her arm across the back of the pew. He stopped. Isabel returned her attention to the front of the church, and Reid studied her profile. She'd twisted her copper-colored hair into a simple bun, but a strand had worked itself free and her fingers shook as she shoved it behind her ear. Her angular jaw was tight with the effort of holding back the tears that shone in her eyes.

Isabel tried to tune out the chaplain's words. He'd begun by saying that Jimmy was a man of conviction. He talked about Jimmy's commitment to his family, specifically the wife he had lost and the son he was raising alone. But when he began to praise the courage and honor Jimmy had displayed in his work, Isabel stopped listening. She didn't want to hear about honor. It had stolen her brother.

She couldn't keep her eyes from drifting to the casket, closed at her request. Hard as she tried, Isabel couldn't banish the image of Jimmy in full dress uniform lying inside. She squeezed her eyes shut.

At a light touch on the back of her hand, she opened them again. Reid's fingertips caressed her wrist in a comforting gesture, but Isabel slid her hand away and folded her arms over her chest. She didn't want comfort today, and she certainly didn't want it from Reid. She wanted to immerse herself in her grief and guilt.

She had stayed away far too much over the years and, she now realized, she had missed knowing her brother as well as she could have. It had been so difficult to come home after her parents died. Everything reminded her of them, and instead of dealing with the pain, she had stayed away. Selfishly, she hadn't thought about whether Jimmy might need her, but instead had accepted his assurances that he was doing okay. Now she wondered how many times he had felt alone, as alone as she now felt. She glanced again at Chase, wondering how she would raise this boy who was virtually a stranger to her.

In truth, even this small display of concern from Reid, this quiet contact, had surprised her. After the day in the hospital, Isabel had seen Reid become emotional only when they sat Chase down and told him what had happened. When his chin trembled with the effort of suppressing tears, Reid had gathered him close, and as she held him tightly the agony etched on her strong features was evident. Isabel wasn't sure which of them had needed the embrace more.

Since then Reid had been quiet and introspective, even more so than usual. She seemed to be far away and offered her opinion about Jimmy's arrangements only when Isabel solicited it. She'd been silent during the ride to the church, staring out the window. This simple touch was the first hint that Reid was aware of her surroundings at all.

The dark walnut pews were filled with crisp uniforms that displayed all manner of rank and decoration. In addition to a full complement of the department, representatives from other cities from across the state had attended. Suddenly Isabel wished she'd been more insistent about her desire to limit the traditional ceremony. The department's liaison officer had made it clear that they would abide by her wishes. But focusing on every detail of the arrangements had overwhelmed her, and in the end she'd simply acquiesced to the routine procedures. It seemed the firefighters needed the closure of this formal ceremony. But just then Isabel wanted nothing more than a quiet moment to mourn Jimmy without the reminder that he had belonged to a whole brotherhood of people who understood him better than she ever had.

The abundance of flower arrangements that filled the front of the sanctuary indicated that many people in addition to those at the funeral would miss Jimmy. Isabel had seen cards that bore the names of local elementary schools where he visited every year for fire-prevention week, of people he had carried out of burning buildings who swore they would never forget him, and of his friends and coworkers. Isabel had never realized how many lives Jimmy had affected, but no one should have to risk his life daily and end it so young, no matter how much good he did for others.

❖

Reid held the door of the black limo open and waited while Isabel, Meredith, and Chase climbed inside. She was about to follow when she caught Joey's eye. The ache that had been throbbing in her chest all day intensified at his sympathetic gaze. She knew he wouldn't say much to her about Jimmy. Instead he'd obviously spent hours assuaging his grief by washing and waxing the engine in preparation for the traditional service. The hose bed had been emptied to make room for the engine to serve as a caisson. The pallbearers would ride on the rig to the cemetery, and Joey and Nathan would stand on the back step.

"Reid?" Isabel gave her a questioning look.

"Yeah, I'm coming," she mumbled. Reaching into the inside pocket of her jacket, she pulled out her sunglasses and slipped them on.

She settled into the plush leather seat and closed the door. As the fire engine slowly drove away, the limo slid in line behind it. The ride to the cemetery was solemn. Chase climbed to his knees to watch the line of vehicles that stretched for miles behind them.

"Chase, please sit down," Meredith requested quietly.

Knowing better than to argue, he spun around and slumped down in his seat.

As they approached the entrance to Mt. Olivet Cemetery, Reid saw two ladder trucks parked on opposite sides of the entrance, their aerials extended skyward and crossed in tribute.

The car followed the narrow, tree-lined road that wound through the shaded grounds. When they stopped, Reid was first out of the car. Out of respect she removed her sunglasses, though she would have preferred to keep them on. The effort of keeping her emotions under control for the past several days had exhausted her. She could feel the other mourners assessing her as if trying to decide if they should approach, and she wanted to hide behind the dark lenses.

She led their small group across the meticulously manicured grass to a row of chairs at the graveside. Isabel settled Chase into the center chair and, along with Meredith, flanked him. Reid remained standing near Isabel's left shoulder.

"Detail, attention," Chief Perez ordered, and Reid snapped to attention. The pallbearers eased the casket from the hose bed. With careful and precise steps, they carried it to the stand and two of them draped an American flag over the top.

"Parade rest."

Rows of uniformed firefighters moved as one, all shifting their left foot so they stood with their feet shoulder-width apart, clasping their hands behind their backs.

Reid forced herself to focus on the prayers and words of condolence the chief offered to the family. She drew strength from the rows of firefighters assembled nearby, but nothing could fill the gaping hole in her heart.

The crowd was silent as the mournful tones of the bagpipes played "Amazing Grace." Resolutely swallowing the sob that lodged in her throat, Reid closed her eyes and imagined that the wailing instrument was releasing the pain building inside her. But when the last notes faded into the somber afternoon, she felt no relief.

The chaplain spoke. "Throughout most of history, the lives of firefighters have been closely associated with the ringing of a bell. As they began their hours of duty, the bell started it off. Through the day and night, each alarm was sounded by a bell that called them to fight fire and to place their lives in jeopardy for the good of their fellow man. And when the fire was out, the alarm had come to an end. The bell rang three times to signal the end. And now our brother, Captain James Matthew Grant, has completed his task, his duties well done, and the bell rings three times in memory of, and in tribute to, his life and service."

"Detail, attention." Once again, men and women reacted in unison. "Present arms." They executed a crisp salute and held it.

The large gold bell was struck three times. As the final vibrations faded away, a lone bugle began to play "Taps."

"Order arms." A sea of hands snapped down, arms returning to their sides.

As the honor guard carefully removed the flag and folded it into the customary triangular shape, Reid stepped forward. This was the one exception to tradition she had requested. Normally the fire chief would receive the flag and present it to the family. Today, Reid would do it instead.

Accepting the flag with one palm on top and one on the bottom, Reid pressed her left toe to the ground and executed a crisp military-style 180-degree turn. She'd once heard that you couldn't cry if you held your breath. *It's worth a try.* She filled her lungs and braced herself. Taking comfort from the feel of the embroidered stars beneath her fingertips, she tried to focus on the rituals she was there to recognize instead of the agony that burned in the pit of her stomach.

Tradition and honor were something Reid could understand. The emotions looming at the edges of her consciousness were foreign to her. This was Jimmy. Half of her soul had been ripped away. And though she put up a strong front because others expected it of her, inside she was bleeding.

Meredith, Chase, and Isabel sat before her. Three pairs of tearful eyes were riveted on her face. Three reasons to be strong. She dropped to one knee in front of Chase's chair. When she extended the flag, he took it and clasped it to his chest. His face was set—harder than his years—and his continued refusal to cry sent a shaft of pain through her.

"Detail, dismissed."

Chapter Three

Reid stood in the doorway of the kitchen—it still felt like Jimmy's kitchen. His thermos sat on the counter waiting for him to fill it with steaming coffee, strong and black. A stack of mail lay on the counter by the back door, waiting for him to sort it. He had a habit of pulling out just the bills and leaving the rest until the pile got so big it threatened to spill onto the floor. Only then would he go through it, and by that time most of the coupons and offers had expired, so he threw them directly in the trash.

Isabel stood at the sink, her back to Reid and her hands immersed in soapy water, but she didn't attempt to wash the dishes. Instead she stared out the window into the backyard.

Reid nudged her aside. "Let me take care of those." Isabel had been standing there for so long, the water had cooled and the soap bubbles had lost their bounce.

Isabel started to argue, but Reid was already plunging plates under the tepid water and had hot water streaming from the faucet. Isabel picked up a towel to dry.

"Has everyone gone?" Jimmy's house had been full of well-meaning friends and fellow firefighters who brought enormous amounts of food and condolences. Isabel had stayed in the living room with them as long as she could and eventually fled to the quiet of the kitchen.

Reid nodded. "I just walked Joey and his wife out."

"She's really sweet."

"Yeah, he sure is lucky she puts up with him. I know today was hard for you. You handled everything well," Reid said softly.

Isabel glanced at Reid, noting the smudges that marred the smooth skin beneath her eyes. At some point she had stripped off her jacket and tie, and the sleeves of her uniform shirt were rolled up, baring sinewy forearms.

Isabel knew Reid felt the loss as acutely as she did. She sighed as the grief of the day weighed heavily on her. "Thank you for helping me out here. And please thank your mother for me."

"Sure. The crowd made Chase cranky, so Mom took him over to the house and he fell asleep. She said to tell you that, if it's okay, you can collect him in the morning."

Isabel had quickly learned that because Reid and Jimmy worked twenty-four hours on and then forty-eight off, Chase customarily spent every third night with Meredith, so he had his own room at Reid's house as well. The unconventional arrangement worked well for them.

"Yes, there's no point in waking him now." Isabel dried and put away the last of the plates. "Are you heading home or can you join me for a glass of wine?" She wasn't willing to admit it, but she didn't want to be alone just yet. And though it had been years since she'd spent any length of time with Reid, her company was preferable to the void left by Jimmy's absence.

"I can stay for a bit."

Isabel picked up a bottle of Riesling and two glasses from the counter and headed for the living room.

As Reid followed, she glanced around the room. Though over the years the house had taken on Jimmy's personality, Reid could still see touches of Jimmy's wife. She remembered Amanda's excitement when they had moved in. She had wandered from room to room rambling about curtains and wallpaper while a bewildered Jimmy carried in boxes and furniture. Reid had grinned when Amanda talked about refinishing the hardwood floors, until Jimmy pinned her with a stern look.

"Don't laugh too hard, Webb. Your ass will be here sanding next to me," he'd whispered behind Amanda's back.

Jimmy and Amanda had spent their first year painstakingly fixing up the house. Reid had expected that she and Jimmy would be doing most of the manual labor and she'd been pleasantly surprised when Amanda had worked alongside them. She was adamant about staying true to the 1940s architecture, so they restored the original molding.

Reid felt nostalgic as she looked at it and the simply styled cherry furniture that Amanda had carefully selected to accent the rich woodwork and the deep colors of the walls.

"Where did you go?" Isabel asked as Reid settled on the opposite end of the sofa.

"I was thinking about when Jimmy and Amanda moved in here."

Isabel smiled and handed Reid a glass of wine. "I remember. Amanda was so excited. She'd been decorating the place in her head since the first time she saw it. I came home from college that weekend to help them move."

Reid frowned. "Oh yeah, you brought that jerk—er—jock you were dating."

"That's right. He was a basketball player and he wasn't a jerk." His face flashed in Isabel's mind. He was a sweet guy—tall, good-looking, and, as it turned out, totally wrong for her. They had dated most of her freshman year. Their breakup, much like their relationship, had been uneventful.

"Whatever. He wasn't good enough for you." Reid dismissed Isabel's defense of the jock with a wave of her hand.

Over the years Isabel had grown accustomed to the protective way Jimmy and Reid treated her. Two years younger, she'd often heard her father instruct Jimmy to look out for her. And, she guessed, Jimmy spent so much time with Reid that it was only natural that she would see her as a little sister, too.

"Something tells me that you and Jimmy never thought any of my boyfriends were good enough." Reid's brown eyes darkened at Isabel's words, and her pupils flared. A moment later Isabel wondered if she'd imagined Reid's reaction. Her gaze was neutral now.

"You know, you're probably right. Jimmy was always saying he wished you would let him fix you up."

"Ha! He probably would've fixed me up with some big, sweaty firefighter."

"Not all firefighters are big and sweaty."

"Really? Well, you're probably right about that. That Nathan guy is pretty cute. What's his story?" Isabel shifted on the sofa and tucked one leg beneath her.

"Nathan? He's not good enough either."

"Really?"

"Besides, I heard he's gay," Reid lied.

Isabel laughed. "He is not. He does have a nice body."

Reid bristled at the appreciative gleam in Isabel's eye. "He's too young for you."

"What?" Isabel swatted at her playfully. "How old is he?"

"I don't know, early twenties," Reid guessed, thinking that though Isabel had nearly a decade on him, he would be lucky to get a woman like her. Isabel was completely out of his league, and Reid wasn't biased in the least.

"Hmm, yeah, that's a bit young."

"And anyway, Jimmy wouldn't have fixed you up with Nathan. He couldn't stand the guy."

Reid watched the teasing light slip from Isabel's eyes. They turned dark gray like storm clouds gathering on a winter afternoon, and Reid wondered what had caused this change.

"Reid, I haven't asked because I wasn't sure I wanted to know, but—what happened in there?"

And just like that the mood between them shifted. Reid went cold. "Please don't ask me that right now." Rehashing the details had been hard enough when she had given the fire marshal a report, but telling Isabel would be agonizing. She was having a difficult time just facing Chase and Isabel, much less having to verbally recount her failure to rescue her partner.

"I need—"

"No, you don't, Iz."

"Isabel."

"What?"

"My name is Isabel."

"I've called you *Iz* since you were five years old."

"Well, I'm not five years old anymore," Isabel snapped back.

"I didn't mean anything by it."

"I need to know what happened to my brother."

"I can't." Reid stood, giving Isabel no chance to argue. "I'll see you later. You know how to reach us if you need anything." Isabel followed, but Reid barely paused on her way out the door.

Wrapping her sweater more tightly around her, Isabel stood on the back porch and glared at Reid's back. She considered letting Reid go without saying anything, but she'd been burying her anger beneath her grief since she'd returned to Nashville, and she was exhausted.

"I asked him to quit, you know," Isabel called out.

Reid froze with her hand on the wooden gate that separated their two yards, but she didn't turn around.

"After Amanda died, I was so afraid of exactly this situation. I told him he needed to find a new career, one where he would be safe. I *begged* him to do it for Chase. Do you know what he told me?"

Reid was silent.

"He told me I couldn't understand. Do you think that's true?"

Several long moments passed.

"Damn it, Reid. I need some answers."

"I'm sorry." Reid's words were clearly filled with anguish, but they weren't enough to make Isabel forget that this woman had walked beside her brother in his last moments. Reid pushed through the gate and was gone.

Isabel sighed. The funeral had drained her and left her emotions raw and exposed. She could take a lesson in control from Reid. Among her fellow firefighters, Reid had been stoic. The only slip in her composure had been the glistening in her eyes as she handed Chase the flag. Later, when a crowd of mourners inundated the house, Reid had been the hostess Isabel was unable to be. She had shuttled casseroles to the freezer and made sure everyone who wanted a drink had one in hand. Isabel could only listen numbly as a seemingly endless stream of uniformed men and women paraded through the house muttering sympathetically about heroism. She was beginning to hate that uniform.

❖

The next morning, Isabel crossed their yards to Reid's back door. She knocked tentatively.

Meredith answered with a smile. "Good morning, dear. Come on in. Would you like some coffee?" Without waiting for Isabel to answer, she opened a cabinet near the sink and took down a mug.

Isabel settled on a stool at the breakfast bar and accepted the full cup. Meredith moved around the kitchen comfortably, pushing sugar and creamer across the bar and within Isabel's reach.

The years had been kind to Meredith, painting her once-dark hair with streaks of gray, but leaving only fine lines on her face. Her ivory skin still glowed and her smile was as warm and enveloping as Isabel remembered. It struck Isabel that Reid would probably age this gently. *She'll be disarmingly attractive well into her later years.*

"Is Reid around?"

"She's in the living room, but you might want to wait a minute before you go in there." Meredith stirred a teaspoon of sugar into her own coffee and studied the young woman who was as much a part of her family as her own daughter.

Meredith's husband had been a firefighter. Despite their eventual divorce, the one thing she could never complain about in those early years was the way he provided for his family, often picking up extra shifts so she could be a stay-at-home mom. Therefore, Isabel and Jimmy had spent many an afternoon at Meredith's house while their parents were both at work. She'd been there for as many of their milestones as she had Reid's.

"Why should I wait?" Isabel settled back onto the stool.

"On a good day, she can be a bit difficult until she's absorbed her morning dose of caffeine. This morning—trust me, give it an extra minute."

Reid had come home obviously upset the night before. This morning she'd been gruff, barking one-word answers when she was spoken to. Meredith watched curiously as a guilty look stole over Isabel's face.

"How are you holding up?" The woman who sat before her barely resembled the girl who had gone off to college years before. The once-shy adolescent had become a confident, successful woman. Though Meredith hadn't seen much of her lately, she would always have a soft spot in her heart for Isabel.

"I've been better," Isabel sighed. She had seen the evidence in the mirror that morning. Fatigue dulled her eyes, and makeup hadn't quite covered the dark circles beneath them.

"You know if you need anything we're right next door, don't you?" Meredith echoed Reid's words from the night before, but hers sounded more sincere.

"I know, thank you," Isabel said. "I feel so disconnected right now."

"Well, sweetie, that's what family is for, to keep you connected."

Meredith's generous inclusion of Isabel in her family nearly brought tears to Isabel's eyes. *God, when did I get so weepy?*

"Good morning." Isabel poked her head into the living room and found Reid sitting on the couch watching Chase play on the floor in front of her. The room was laid out similarly to Jimmy's living room, just as Reid's life was basically similar to his. And here, too, Reid had kept the integrity of the original woodwork. But instead of the bold colors, Reid had shown her individuality by decorating in neutral tones accented with sparing touches of navy blue. The microsuede sofa that faced the stone hearth was new, as was the matching chair set at an angle nearby.

Isabel missed the familiarity of the old couch and chair on which she had sat so many times while she was growing up. A television, also new, was tucked into a corner beside a wooden chest that housed some of Chase's toys, and Isabel recalled how often she'd come over after school and watched *Scooby-Doo* while Reid and Jimmy played outside. She had sometimes stood and watched them through the large windows that opened up the cozy room and let in a good amount of natural light. For a time she'd been envious and had wondered if they might let her play with them if she learned to throw a football or hit a baseball. But back then they'd shared interests that Isabel never would, and that hadn't changed over the years.

Reid glanced at her. "Morning," she grumbled.

Isabel ventured into the room and settled on the other end of the sofa, keeping in mind Meredith's warning. She briefly noted the empty mug on the coffee table.

Isabel watched Chase push his toy cars around on the floor nearby. Then he carefully constructed a bridge from his blocks, his head bent in concentration as he did so. "How do you look at him and not see Jimmy?"

"Jimmy once asked me the same thing about Amanda, shortly after she died. I guess Chase just had the good fortune to get the best of both of his parents."

Reid was right. Chase had inherited his strong chin and slightly crooked nose from his father. A wide grin held traces of Jimmy that made Isabel's heart ache. But when she studied Chase's naturally curly brown hair and large, chocolate-colored eyes, she remembered his mother's gentle face. Amanda's nurturing nature was undoubtedly responsible for the tenderness in those eyes that superseded even the rough edges of boyhood.

"I'm sorry I upset you last night," Reid said quietly.

"It's okay," Isabel murmured as she watched Chase wrap his fist around a fire truck and imitate a siren. She winced. "Your father was a firefighter. It's all I can ever remember you wanting to do."

"It's all I've ever wanted." Reid carefully controlled her tone. She refused to apologize for her chosen profession.

"I know. It's what Jimmy wanted, too."

Reid didn't think she was imagining the blame in Isabel's tone. *Because of me. Jimmy wanted it because I wanted it. Is that what you're trying not to say?* "Iz, if I had known—"

"What, Reid? What would you have done? Would you have talked him out of becoming a firefighter all those years ago?"

"I don't know." Even as she answered she couldn't convince herself that it was even half-true. She wouldn't have. It was what they were meant to be, and even if her own fate was the same as Jimmy's she couldn't change who she was. She didn't have the right to trade the lives she'd saved for her own. She owed Isabel so many truths and she made herself grant this one. "No. I wouldn't have."

"Reid, I'm just trying to understand why this happened."

"Well, let me know if you come up with anything." Glancing at Chase, Reid was careful to keep her voice low. "Because I sure as hell can't find any logic in it." She tried unsuccessfully to block the image of Jimmy's face just before he fell. She'd been dreaming about it for days, but it had begun to haunt her waking moments as well.

Isabel must have sensed the topic was closed. "There's so much to do," she muttered. "When we get to Knoxville, the first thing I'll do is look for a two-bedroom apartment."

"What?" Reid stared at her, hoping she had heard wrong.

"Well, my one-bedroom place isn't going to be big enough for Chase and me."

Chase looked up. "I don't want to move," he declared stubbornly.

"Honey, it'll be okay. You'll make lots of new friends and be settled in no time."

He surged to his feet and ran to Reid's side. "I don't want to move away from you."

"Chase," Reid began.

His eyes filled with tears and he clung to her hand.

"Chase, it's time for breakfast," Meredith called, coming in from the kitchen. Seeking refuge, Chase ran to her and flung himself against her legs. By now he was sobbing.

"I don't wanna move away," he wailed.

"Come eat your cereal, sweetie. We'll leave Reid and Isabel to work it out." As Meredith guided him into the kitchen, she rubbed her hand gently over his back.

"Am I a horrible person?" Isabel asked, massaging her temples.

Reid's first instinct was to insist Chase was not going anywhere. She struggled to keep her opinion to herself, reminding herself that Isabel was Chase's guardian and she had to respect that.

"Just give him some time. Um—kids are resilient. He'll adjust." Reid felt like she was just spouting platitudes. Did she really believe that taking Chase away from the only home he'd ever known was the best thing for him right now? Shouldn't she fight for him?

"You really think so?"

"I don't know," she admitted. "Maybe I'm not the best person to ask about this."

"Why?"

"Well, I've kind of gotten used to having him around," she hedged.

"Reid." Isabel sighed. "I know it's been a while since we've really spent a lot of time together, but I've always gotten the impression that you didn't hold anything back."

Ironically, Reid felt like Isabel was someone she did have to censor herself around. Over the years Isabel had come home less often. When she missed an important holiday, Jimmy shrugged off her absence, saying Isabel worked hard. But when she did come around, Reid found the impact of her nearness hadn't lessened. And that attraction was something she kept very carefully concealed.

"I keep wishing Jimmy would walk through the door, pick Chase up, and swing him around. I just lost him. I don't want to lose Chase, too." Reid tried to harden herself against the loneliness already creeping into her heart. "But you should do what's best for the two of you. We all have a lot to adjust to right now."

"And it's going to be even harder for Chase to adjust if I keep throwing more changes at him," Isabel added.

"Maybe you should sleep on it. It's been an emotional couple of days, and this is probably not the best time for you to make any important decisions."

"You're probably right. I've already arranged to be here for a few days anyway, so I can take some time to work things out."

Reid slumped back on the sofa and wondered how much more she could handle. The very vocation to which she had committed her own life had stolen Jimmy from her. And now Isabel might take Chase. She nearly laughed at the irony.

CHAPTER FOUR

As Reid stepped inside the Blue Line Bar and Grill, she noticed how the grimy windows blocked out the late-afternoon sun. She would have put money on the fact that the few occupants were regulars. Why else would they be bellied up to a bar on a weekday afternoon? The Blue Line was a well-known cop hangout, owned by a retired detective. Over the years a fair number of firefighters had lifted a glass; in fact, they possibly made up the majority of the patrons.

Reid glanced at the two men playing pool in the back and dismissed them immediately. The man she sought would be perched on the second stool. Like clockwork.

"Hey, Billy," she called out to the bartender.

"Hey yourself, Reid. What can I get you?"

"Nothing today." She slid onto a stool next to the man hunched over his drink. "Hi, Pop."

Her father looked older than the last time she'd seen him. The lines on his face were deeper, and his gray hair, once as thick and dark as hers, was thinning on top. His eyes were bloodshot, his expression flat. Every time she saw him, she had to look more closely for the man she'd admired as a child, now destroyed by the demons he chased from atop his bar stool.

"I heard about Jimmy. He was a good kid."

"You didn't even come to the funeral."

He shrugged.

"He was a firefighter, Pop. You should've been there." In addition to Reid's personal relationship with Jimmy, as a retired district chief, her father was expected to attend the funeral of a line-of-duty death. Jimmy was like a brother to Reid. And though she had thought her father's neglect could no longer hurt her, his casual dismissal of Jimmy opened a fresh wound.

"It's too late now." He lifted the glass of amber liquid in front of him. Scotch, no ice. He was so damn predictable.

"I don't even know what I'm doing here," she mumbled.

As she swung around to leave he grabbed her arm. "What do you want from me, angel?"

The childhood nickname that had once made her feel special sounded hollow. But she was vulnerable now, and the endearment snuck through her armor. She hadn't been Daddy's little girl in a long time, but enough of the memory lingered to make her yearn for those days. She could still remember what her father looked like in his uniform.

Back then, she'd touched his shiny badge much the same way Chase had touched hers the other day, and from that moment she'd known what she wanted to be, who she was. She could almost hate her father for sullying that destiny, for not still embodying the qualities she'd held so dear.

"I wanted you to be there." *So many times I've wanted you to be there.*

"Well, I can't go back in time, can I?"

Reid silently counted to ten. What good would it do to blow up at him? He was impervious to her attempts to get him to listen. "Did you ever lose anyone?"

He was quiet for so long she thought he might not respond. "Twenty-five years. Yeah, we lost a couple."

"How do you keep going?"

"What do you mean, how? It's the job. What else are you gonna do?"

"Sit around on a bar stool all day," Reid mumbled.

"What?"

"Nothing, Pop." She stood. "I've got to get going. I'll see you later."

When she left, he didn't try to stop her.

As she stepped out onto the sidewalk, she tried to shrug off the weight of their exchange. She shouldn't have come here. She hated the weakness that kept her seeking her father's affection and support. *No more.* She vowed to banish the unfulfilled need that made her stomach queasy.

❖

Isabel entered the living room to find Chase in the same place he'd been for the past two hours. He sat cross-legged on the floor in front of the television with a video-game controller in his hand. She glanced at the screen and winced as two characters clashed, slashing at each other with swords. When Chase's player beheaded the other with a mighty swipe, he pumped his fist in the air.

"Did your dad let you play this game?"

"He bought it for me." Chase's attention remained riveted on the action.

"Well, you've been at it for a while now. Time to put it away. Dinner will be ready soon."

"I gotta finish this level."

"Chase," Isabel warned.

"I can't save it until I finish this level."

She strode back into the kitchen wondering what she'd gotten herself into. She knew nothing about parenting. She felt sorry for Chase. After all, he'd just lost his father, and she wanted to coddle him. But she knew she couldn't do that for the rest of his life. At some point she'd have to figure out when to discipline him.

When he finally joined her she was halfway through her own dinner. He picked up his fork and toyed with his spaghetti, not really eating any of it.

"Chase, eat your food," she snapped after listening to him scrape the tines on his plate for several minutes.

"I'm not hungry."

Forcing patience, she set down her own fork. "Why not?"

"I dunno."

"What's wrong?"

"I'm just not hungry."

"Chase," she began. When he merely continued to push his food around on his plate, she plucked the fork out of his hand. She waited until she had his attention before she continued. "Do you want to talk about it?"

He remained silent.

"This is a hard time for you. I know—"

"No, you don't." He pouted.

"Yes, I do."

"You don't even live here."

He didn't respond to any more of her prodding. Eventually, she gave him back his fork and he returned to twirling it idly through his spaghetti.

Isabel stared at her plate. She *didn't* live here, and his sulking reminded her that she wasn't a substantial part of his life. It would take more than a few days and a plate of spaghetti to change that.

❖

Reid lay awake and stared at the ceiling, one hand tucked beneath her head, the other flung across the empty side of the bed. After waking up in the early hours with the edges of a nightmare pounding in her head, she'd given up on sleep. Frustrated, she'd flung off the covers, but then a chill chased across her sweat-soaked skin.

She glanced at the clock on the nightstand, the glowing numbers telling her she had managed to sleep for three hours.

"Two more than yesterday," she muttered as she crawled out of bed, wincing as her bare feet touched the cold floor. After hurrying through a shower, she tugged on navy BDU pants and a navy T-shirt bearing the department's logo.

Downstairs she grabbed a mug from the cupboard. The coffeemaker was halfway through its morning cycle, so she slid the carafe out and quickly replaced it with the mug. She swallowed as much coffee as her throat would allow and waited for the caffeine to calm her jitters.

As she consumed three cups, she stood at the sink and watched the sun rise through the kitchen window. Her stomach, already edgy from lack of sleep, protested the third cup. After searching the pantry for something to settle it, she dug up a box of strawberry Pop-Tarts her mother kept for Chase. She tucked a package of them in her bag, cringing as she considered what the sugar rush would probably do to her system that early in the morning.

She rinsed her mug and left it in the sink. Grabbing her leather jacket from the hook by the door on her way out, she headed for the garage and fished her keys out of her pocket.

"Come on, damn it!" When the motorcycle refused to start, Reid fought the urge to kick it. "Just fucking great," she muttered. She'd been having problems with the bike for months. She and Jimmy had been talking about pulling it apart and locating the problem, but they'd just never got to it. Now she was going to be late on her first day back to work.

"Do you need a ride?"

Reid turned at the voice from behind her. Isabel stood on Jimmy's front porch and clutched a white terry-cloth robe tightly around her. Bare, shapely legs peeked out from beneath the hem. She was braless, the robe clung to her breasts, and arousal quickly edged out Reid's frustration.

"I'm sorry if I woke you." Dragging her eyes from Isabel's chest, Reid glanced pointedly at her sock-clad feet. "You're going to get sick." Though it was only mid-October, winter seemed in a hurry to arrive.

"Speaking of which, it's a bit cold to be riding to work, isn't it?" Isabel eyed the big black motorcycle dubiously.

"Well, Jimmy and I usually carpooled, so…" Reid fiddled with the machine. They had usually taken Jimmy's old pickup and left Reid's Jeep for Meredith. In addition to watching Chase and taking care of Reid's house, Meredith volunteered at the senior center several days a week and needed a way to get there and to the grocery store. During the summer months Jimmy and Reid had both pulled out their motorcycles, often going the long way to work in order to eke out a few more moments on the road.

"Do you want to take his truck?"

Reid glanced toward the garage. "I don't think I can." A twinge of pain tore through her chest at the thought of being in Jimmy's truck. Joey had driven it home from the station and parked it in the garage, and no one had touched it since. She returned her attention to the bike.

"I can drive you." Isabel had just made the offer when the engine caught and roared to life.

"Thanks anyway," Reid called over the rumble. No doubt, the image of Isabel in her robe would linger for the rest of the day, and she didn't need even ten minutes close in the cabin of a car to make things worse. She pulled on her helmet, threw her leg over the bike, and settled into the seat.

Fifteen minutes later, she strolled into the truck bay of Station 9. It was outfitted similarly to the other forty fire stations in the city. Each possessed the basic work areas, vehicle bays, storage space for equipment, and personal areas that included kitchen, sleeping quarters, and a living room of sorts furnished with a garage-sale assortment of furniture and a television.

Everything felt different. Maybe she was imagining things, because nothing seemed to have changed. The engine was parked in the left bay and the ladder truck in the right. Along the wall a row of turnout coats hung on hooks with their respective helmets on the shelf above. The boots stood on the floor with pants folded down over them, all ready for the firefighters to step into and go.

But midway down the row was an empty space. Things *were* different. Jimmy's gear was missing. His helmet now held a place of honor on a shelf in Chase's room. Reid had been touched when Chief Perez gave it to him after Jimmy's funeral.

As she rounded the corner of the engine, Joey clapped her on the back. "Hey, Reid, welcome back."

"Thanks." She squeezed his shoulder as they walked into the station side by side.

"The chief wants to see you," Nathan called out from the kitchen.

"Yeah. Thanks, Brewer," Reid muttered, heading for the offices.

She knocked once on Perez's door before she pushed it open.

"What's up, Chief?"

"Sit down, Reid." Perez leaned back, regarding her across the expanse of his scarred wooden desk.

Reid saw kindness in his eyes and sympathy on his expressive features. He folded his hands together over his sizeable belly and didn't say anything until she was settled in the chair.

"How are you doing?"

"I'm okay."

"How are the ribs?"

"Fine." She still had some soreness but it was nothing she couldn't handle. And she certainly wasn't going to risk being put on light duty by admitting it.

"Good. Are you sure you're ready to be back?"

Reid tensed, suddenly feeling defensive. She'd already been off for more than a week, and it wasn't going to get any easier to return.

"I'm ready."

"Listen, nobody would blame you if you took a few more days."

"To do what, Chief? I just want to get to work."

"Okay. If you need anything, my door is open." She stood but he stopped her. "Reid, headquarters is assigning a rookie to your crew."

"Chief," Reid started to argue. The last thing they needed to worry about was training a rookie.

"This decision comes from higher up, Reid. It's a done deal. She starts today. And there's one more thing." He hesitated. Reid waited. "You know you were the next one in line for a promotion. Effective immediately, your rank is captain. And they decided to keep you with your crew."

She was stunned. She had known she was near the top of the list, had been for six months. Jimmy had helped her study for the test, and when they had posted the results he had helped her celebrate. They had sat on his back porch, each holding a beer, and he congratulated her. She'd argued that she had only ranked seventh.

"But the list is good for a year. They'll definitely make that many captains in a year. You are so *in,* Captain Webb," he'd said with a grin.

He'd been right. They had promoted everyone ahead of her and she had been next in line for over a month, but to get promoted like this felt tainted. She didn't want to take Jimmy's place on the crew, and she didn't want some rookie coming in to take hers. She wanted things the way they had been.

Isabel settled on the sofa with her open laptop. The early-morning sun stretched across the hardwood floor. The spacious feel of the living room, which boasted large windows on both exterior walls, was one of the features Isabel liked best. It helped keep her from feeling totally closed in by the recent upheaval in her life.

She hadn't been sleeping much the past few days. When she'd found she was irrevocably awake at five a.m. she forced herself to lie in bed a bit longer. By the time she heard Reid outside cursing, she was certain sleep wasn't going to come. She'd heard Reid's failed attempts to crank the engine and, after putting a robe on over her silk nightshirt, had gone outside. When she'd offered the use of Jimmy's truck, she had seen pain wash over Reid's face, her mouth tight and her eyes sad. The unexpected flash of vulnerability had pulled at Isabel, momentarily overshadowing her resentment and anger. Without thinking, she had offered to drive her and was actually relieved when Reid refused. After watching Reid ride away, Isabel had come back inside and proceeded to stare listlessly at the morning news.

Having finally decided to get some work done, she stuck a pen behind her ear and laid an open file next to her computer. She quickly scrolled through her e-mail, responding to a few urgent messages. Then she consulted the notes she'd taken the previous day and began to methodically research a series of new investment options.

Before long her mind wandered away from the figures in front of her. She had been having a hard time putting things in perspective lately. Less than two weeks ago she'd had a routine. Her life had been structured and she was reaching all of her goals. She had worked quite hard to get to that safe place after the last time her life took a sharp turn.

Isabel had been a student at the University of Tennessee in Knoxville when her parents and Amanda died. After that, she had spent several weeks clocking over a thousand miles a week driving back and forth from Nashville to school in order to be with Jimmy, who was left alone with a newborn.

But when she began to talk about dropping out and moving home, Jimmy refused to consider it. He had argued that Reid and Meredith lived just next door and were willing to help him out, and she was torn between wanting to be with Jimmy and Chase and the urge to run away from her grief at losing her parents. In the end, when he reminded her tearfully how proud their parents had been when she'd been accepted to UT, she gave in.

She had been lonely during that first year back in school. She knew Jimmy felt responsible for her and was working double shifts to pay her tuition. She felt guilty and missed her parents terribly. Every time she went home she felt the emptiness in her heart more acutely than she had during the last visit. As the months dragged by, she made more excuses about why she couldn't make it home during each break.

When she graduated and a Knoxville-based financial-planning firm offered her a prestigious job, she had accepted. During her three years at Becker, Strouse, and Baxter, Isabel worked hard and built her reputation. So when she decided to establish her own consulting business, several of her clients followed. She loved the independence that being her own boss gave her. After her initial meeting with each client to determine their financial needs, she could work primarily from home by phone or computer.

Now all of that had to change. Remembering how devastated she had felt after her parents' death, Isabel couldn't even imagine experiencing that loss at Chase's age. That fire had changed all of their lives, but no one was more ill-equipped to handle the trauma than Chase. Everything else in her life would have to take a backseat to a seven-year-old boy—a boy, it seemed, who didn't even want her around.

In the few days since Jimmy's funeral he'd been sullen and distant with her. She, in turn, felt awkward with him. She had no idea what to say or do, and every time she tried she got it wrong. He clammed up every time she talked to him about Jimmy. But when she avoided talking about Jimmy, Chase didn't behave any better. Today, his first day back in school, he'd been grumpy at breakfast because she put too much milk on his cereal. When she'd dropped him off at school he took his lunch money from her and climbed out of the car silently.

Regardless of whether either of them liked the way things were, Isabel was his guardian now. And she wouldn't turn her back on that responsibility. She would act in his best interest, just as Jimmy had acted in hers.

She picked up the pen and notebook from the coffee table and began to make a list. She could always think more clearly if she had a list. She wrote down the pros and cons of forcing Chase to relocate. Her client base was in Knoxville, and she wasn't sure how many accounts she would risk by moving to Nashville. Knoxville was her home now, and if Nashville had reminded her of those she'd lost before, it would probably be worse now, living in Jimmy's house.

But Chase was a just a child. And everything he knew was here. He lived in a house with a yard, and her apartment was in the city. In Knoxville she would be raising him alone. Here Chase would still have Reid and Meredith, whom he relied on so heavily. He had just lost his father. *Is it really fair to take him away from the rest of his family and friends just because I'm afraid to stay in Nashville?* She knew the answer even before she asked, but that didn't make the realization that her life was no longer entirely her own any easier.

❖

"Come on, Moss. You mean to tell me you actually like this stuff?"

Nathan and Joey sat side by side on the faded and sagging couch, their feet propped up on the coffee table in front of them. The television was tuned to a popular custom-truck repair show.

"Do you have to give me a hard time every day, Brewer?"

"Hey, go easy on him, Joey," Reid warned from the armchair nearby. "You know he'd rather be watching his soaps."

Chief Perez cleared his throat from the doorway and cut short whatever comeback Nathan was about to spout. They all looked up at the woman who stood next to Perez. She definitely had Reid's attention. Taller than the chief by several inches, she had a smooth caramel complexion, a smile that warmed her dark brown eyes, and her braided hair in a ponytail at the base of her neck. Her blue uniform showed off a solid physique. *Uniform?*

"Meet the newest member of your crew, Megan Edge." Perez moved aside and ushered her in. "That's Joey Moss, the engineer. Over there is Nathan Brewer. And our newly promoted captain, Reid Webb."

"What? Captain? Way to go, Reid." Joey reached across Nathan to shake her hand.

"You didn't tell them?"

"Ah, no, Chief, I hadn't gotten around to it yet." She'd been waiting for the promotion, but now she almost wished they had moved her to another station with the change in rank. Stepping into Jimmy's shoes was just going to be too hard.

"No time like the present. Why don't you give Edge the rundown on this place and show her where to stow her gear."

Minutes later as Reid led Megan through the truck bay, the newcomer ventured, "I get the impression you aren't pleased with your new title."

Reid ignored her words. "You can put your turnout gear over there." With some effort, she indicated the empty hook where Jimmy's coat used to hang. She wished she could leave it empty, but they were already pressed for space.

Megan made another attempt. "I'm sorry, have I done something wrong?"

At least she's direct. That was one point in her favor. Reid waited while she stowed her things.

She had stopped checking Megan out the moment the chief uttered the words *crew member*. She had learned her lesson about getting involved with women at work. She still felt awkward when she ran into Susannah, and they weren't even on the same crew. Her relationship with the paramedic from Station 12 had ended badly. After dating for several months, Reid could tell their relationship wasn't going anywhere. Unfortunately Susannah didn't see things the same way, even after Reid broke it off.

"It's not you," Reid responded neutrally. Though Reid resented Megan's presence, this was Reid's issue and she would deal with it.

The station speakers echoed throughout the truck bay with the dispatch information: a vehicle was on fire on the side of I-24. Reid stopped next to the row of jackets hanging on the wall and shoved her feet into her boots. She grabbed the turnout pants that were folded down over the tops and yanked them up over her hips. As she began to move, she looped the suspenders over her shoulders and the rest of her crew ran by in various states of dress, headed for the engine. Reid hesitated for only a second before she tossed the rest of her gear on the floorboard of the passenger seat, then climbed in beside Joey.

When they arrived, the front of the SUV was completely engulfed in flames. The driver had maneuvered to the side of the road, but traffic was still backing up as motorists slowed to get a look. Joey positioned the engine a safe distance from the car, angled to force the flow of cars away from the scene.

"Brewer, Edge, get on that line."

Reid forced herself to stand back and watch her crew work. Though it went against her work ethic, she would do it whenever possible over the next few weeks. She needed to get a baseline of Megan's skills. And it was important that Joey and Nathan see what she could do. Any one of them could be forced to rely on those skills someday, and they wouldn't have time to second-guess.

Megan and Nathan started pulling hose. They were both able firefighters, and to the casual observer they would appear to work well together. But to Reid they looked awkward. The difference was subtle but clear to the trained eye. She was used to a crew who could anticipate each other's actions. That effortlessness was missing now.

A tall man in a pin-striped suit stood nearby, watching the firefighters smother the flames. The tail of his jacket flapped behind him as he paced up and down the side of the road, apparently talking to himself and gesturing wildly. When he turned around and shoved his hand through his thinning hair, Reid caught sight of the wireless headset tucked around his ear. It figured. Reid had a cell phone, but she didn't understand so many people's compulsion to be in constant contact. She used hers only when necessary.

"Hey!"

Reid looked up to find the man striding toward her. *What the hell?* "Sir, you should step back over there."

"Why aren't you working?" Despite her warning he kept coming, drawing up several inches from her.

"What?"

"While you're over here lounging against your fire truck, my car is burning up. You need to get off your ass—"

"We have this under control. You need to step back, sir." Reid remained calm despite the fact that the man was jabbing his finger in her face. In her peripheral vision Reid caught the arrival of the police officer she had requested for traffic control.

"What the hell are you going to do about my car? I want to talk to your boss."

Reid flinched as he punctuated his words with a sharp poke in her shoulder. She tensed and stepped forward, not backing down. She was mentally weighing the number of days she would likely be suspended for punching him versus the measure of relief she would feel. She had been itching for an excuse to let off some steam, and this idiot just might be the ticket.

"What seems to be the problem here?" The even alto of the officer put an end to Reid's dilemma.

The man glanced at the officer behind him. "I'll tell you what the problem is. I don't pay my taxes so she can stand around."

"Well, sir," the officer smoothly steered the man away from Reid, "it looks like the fire is out. I need you to step over here and talk to the tow-truck driver so we can get things moving again out here."

Reid was stowing hose when the officer returned.

"What an ass, huh?" The officer propped herself against the engine.

Reid glanced up to find sharp eyes watching Megan and Nathan work nearby. She'd be willing to bet those eyes didn't miss much. Of course, being observant was definitely part of the police officer's job. Reid remembered her from the night of the fire, but she hadn't paid her much attention at the time. She'd sat silently in the passenger seat all the way to the hospital, fighting the feeling that she would arrive too late.

The officer's dark hair was pulled into a trim bun, and her uniform was neatly pressed. She was taller than Reid by a few inches and walked with a confident swagger.

"Thanks for handling that, Officer. I would've hated to have to punch him." Reid puffed her chest out with false bravado.

"No problem," the officer replied with a friendly smile. "And I sure wouldn't want to be the one who witnessed you assaulting a citizen."

"He would have deserved it," Reid replied stubbornly. "I appreciate your help, though." She pulled off a glove and stuck out her hand.

The officer shook it firmly. "Listen, I was real sorry to hear about your partner." She shifted from foot to foot.

"Yeah, thanks." *Damn, can't I get through even a day without talking about him?* Reid's pain over Jimmy's death seemed almost as powerful as the day she'd lost him.

Chapter Five

Isabel inched her Honda Accord forward in the long line of minivans and SUVs that filled the circular drive looping in front of Chase's school. Jimmy had insisted Chase attend a private school and had chosen Saint Catherine's for a number of reasons. Aside from having a solid reputation, it was set on a quiet block only minutes from their house.

The school was housed in a long, L-shaped building adjacent to the parking lot at the back of the stone cathedral, which held a place of honor amid the meticulously groomed lawns. It was exactly what Isabel pictured in a Catholic school. Isabel and Jimmy had gone to public school. She remembered how the private-school kids acted like they were better than them, and she wondered if that was why Jimmy chose this one.

When Isabel finally got to the front of the line, she spotted Chase slouched against the wall outside the school. He sauntered over to the car, and from the pout on his lips, she guessed he wasn't happy. He yanked open the back door and threw his backpack on the floorboard.

"Put your seat belt on, please."

He did as she asked, then slumped down in his seat.

"What's wrong?" she asked, but he didn't answer. "What are you so grumpy about? You're going over to your friend Eric's house later. You guys are going to have a great time." She checked his reflection in the mirror as she eased through the rest of the drive and onto the street.

"Everyone got to go on a field trip to a museum today, and I had to stay at school with the stupid guidance counselor."

"The guidance counselor is not stupid. Now, why didn't you get to go?" Isabel couldn't understand what had happened. If someone at the school had treated him unfairly, she would just turn the car around and go have a talk with his teachers.

"Because I didn't have a permission slip."

With a flash of guilt, Isabel remembered when he'd brought home the form. She had set it aside to fill out later and completely forgotten about it. *She* was the reason he didn't get to go to the museum with his classmates.

"Oh, Chase, I'm so sorry. I totally forgot. It won't happen again." She didn't know what to say to make it up to him.

Obviously still upset, he was silent for the rest of the drive home and Isabel mentally kicked herself. She could balance a number of complicated accounts and spout percentage rates in her sleep, but she couldn't remember to sign a damn permission slip. She was already failing miserably at this parenting thing.

"Mom, I'm home," Reid called out wearily as she entered the front door. After pulling an extra twelve-hour shift, all she wanted was to fall into bed. She dropped her keys on the table by the door and picked up a stack of mail, flipping through it as she wandered into the house.

"I'm in here, honey." Her mother's voice drifted out from the kitchen.

"Something smells good." Reid sniffed appreciatively and immediately identified the aroma of her mother's lasagna. The kitchen was definitely not Reid's domain. She couldn't handle much more than the simplest recipe.

When Reid had been fixing up the house and they started outfitting the kitchen, she had solicited her mother's advice.

Following Meredith's instructions, Reid had purchased quality cookware and appliances with stainless-steel facades so they would last. Over the years, Meredith had added her own touches, such as the wrought-iron pot rack that hung over the bar and the large spice rack that was tucked in the corner near the sink. Reid liked the feeling of permanence they provided.

"I'm going to be picking up some extra shifts in the next few weeks."

"Why?"

Reid shrugged and slid onto a bar stool. "I could use the overtime."

"Do we need the money? We're doing okay, aren't we? I can give you more if you need me to." Though Reid had tried to refuse her mother, Meredith insisted on handing over a portion of her social security check each month.

"No, Mom. We're okay. I just figured it wouldn't hurt to save some. Plus, I've been wanting to do some more remodeling around here. If I work extra through the winter and put some money away, I can get started on that in the spring."

"How much extra do you plan to work?" Meredith, bracing herself against the kitchen counter, studied her daughter. Reid looked exhausted and Meredith guessed it had to do with more than just work. But as usual Reid was difficult to read. She got that trait from her father, along with her stubbornness. Those two characteristics had been part of the reason Meredith had divorced him.

"As much as I can."

"Chase will miss having you around."

"Mom, we don't even know if he's going to be here or in Knoxville. I know it might not be the best time, but one of the guys on A shift is out sick so they need some more coverage."

"Well, we might find out something tonight. Isabel's coming for dinner. Chase is eating at a friend's house, and she said she wanted to talk to us."

"Did she say what about?"

"No."

"Well, what could it be?" Reid folded her hands together and tightened, then relaxed them repeatedly.

"I don't know, Reid. I guess we'll find out when she gets here," Meredith said in a tone intended to calm Reid.

"Do you think she's going to tell us she's taking Chase back with her? I sure hope not."

"Honey, whatever it is, we'll deal with it."

"She blames me."

Meredith looked at Reid and found eyes filled with guilt. "I'm sure she doesn't blame you. She knows the dangers of the job as well as all of us."

Reid shook her head. "She as much as told me she holds me responsible. And I don't know if I disagree."

Meredith's heart broke at the idea of her daughter carrying that kind of burden. She hoped Reid was wrong about Isabel. Reid already took on far more than she should. She certainly didn't need anyone else adding to her guilt.

"Sweetheart, you know it's not your fault."

A light tap sounded on the glass pane of the back door. Reid glanced over and Isabel offered a small wave. Reid motioned her inside.

"I brought dessert." Isabel presented a square bakery box.

Reid took it and flipped open the lid. "Mmm, chocolate cake."

Because Reid's tone sounded a bit forced, Isabel wondered if she'd interrupted a difficult conversation between mother and daughter.

Just then Reid reached into the box, but jerked her hand back when Meredith swiped it from her. "You'll ruin your dinner."

When Meredith turned to place the cake on the counter, Reid scowled at her with childish playfulness. And when Reid withdrew her hand from behind her back and stuck a finger full of frosting in her mouth, Isabel couldn't help but smile at the twinkle in her eyes.

"You girls go set the table. Dinner will be ready soon."

Meredith gestured to the plates and flatware stacked on the corner of the bar and began slicing cucumbers for the tossed salad.

In the dining room, Reid moved around the heavy pine table placing the plates and linen napkins, and Isabel followed with the utensils. Meredith brought in a large salad and a basket of bread. When all the food was on the table, they sat down.

"Everything looks great, Meredith," Isabel said as they all served themselves.

While Isabel chatted politely with Reid's mother about Chase's school and his soccer team's schedule, she noticed that Reid's attention was elsewhere and wondered why. Maybe she was impatient to know the reason for Isabel's visit but also didn't want to bring it up, afraid that it was bad news. Instead she pushed her lasagna around on her plate like Chase had done with his spaghetti and gave one-word answers when she was spoken to.

They were lingering over coffee and cake when Isabel finally raised the subject that was obviously on Reid's mind. "Well, there *is* a reason I wanted to talk to the two of you."

Though it went against her nature to ask for help, Isabel would do it. She knew she couldn't raise Chase alone, and Reid and Meredith were already an integral part of his life. She was willing to keep whatever resentment she felt toward Reid between them. She couldn't allow it to affect Chase.

"I've been giving this a lot of thought. Because I do most of my work from home, it really wouldn't be that hard for me to relocate. I should have no problem keeping my current clients, and I could cultivate some new ones."

Reid's head snapped up. "You're moving here?"

"Chase has been through so much. You're both his family, too. With everything else he's lost, it just feels cruel to take that away from him now. But I'm going to need some help."

"What can we do?" Meredith asked.

"For starters, it's going to take several days for me to go back and get things in order. I need to pack and arrange for movers. I also need to contact my clients. I was wondering if Chase could stay with you while I'm gone so he won't have to miss school."

"Of course he can. He's welcome anytime."

"When I get back it'll take me some time to get settled. But once I do, my schedule should be fairly flexible. Hopefully, I'll be able to do most of my work while he's in school. Then you won't have to spend as much time watching him."

"I don't mind at all. I enjoy having him around here," Meredith assured her.

"Sounds like you've got it all worked out," Reid said.

"Sure, in theory." Isabel felt some of the pressure in her chest ease and the tension left her. She'd made the right decision, and for the first time since Jimmy's funeral she felt like she didn't have to handle everything on her own.

The next morning, after Isabel took Chase to school, she put an overnight bag in the trunk of her car, slammed the lid, and went back to the house to lock up. Everything was arranged. Reid would pick up Chase after school.

Isabel had already made a list of things she needed to do when she got to Knoxville. It was going to cost her to get out of the lease on her apartment, so she would have to dip into her savings. But since Jimmy's insurance was paying for the mortgage on his house, it wouldn't take long to replace the money.

She returned to the car and put her briefcase in the passenger seat. A glance at her watch told her she could be in Knoxville by ten a.m.

"Hey," Reid called from the backyard, pushing through the gate.

"Hi."

"You all ready to go?"

"I think so." Isabel reached inside the open door, started the car, and cranked up the heat before she turned back to Reid.

"You'll call when you get there?"

"Yes." Isabel rolled her eyes. "Did you inherit my brother's responsibility for me?"

"He'd want us to look out for you."

Isabel felt tears well up and wondered when she would finally be able to get through a day without crying. She bit her lower lip but was unable to stop a small sob and the tears that spilled over.

"Hey, come on, don't do that." Reid gathered her close.

When strong arms encircled her, Isabel briefly struggled against them. She didn't want comfort; she wanted to hang on to her anger at Reid. She couldn't let herself forget that if not for Reid, Jimmy would never have been inside that building.

But as she fought her tears and the embrace, the arms around her tightened. And it felt so good to be held that eventually she relaxed. She just needed a minute. Jimmy had grounded her and provided the one remaining safe place she had always known she could return to if life got too overwhelming. She hadn't appreciated him enough, and now he was gone. She had tried to be strong for Chase and because she was afraid of letting go, but now she was exhausted. Reid's compact body was solid against hers, and for a moment she didn't feel quite so alone.

"Better?" Reid asked when Isabel's tears slowed.

Isabel nodded. "Yes, thank you," she rasped close to Reid's ear. She drew back slightly. The concern in Reid's eyes was mixed with something else that Isabel didn't understand, but her body responded with a flush of warmth and she couldn't keep from staring at Reid's mouth. Suddenly she wanted very badly to see how those lips would feel against hers. Instead, before she could stop herself, she pressed a kiss to Reid's cheek.

"Okay, drive safely, then." Reid released her quickly, opened the car door, and waited while she climbed inside.

As Reid closed the door Isabel met her eyes and found the expected compassion, but also a degree of distance. She'd felt the tightening of Reid's arms and heard the indrawn breath as she'd brushed her mouth against Reid's cheek. But she hadn't expected the twinge in her own stomach. Suddenly she was glad she would have a couple of days away to settle her emotions.

❖

"Damn it!" The wrench slipped off the nut and Reid's knuckles slammed against the motor. She sucked a breath through her teeth and shook her hand, waiting for the blood flow to return to her tingling fingers.

A full day of running every errand she could invent and fixing everything in the house in an attempt to distract herself hadn't done any good. Her mind kept conjuring up the feel of Isabel in her arms and Isabel's lips against her cheek. When Isabel had started crying, Reid had been intent only on comforting her. She had felt protective and Isabel's vulnerability tore at her. But the brief kiss had changed everything. For a split second she'd registered the feel of Isabel's body pressed against hers. *Get over yourself, Webb. I'm sure she didn't give it a second thought.*

"Whatcha doing?" Chase said from behind her.

Bracing his hand on her shoulder, he watched as she stubbornly applied wrench to nut once more.

"Trying to fix my bike."

"What's wrong with it?"

"I'm not sure yet, buddy. What are you doing?" Reid laid down the wrench. If she kept at it she'd be cursing again, and she tried to watch her language around Chase.

Chase shrugged. "I've got a soccer game this weekend."

"Yeah?"

"Yep." He hesitated. "Dad always helped me practice."

"Well, come on. Let's see what you've got." She pulled a rag from her back pocket, wiped her grease-smeared hands on it, then tossed it on the nearby workbench.

While Reid wandered across the lawn, Chase ran next door to get the soccer ball from his garage. It was just cool enough for the sweatshirt she'd pulled on that morning, but the sun shone brightly in a clear blue sky. She drew a deep breath, filling her lungs with crisp autumn air.

As Chase dribbled toward her, Reid gave him her attention.

"That tree and that big rock over there," Chase called out, pointing to establish the makeshift goal posts.

Reid nodded and moved into position between them. Chase dribbled toward her, faking around invisible defenders. With only a year of experience, Chase was already showing promise. Reid had been to several of his games. At an age when most of the other kids were running haphazardly around the field with little knowledge of the mechanics of the game, Chase displayed a level of skill above that of his teammates. If he stayed interested, he would be a talented player someday. However, Reid suspected he'd heard enough of his father's old football stories that his focus would most likely swing that way eventually.

Wherever his interests lay, Reid was sure he would excel. He had his father's heart, and when he put his mind to something he succeeded, as evidenced by the stinging in her hands after she deflected about a dozen of his shots, not to mention the ones that flew past her.

Thirty minutes later, when Meredith stuck her head out the front door and called them for dinner, Reid was actually relieved for the break.

"Let's go wash up." She abandoned her post in front of the goal.

Chase spun around and kicked the ball across the driveway, where it came to rest in his yard.

"Put it away," Reid admonished when it became clear he was going to leave it there. She didn't miss his scowl as he trudged toward the ball, but he obeyed. She sighed. She knew Chase was having a difficult time, but his attitude had become increasingly worse. He had been more distant than usual with her, and she had watched him shut out Isabel as well. She ached for him but realized that as much as she wanted to, she couldn't fix everything for him. She couldn't give him back his father.

❖

Isabel picked at her salad, barely tasting the bite she forked into her mouth. As soon as she had returned to Knoxville she had begun calling her clients. Several were uncomfortable with staying with her after she moved, and she told them she completely understood. People tended to get nervous about their money and wanted someone local. So she offered to make a referral, and three out of the four accepted. She'd wished the fourth luck and promised to send over the necessary papers for them to go to someone else.

She'd invited her friend and colleague Anna Hill to lunch to discuss taking on the other three. Anna now sat across from her at a downtown café known for great soup and salads.

"Are you sure about this?" Anna asked, concern evident in her blue eyes. She'd remained silent while Isabel explained her plan to relocate.

"I think it's the best thing for Chase."

"We'll miss you."

"I'll miss you, too."

"How are *you* doing?" Anna covered Isabel's hand with hers.

"I don't know," Isabel admitted. "It hasn't sunk in yet. I'm walking around in a daze." Isabel felt comfortable talking to Anna, who was one of the few people she fully trusted. When they'd met in college they'd bonded over their shared misfortune in ending up in an especially difficult English lit class.

Complete opposites, they were an unlikely pair. Anna, with her blond hair and small, shapely figure, was outgoing and friendly. Isabel, taller and lithe, was shy and tended to linger at the edges of the action. But they balanced each other and had remained friends, even when after college they'd accepted jobs at competing firms.

As Isabel carefully sorted her thoughts, she outlined the events since Jimmy's funeral. She talked about the challenges she hadn't expected when she assumed Chase's care, about how he resented her authority, especially when it conflicted with those areas Meredith or Reid usually dealt with.

Isabel had discovered a dynamic among the three adults in

Chase's life that she hadn't been aware of, a strange team effort that had worked quite well until Jimmy's death had upset the balance.

She also described the shift in her relationship with Reid, carefully steering clear of the animosity she couldn't voice. "It's so weird because I feel like I'm coparenting with someone I don't even know. I haven't spent that much time around her since we were kids."

Since the episode at her grandparents' house, Isabel had kept a marked distance between herself and Reid. She flashed on Reid as a child who followed Jimmy everywhere, and she pushed aside a kernel of resentment. She already had enough to deal with, and it wouldn't do any good to rehash her childhood antagonism toward Reid. When she did, she only succeeded in getting those old feelings twisted up with her new anger over Jimmy's death. "Aside from socializing with her during a few family holidays, the most I know of who she's become as an adult is what Jimmy told me."

"Which is?"

"She's very committed to her job and family."

"That's good." Anna paused as the waiter approached and they both ordered coffee. "Isn't it?" she asked when Isabel remained silent.

"I guess."

"What are you not telling me?"

"Nothing." Isabel's mind flickered briefly to the feeling of being in Reid's arms and her skin, surprisingly soft beneath Isabel's lips as she kissed her cheek.

Caught off guard by the direction of her thoughts and needing to focus on the task at hand, Isabel flipped open the first of the three portfolios. "Jack and Erica Simms. They're in pretty good shape and they're easy to work with."

For the next thirty minutes she went through each of the three folders and outlined the contents. Anna took notes and promised to call the people in question later that day to discuss their accounts. By the end of lunch Isabel was confident her clients were in good hands and was ready to head back to Nashville and deal with the situation there. She just hoped Reid would let that kiss go unaddressed, because Isabel still didn't understand the reaction the brief contact stirred in her.

Chapter Six

Saturday afternoon, Reid pulled into Saint Catherine's lot and parked her motorcycle next to Isabel's car. She stripped off her leather jacket and laid it over the seat. Though it was a beautifully sunny day, she had needed the jacket while she rode. As she neared the stand of bleachers occupied by the home team's cheering section, she waved in response to greetings from the parents of several of Chase's teammates.

"Eddie, get in the net. Guys, take some shots, but take it easy on him, please."

Reid grinned at the warning from Chase's coach. She had been to enough practices to know that without his warning they would pummel the young goalie, all firing shots at once.

Isabel stood to one side of the cluster of parents, her arms folded across her chest as she watched the boys warm up. She merely glanced in Reid's direction before she resumed tracking Chase across the field.

"Hey," Reid called as she approached.

Isabel lifted her chin in greeting. They stood side by side for a moment, both watching Chase as he practiced dribbling the ball against one of his friends. He faked a move right, then cut left when the other boy went for the ball.

"He's a natural." Reid smiled proudly and looked at Isabel for confirmation.

Isabel didn't respond and her attention didn't leave the field.

"Okay, well, enjoy the game." Irritated, Reid turned away. She didn't need to stand there and be ignored.

Realizing Reid was angry at her distraction, Isabel put a restraining hand on her arm. She was still of two minds where Reid was concerned—torn between anger and a growing awareness of Reid's very physical presence that still confused her. But she couldn't deny how much Reid cared for Chase, often putting his needs ahead of her own. Just that morning Reid had come home from a twenty-four-hour shift and, instead of going to bed, had helped Chase warm up for today's game.

"Will you watch with me? I don't really know anyone else here."

Wordlessly, Reid returned to Isabel's side. As the game began, they stood, shoulders almost touching, and cheered Chase on, often smiling at each other when he made a quick move around an opponent.

Well into the first half Chase dribbled down the field and was challenged by a shorter, wiry boy. Chase lunged to the left and, expecting the other boy to go for his fake, he flicked his right foot to push the ball around his opponent. The boy saw it coming and jabbed his own foot forward to swipe the ball from Chase. Before Chase could recover, the other boy was several strides away and heading for the goal.

"It's okay, Chase," Isabel called out, clapping.

"Get back in there," Reid chimed in.

Chase caught up with him just as he took a shot that went wide of the goal. One of Chase's teammates kicked the ball into play and the game was back on. Determination set on his features, Chase raced down the field. Just past midfield he cut sharply to the inside, edging out an opponent in time to receive a pass from his teammate. A burst of speed kept him ahead of the other player long enough to get him in range for a shot. The ball sailed past the goalie and hit the back of the net.

"All right, Chase!" Reid yelled, pumping her fist.

Isabel screamed and, jumping up and down, flung herself against Reid, who barely managed to catch her. Her arms wrapped around Isabel and kept them both from toppling to the ground. Caught up in the excitement of the game, Isabel pressed against Reid for a moment. Then she realized what she was doing, pulled back, and tugged down the hem of her shirt where it had ridden up.

"I'm sorry."

"It's okay."

Neither of them said anything more. When they returned to the action on the field, Isabel shifted slightly to put more space between them. She glanced around but no one seemed to be paying them any attention. She'd been so thrilled by Chase's goal. It was that simple. The fact that the hard lines of Reid's body seemed imprinted against hers shouldn't bother her. And the slight breeze that stirred around them no doubt carried the lingering smell of Reid's clean scent. *This is ridiculous. What exactly am I trying to talk myself out of here?*

Rushing over at the end of the game after his coach had excused them, Chase called, "Did you see? Did you see my goal, Reid?"

"I saw it. That was awesome," she exclaimed, giving him a high five.

"It was very impressive, Chase," Isabel said. She'd never seen him play before. He really was very good.

"Thanks."

"Do you have all of your stuff, Chase? We're going to head home."

"Yeah, I've got it." He hefted the backpack higher on his shoulder and asked Reid, "Are you coming over for dinner?"

She glanced at Isabel. "Uh, I don't know."

"Come on," he pled.

"It's okay. We've got plenty," Isabel added quietly. "You can invite your mother, too."

"Tonight is her poker night. I was going to be on my own."

Reid couldn't tell if Isabel was sincere or if the invitation was for Chase's benefit, but she decided to take advantage of the situation. "So, if you're sure, I'd love to."

"I'm sure. It's fine."

"Can I ride with you?" Chase tugged at Reid's hand as they approached the parking lot. He loved being on the back of a motorcycle and had been riding with Jimmy since he was small enough to fit on the gas tank in front of him. Amanda had hated it, but it was one of the few arguments she never won with Jimmy. He'd loved having his boy with him on the bike and always drove with extra care when Chase was along.

"Sorry, buddy, I didn't bring an extra helmet. I'll meet you there." She waited while he climbed into the car, then spoke to Isabel through the open window. "Do you need me to bring anything?"

"Just you," Isabel replied, and Reid wondered if she imagined the slightly husky quality in her voice. *Of course I did.* She convinced herself quickly because if she didn't, she was afraid she would start seeing flirtation where none existed. She'd carefully constructed defenses against Isabel's indifference over the years, and the crumbling of those walls would only increase her emotional stress.

Isabel was pulling the spinach-and-cheese casserole she'd made earlier from the oven when she heard Reid's bike in the driveway next door. She'd been back from Knoxville for two days, but before the soccer game she hadn't spent time with Reid except in passing. Meredith said she'd been working extra shifts, and Isabel decided it was probably for the best. Things were a lot less complicated when she wasn't around Reid.

She cringed as she recalled the awkward tension that had followed their embrace earlier at the game. God, she had literally thrown herself into Reid's arms. Then she had counted the minutes until the game was over so she could escape. But Chase had issued the dinner invitation, and Isabel couldn't think of a feasible reason not to include Reid.

Chase ran to the front door and flung it open just as Reid climbed the steps.

"Aunt Isabel made spinach," he complained as he followed Reid into the kitchen. He wrinkled his nose, clearly disapproving of her choice of entrée. "Can I have a bologna sandwich?"

"Yes, Chase," Isabel said. As she pulled lunch meat and cheese slices out of the refrigerator, she said to Reid, "I've given up trying to feed him anything but bologna lately. Good thing he eats at your house several times a week. Meredith doesn't seem to have any trouble getting him to eat."

"Well, he and Jimmy had dinner over there most nights anyway. When Mom left us to our own devices, Jimmy and I would take him out for pizza."

Reid stood hesitantly in the doorway. She wasn't certain Isabel wanted her here and thought maybe she'd been included only to appease Chase.

"Will you get Chase a glass of milk?" Isabel asked as she spooned casserole onto two plates. "And help yourself, too. I have milk, water, soda, or beer."

After they had gotten drinks and set the table, Reid noticed Isabel watching her.

"What?" she asked.

"Nothing." Isabel picked up her fork, but she waited.

Reid took a bite of the casserole and paused, then looked up to find Isabel's expectant gaze still on her. She forced herself to chew and swallow.

"It's good," she lied.

Satisfied, Isabel took her own bite, then raised an eyebrow at Reid as she laid down her fork. "So you really like it?" she challenged.

"Um, yeah."

"Well, then, eat up because there's plenty more for seconds." Isabel smiled as she watched Reid's expression change. "It's bad, isn't it?"

"No, it's—um…" She grinned. "It's a good thing my mom can cook."

"Why?"

"Because if it was up to you and me, Chase would starve."

Isabel laughed and pushed her plate away. "I must have done something wrong with the recipe, because this is horrible."

"Do you have any of that bologna left?"

For the first time in a long while, Isabel shared a laugh with Reid, and the release made her feel lighter. In that heartbeat, no guilt or responsibility intruded between them. And though she knew reality would return, she absorbed the feeling and locked it away.

❖

After they'd eaten their sandwiches, Reid had helped Isabel clean up. Still in the kitchen, Chase asked Reid, "We rented a movie. Will you stay?"

She glanced over his head at Isabel, who paused in the middle of pulling a bowl from the cabinet and shrugged. "I'm making popcorn."

"Well, if there's going to be popcorn how can I say no? But"—she crossed to Isabel and took the bowl from her—"you'd better let me make it." She grinned and sidestepped quickly to avoid Isabel's playful slap.

When the popcorn was ready, they settled on the sofa with Chase between them, the large bowl in his lap. Three glasses of grape soda sat on the coffee table in front of them, despite Isabel's argument that it was too late for Chase to have any. When both Chase and Reid insisted they couldn't eat popcorn without it, she'd relented. Reid wasn't sure who her muttered "spoiled" was directed at, but when she saw the small smile that accompanied it she didn't care.

The movie had been chosen for Chase's benefit, and Reid found her attention wandering from the animated film. She probably should care if that little clown fish was reunited with his dad, and under other circumstances she might have. But with Isabel so close, Reid just couldn't summon the interest.

Despite the less-than-stellar dinner, it had actually been a nice day. She'd enjoyed watching the game with Isabel, apart from a bit of awkwardness. Spending the evening with Chase and Isabel had been comfortable—she was surprised at just how comfortable. Chase was tucked against her side, his eyes riveted on the screen.

On the other side of him, Isabel also appeared to be watching the movie. In the darkened room, the light from the screen flickered across her features and added a sharp edge to the planes of her face. The intimacy of the moment made it easy for Reid to forget that Isabel most likely didn't want her around.

The reminder of the animosity that usually emanated from Isabel was enough to break whatever spell Reid was under, and she returned her attention to the movie. By the time the credits rolled, Chase was asleep. He leaned against Isabel with his legs draped over Reid's lap.

"He's out cold." Isabel stroked his soft bangs back from his forehead. He looked angelic in sleep, his thick lashes resting against his cheeks. "And he needs a haircut."

"The shaggy look is in again," Reid said with a grin. She shifted from beneath his legs. "I'll put him to bed for you." She scooped him up and held him against her chest. "It won't be long before he's too big for this," she grunted as she disappeared down the hallway.

"He already is," Isabel mumbled, glad for the physical fitness required for Reid's job. Chase had inherited his father's height and, if it hadn't been for Reid, Isabel probably would have had to wake him instead of being able to heft him up the stairs.

When Reid returned, Isabel had cleaned up the remnants of their snack, turned off the movie, and was flipping through channels to find something on television.

"You've been working an awful lot lately," Isabel said as Reid settled back on the opposite end of the sofa.

"I have to pay the bills."

Isabel suspected the reason had little to do with needing the money. "Are there any limits? You look exhausted. Yet you stayed to watch the movie."

"Chase wanted me to."

"He's been having such a hard time. It probably doesn't help that I'm hopelessly lost when it comes to him. I don't know how much to push him to talk. And even if he did, how would I explain why any of this happened?"

"Bad things happen to good people," Reid muttered with a shrug.

Isabel stared at her.

"What?"

"It's that easy, huh?" Isabel challenged, then rushed on without waiting for an answer. "No emotions, just cut-and-dried."

"Give me a break, Iz."

Isabel bristled at the abbreviation of her name, but she remained silent.

"I'm trying to hold everything together here. Work, my crew, Chase."

"Yourself," Isabel supplied.

"What?"

"You forgot to mention yourself. Reid, you're so busy worrying about everyone else. What about you?"

"I'm fine." Reid waved off Isabel's words.

"You're exhausted. You should have gone home and gone to bed. But you stayed because Chase wanted you to."

"I'm not sleeping that well anyway."

"Why not?"

Reid shrugged. "I don't know."

Isabel didn't have much frame of reference prior to Jimmy's death, but since then she'd seen Reid try to be everything to everyone. She'd been the support for each of them, but tonight lines circled her eyes, which were dulled by fatigue. Reid didn't strike her as the type that opened up to just anyone. And, Isabel realized, she'd just lost her best friend who was, aside from her mother, the one person she could talk to. Isabel felt the carefully cultivated distance between them crumbling.

"How are you really doing, Reid?"

"I'm fine," she repeated.

Isabel studied her for a moment longer, trying to gauge how likely she was to disclose anything further. Finally, she decided on a different approach.

"Come on. Give." Isabel patted her lap in invitation. Reid gave her a blank look. "You need to learn to relax. And this is your first lesson." Isabel grabbed Reid's feet and pulled them into her lap.

"I know how to relax," Reid protested. She groaned as Isabel began to knead the ball of one foot through her sock.

"Sure you do."

"You have strong hands," Reid said, obviously already giving in to the pleasure that Isabel's fingers produced.

"You sound surprised," Isabel teased.

Reid moaned softly as Isabel dug her talented thumbs into her arch.

"You don't see me as the strong type?" Isabel asked without feeling a trace of defensiveness.

"Mmm…I don't see you as the manual-labor type."

"Well, normally I'm not," Isabel confessed. "But in this case, it's warranted. When was the last time you let go and allowed someone to take care of you?"

"I don't remember. But it's not like I have any complaints."

"No?"

Reid murmured something unintelligible.

"You don't have to do everything by yourself," Isabel said quietly.

When she received no response she glanced at Reid's face. Her eyes were closed, her features relaxed, and her breathing had deepened. Isabel pulled the throw from the back of the couch and spread it over them.

She settled back to watch television and continued to massage the feet in her lap. *How is it possible to have so many conflicting feelings at once?* She wanted to blame Reid, she *did*, because it was easier than blaming Jimmy or, worse, accepting that no one was culpable. She wanted to cling to the tight fist of anger in her heart.

Yet she sometimes felt that she could see Reid's heart, and she sensed Reid would give anything to change the outcome of that horrible fire. Looking at Reid beside her, so exhausted she couldn't stay awake, Isabel found it difficult to harden herself against the tenderness she felt.

Chapter Seven

Reid awoke disoriented. She tried to stretch and felt a weight pin her down. Rubbing her eyes, she waited for her vision to clear. It took only a second to determine that she had slept on Isabel's couch, but, more surprisingly, Isabel appeared to have done the same. She was tucked alongside Reid, her upper body and one leg on Reid, her head on Reid's chest. Reid's hand rested in the small of her back, her fingers in the gentle dip of Isabel's spine. Isabel's soft curves yielded to hers, fitting together like pieces of a puzzle that didn't appear to match until they slipped into place so perfectly.

She lay there for a moment longer, enjoying the feel of Isabel's warmth against her. She guessed Isabel had innocently fallen asleep next to her, and then they'd both shifted in their sleep to end up in this position. That was probably the only way she would find herself so close to Isabel.

Not wanting to face the awkwardness that would no doubt accompany Isabel waking while sprawled atop her, Reid began to extricate herself. Isabel's arm tightened around Reid's waist and she nuzzled Reid's neck. Isabel's breath fluttered across Reid's sensitive skin and Reid stifled a groan. She waited for Isabel to relax again, then slowly shifted toward the edge of the sofa. Unfortunately, at the same time Isabel rolled away, pushing against her. Unprepared for the sudden movement, Reid smothered a curse as she fell off the edge and hit the floor between the sofa and the coffee table. She rubbed a sore hip as she limped toward the kitchen.

The predawn horizon, tinged with pink, cast a pale glow through the window. She started making a pot of coffee, more to have something to do than out of necessity. For the first time in months, she had awakened feeling rested and without the compulsion for caffeine clawing at her.

When she carried two steaming mugs into the living room, Isabel was just waking. She sat up, wrapped in the blanket, and tried to straighten her hair. She looked adorably disheveled.

"Good morning." Reid handed Isabel one of the mugs and settled down next to her. "I'm sorry I fell asleep on you last night. You should've made me wake up and sent me home."

"Obviously, I fell asleep before I meant to as well." Isabel sipped carefully. She eyed Reid's still-full mug and decided that, considering her mood, she must've had a cup already. Reid's clothes were rumpled and her hair stood on end, but her full lips were quick to smile. "I'm sorry if I drooled on you," Isabel joked.

"Well, that *would* explain this wet spot on my shirt," Reid teased, tugging at the shoulder of her shirt.

"Would you like some breakfast?" Isabel said, standing and heading for the kitchen. Reid followed.

"No thanks. I don't usually eat until I get to the station."

"Are you working today?"

"Yeah."

"No rest for the wicked, huh?" Isabel studied her across the kitchen. She sometimes yearned for this kind of interaction, talking with someone about plans for the day over morning coffee. The warm feeling of knowing she had slept next to that person the night before, comforted by their solid presence. It had been some time since she'd experienced the sensation, and certainly never with a woman. So why did it feel completely natural to be sharing her waking moments with Reid? She told herself it was not that surprising, considering how emotional she was these days.

She faintly recalled waking sometime in the middle of the

night tangled up with Reid. But since Reid had been gone when she awoke, she wasn't sure if it had been a dream. It was quite possible they'd slept on opposite ends of the sofa, wasn't it? Looking at Reid's face, still flushed from sleep, she preferred to think they did. She didn't want to examine the quickening of her heart at the image of her sleeping in Reid's arms.

"Do you want a refill?"

"No, thanks, I'm good. I'm going to take off before Chase gets up."

"Why? It's no big deal if he knows you slept on the sofa."

"We just won't tell him that you slept with me, huh?" Reid only realized how her words sounded as they came out. But before she could correct them, Isabel was speaking.

"It was completely innocent," she argued, despite the flush creeping up her neck.

"I know." *Innocent? There was nothing innocent about the thoughts I was having just before you pushed me off the sofa.*

"You're probably right. I need to get him up and dressed anyway, and he won't be as accommodating if he's distracted by you."

"Now why would you assume I would be a distraction?" Reid called over her shoulder as she walked out, not waiting for an answer. *Because you sure as hell distract me.*

After Reid left, Isabel headed upstairs to Chase's room but found herself in Jimmy's bedroom next door instead. She'd been living in his house, sleeping in the guest room because she couldn't bring herself to disturb his things. It looked the same as she remembered. Their mother had made the threadbare quilt that covered the full-sized bed in the center of the room. She'd spent months collecting just the right fabrics for the double-wedding-ring pattern as a gift for Jimmy and Amanda.

Isabel lightly touched the top of the mahogany dresser and let her fingertips trace through a thin layer of dust, the only evidence of the occupant's absence. The surface was littered with pieces of Jimmy—the ever-present scatter of loose change, a movie ticket stub, and one of Chase's toy cars.

Three framed photographs testified to what Jimmy had valued most in his life. The first had been taken fifteen years before, but Isabel remembered the occasion like it was yesterday. Her mother had wanted a family picture for their Christmas cards. Teenagers Jimmy and Isabel couldn't have been less interested in sitting for a portrait. Wanting to make their mother happy, their father had put his foot down. Jimmy begrudgingly put on a tie and Isabel donned her best Sunday dress. They all pasted smiles on their faces long enough to take the photo. Isabel remembered being irritated because her friends had been going to the mall and she'd had to accompany her family to the portrait studio instead.

The second was a candid shot, with nothing posed about it. Amanda stood on a beach squinting against the bright sunlight. The sundress she wore couldn't hide the roundness of her stomach. She was near the end of her pregnancy, and from Amanda's wide smile and the love shining in her eyes, Isabel guessed that Jimmy had been behind the camera. She then spied a wallet-sized photo tucked into the corner of the frame. Isabel knew it was Chase's latest school photo because she'd had the same one sitting on her desk in Knoxville. Seeing Amanda's and Chase's faces so close together made the resemblance between mother and son even more apparent.

The final photograph was similar to the one that held a place of honor on Reid's mantel. Reid and Jimmy stood in front of a fire engine, but in this shot they were clowning around. They'd both pushed up the sleeves of their T-shirts and were flexing their arms. Jimmy was an ox of a man, thick and solid all the way around. He was at least six inches taller than Reid, and his broad shoulders and chest made her look petite. But Isabel knew Reid was both compact and strong, because the bicep that protruded from her sleeve was firm and round.

Though Isabel hadn't been there at the time, it took little effort for her to picture the moments before the photo was taken.

Their wide grins held traces of their shared laughter. Looking at this picture, Isabel realized again what Reid had lost and that she and Jimmy had shared a connection as strong as any blood tie. *In fact, it was stronger than the one between Jimmy and me,* she thought with resentment.

❖

Reid steered her motorcycle into the parking lot of the station and scowled at the muddy tire tracks that crisscrossed the concrete in front of the truck bay. She took off her helmet and rested it on the gas tank against the crook of the handlebars. As she stepped inside the station, she slipped off her sunglasses.

Joey stood in front of the stove making his trademark Southwestern omelets. The pungent odors of cheese and jalapeños filled the kitchen, and a gentle sizzle rose from the skillet. He transferred freshly cooked bacon to a plate and put it on the table.

"Where's Nathan?"

Joey jerked his chin toward the archway that led to the living room. Nathan was sprawled on the couch leafing through a magazine.

"Good morning," Megan called out as she came in. "Mmm, Joey, something smells great." She dropped into a chair at the table.

"Got a job for you," Reid called to Nathan. She folded her arms over her chest.

"Yeah," he drawled, not looking up.

"I need you to go hose the mud off the concrete out front."

He didn't move.

"Now, Brewer. We've got a Cub Scout troop coming for a tour this morning and I want that cleaned up."

He lifted his eyes indolently. "Are you forgetting I'm not the rookie anymore? Isn't the grunt work someone else's job now?" He cast a pointed look in Megan's direction.

Megan stood and reached for her coat.

"Sit down, Megan," Reid said over her shoulder.

"I don't mind—"

"No. Nathan will do it because I'm pretty sure if I go outside and look at the tires on that jacked-up redneck truck of his, I'll see the treads loaded with mud."

With a dramatic sigh, Nathan slapped his magazine down on the coffee table and headed for the door. As he passed Reid he grumbled under his breath about fairness.

"Keep it up and you'll be mopping the truck bay, too."

He slammed the door behind him.

"It's like fucking kindergarten," Reid muttered.

"Here you go, boss."

As Reid sat at the table, Joey slid a plate full of food in front of her. She glared at him. He'd started calling her *boss* when he'd found out about the promotion. The term aggravated her and he thought it was funny.

"Megan, could you check the storeroom and see if you can find the coloring books? I want to hand them out to the kids."

Reid waited until she was out of earshot before she spoke again. "Man, I don't know what I'm doing here." She never would have admitted it to anyone else. But Joey had seen her at her most unsure, years ago as a scared rookie herself. The first time she had carried a lifeless body from a building, he had stayed up all night talking to her when they got back to the station and she couldn't sleep. Many times he was more like a father to her than her own father. He had mentored her and Jimmy, which had been part of the reason they had turned into the firefighters they were.

"You're doing fine, Reid. Things feel weird to all of us," Joey said.

When she had asked him once why he didn't take the test for a promotion, he'd told her that he didn't want to be a supervisor. He liked being an engineer and took great pride in the presentation and operation of his engine. And she respected him for that decision.

"I wish I could ask Jimmy for advice."

"I know." Joey briefly covered her hand with his large callused one. "It's only been a couple of weeks. Give it some time. Now eat your omelet before it gets cold." He stood and carried his plate to the sink.

After breakfast, Reid took her crew outside to get things ready for the tour. Joey pulled the engine out onto the apron where he and Reid could wash it. She asked Nathan to lay out some equipment to show the kids and Megan to sweep the truck bay.

After Reid and Joey finished washing the engine, they polished the chrome.

"Edge is catching on pretty quick," Joey said from the other side of the truck where he was cleaning the panel that housed the pump controls and gauges.

"She's smart. But she and Nathan seem to be rubbing each other the wrong way," she commented, pausing in the midst of polishing the front bumper to watch Megan push a broom across the floor of the empty bay.

"Yeah," Joey said. "Why do you suppose that is?"

"They're both young, in their careers even more than in years. The difference is Megan seems willing to learn, whereas Nathan thinks he already knows everything. Why does it seem like Jimmy did a better job of keeping him in check?" Reid circled the front bumper and went to work on the steps on the driver's side.

"Because he did."

"Thanks," she said wryly.

"Nathan's like a lot of the other guys in the department. He's got that macho male mentality."

"Then why is he the only one I have a problem with?"

"Because the rest of us know you could probably kick our ass," Joey joked, pretending to flinch when she took a step in his direction. "We've all seen you in action and respect you. And anybody who hasn't knows how much Jimmy thought of you. They respected him, so they figure you must be okay."

Frustrated, Reid threw the rag down on the running board. "Nathan and I never had any issues before."

"You weren't his boss before."

"So he's a fucking caveman? He can't deal with a woman boss?"

Joey shrugged. "I didn't say it made sense."

The fact that Nathan's insecurities were now Reid's problem was one example of the kind of things she would have to deal with as a captain. She couldn't shove aside the issues within her crew just because she had far more than she could deal with at home as well. So she would simply have to bear down and figure out how to handle it all.

CHAPTER EIGHT

Isabel stood in the middle of the garage surrounded by boxes. She'd had the movers deposit them there to deal with later. And now it was later. The boxes had been sitting undisturbed for over a week while she had spent her days trying to cultivate local clients, sending e-mails and meeting with potential clients. She had gotten three confirmed new accounts and had solid leads on half a dozen more. Nashville was proving to be more lucrative than she had originally planned.

However, she was still practically living out of a suitcase. She had unpacked the clothing she would need, and the rest of her belongings sat in these boxes. So she had granted herself two days to organize things. Today she would figure out what she needed and the rest would go into a storage unit. Then she would set up an office for herself. She'd been working from her laptop and briefcase, but she really needed an established space to work in. Determined to accomplish her goals, she began separating the boxes into stacks according to the descriptions written on the outside.

By midafternoon she had sorted all of the contents and carried a stack of cartons into the empty downstairs bedroom that would become her office. She loaded the ones bound for storage into the back of Jimmy's pickup, intending to take them later. She was pulling the garage door down when Meredith pulled into the driveway next door.

"Good morning," she called as Meredith began to remove plastic grocery bags from the back of the Jeep. "Let me help you with those." Isabel grabbed the remaining bags and followed Meredith into the house.

"Thank you. I saw Reid briefly this morning and she mentioned that Chase won his game on Saturday."

"Yeah. He's pretty good."

"Well, Jimmy was very athletic. And if I remember correctly, didn't Amanda excel at basketball in school?"

"Her college team won a regional championship and she held the school scoring record for quite a while." Isabel began to unpack the bags and Meredith put the groceries away.

Meredith paused with the pantry door open and glanced at Isabel. "Reid also mentioned that she spent the evening with you and Chase."

"Yes, we had dinner and then watched a movie." Unsure how much Reid had said, Isabel didn't volunteer anything more.

"I appreciate your including her. She has a tendency to spend too much time alone when she's upset."

Isabel shrugged. "That's just how she deals with things, I guess."

Abandoning the groceries altogether, Meredith rounded the counter and stood near Isabel. "Reid takes too much responsibility for things that aren't her fault, especially when she can't bear to place the blame where it really belongs."

"What do you mean?"

"That day at your grandparents' house, for example."

Surprised by the reference to the event from so long ago, Isabel set down the jar of peanut butter she'd just unpacked and gave Meredith her full attention. She didn't need any more details to know that Meredith was referring to the day she had fallen out of the tree. She knew her grandparents had recounted the story to her parents and they, in turn, had told Reid's parents, but she'd never talked about it with Meredith.

"What about it?" She kept her expression neutral though her stomach churned with an echo of latent fear.

"Reid blamed herself for leaving you there to climb the tree even though, as I understand it, Jimmy was the one who left first."

The memories Isabel had so often suppressed surged into her head. Her grandfather had called an ambulance and, after she spent the night in the hospital, she had been fine, aside from her broken arm and concussion. But the whole incident had scared her badly and had sparked a string of nightmares that lasted for months.

She had blamed Reid for her fall, because when Jimmy was with Reid, he acted different. He and Reid were always trying to outdo each other, to prove who was tougher. For Jimmy that meant he didn't want his *little* sister tagging along because she slowed him down. She'd tried to climb that tree to show Reid that she was as strong as they were.

That night in the hospital, when the throbbing in her head kept her awake, Isabel had replayed what she could remember of the day and decided that Reid had taken her brother from her. And since she couldn't compete, she'd stopped trying. But it had hurt even more when Jimmy and Reid didn't seem to notice the change in her. They seemed to think that she had just become more interested in girly things.

Isabel shoved aside feelings she didn't want Meredith to see. "We were just kids—"

"But she's still that way." Meredith touched Isabel's shoulder lightly before returning to the groceries. "All I'm saying is that Reid doesn't like for anyone to know she's hurting, so it's not always easy to tell when she needs something. But she's having a tough time without Jimmy, so I appreciate you and Chase keeping her company last weekend."

"Okay."

Isabel finished helping Meredith, then excused herself to get back to work on the office. The entire time she emptied the cartons in her office, Saturday night replayed in her mind. It wasn't easy to see what Reid needed, that much was true. And she did take on too much. Isabel had accused her of as much when she insisted that Reid put everyone else before herself. But she'd sensed a wave of relief in Reid as she had closed her eyes and gone to sleep with her feet in Isabel's hands. And, Isabel realized, that unguarded moment was special because it was so rare.

❖

Twenty minutes later, after receiving a phone call from Chase's principal, Isabel walked down the hallway at St. Catherine's. She checked the nameplate on each door until she found the one she was looking for. The door to the reception area was open.

Isabel smiled at the young woman behind the counter that bisected the small room. *Times have sure changed.* This was not the matronly secretary of Isabel's youth. She was a cute brunette who barely looked old enough to be out of school and most likely referred to herself as an administrative assistant. *Ah, well, face it, Isabel, you're getting older.* When the woman gave her an expectant look, Isabel offered her name.

"The principal will be with you in a few minutes."

Isabel settled into a chair along the wall next to a sullen-looking boy. The dark fringe of hair that fell past his eyebrows didn't hide the bruise that was forming high on his cheek. His left eye was swollen and he would have a nasty shiner by the next morning. He stared at his lap and swung feet that didn't reach the floor.

"What are you in for?" she asked.

Before he could answer the receptionist said, "He'll see you now."

Isabel was led to a sparely decorated office just large enough for the glass-topped desk and a couple of leather chairs. The surface of the desk overflowed with papers, leaving only a corner for a computer. The man behind the desk looked out of place in the clutter. His dark hair was meticulously cut and slicked back. A neat half-Windsor knot nestled in the collar of a crisp pale lavender shirt. He studied the computer screen and twirled a pen between slender manicured fingers. Isabel guessed him to be close to her own thirty years of age.

She tapped lightly on the door as she stepped inside, and he glanced up. "Ms. Grant?"

"Yes."

"I'm Chase's principal." He stood and extended a hand.

When Isabel moved inside to shake his hand, she noticed Chase sitting slumped across the desk from him. "Chase?" He turned to her and she sighed. His lip was split and already swelling. "Oh, Chase. What happened?"

"He started it," Chase began.

She remembered the boy with the black eye. "You got in a fight with that boy out there?" *This is just what I need.*

"Chase, why don't you wait outside while I talk to your aunt," the principal suggested.

"Yes, sir." Chase stood and trudged to the door.

"And don't say a word to that boy," Isabel warned.

The principal waited until Chase closed the door before he spoke. "I was very sorry to hear about Chase's father." He indicated the empty chair across the desk from him.

"Thank you." Isabel sat down. She knew the guidance counselor had met with Chase shortly after Jimmy's death. And the principal had obviously been filled in as well. "What happened with Chase?"

"I honestly don't know. Neither of the boys will talk. All Chase will say is that the other boy started it, and he won't utter a word." He paused, his expression sympathetic. "I'm going to have to suspend them both for a day."

"Isn't there anything else you can do? That's the last thing he needs right now."

"I'm sorry. It's obvious from their faces that both of them threw at least one punch. I believe Chase was provoked, but since he won't tell me what the other boy did, I have to punish him, too."

"I understand. I'll try to talk to him." Isabel stood.

"Good. If he needs anything, please don't hesitate to call." He stood as well. "And if it will help, I can give you the name of a good grief counselor."

"Thank you. I'll let you know."

Returning to the outer office, she found the two boys sitting side by side glaring at each other. They looked so cute, one with a black eye and the other with a fat lip, both trying to look intimidating, that she had to remind herself she was angry.

"Let's go." She held the door open and Chase didn't meet her eyes as he rounded her to exit. He still clammed up when she tried to talk to him about anything serious. Isabel hoped she could figure out how to get through to him before things got any worse. Her world was spiraling out of control, and she hated the dizziness.

When they got home, Isabel lifted her fist to knock on Reid's back door, but Chase pushed it open and said, "We don't have to knock."

"He's right," Reid said. She didn't look up from the newspaper spread out on the dinette table in front of her.

"Chase, go in the living room and work on your reading assignment." Isabel picked up the coat he dropped on the floor just inside the door and hung it on the back of a chair. "And no television."

"Who busted your lip? That little blond girl?" Reid asked as he passed. He stuck out his tongue at her, wincing as it poked against his injured lip. When he continued into the living room with no reply, Reid glanced at Isabel. "What happened? Did you finally lose your temper and smack him?"

"Funny." Isabel sat down opposite her and extracted the business section from the center of the newspaper.

"Hey, I have a system here," Reid protested, indicating the stack to her left. "Those are fair game, these I haven't read yet."

Isabel tilted her head, trying to decide if she was being serious.

Protectively Reid pulled the unread pile closer.

She is. Isabel made a show of opening the pilfered section and pretending to scan it.

Reid's eyes narrowed. They stared at each other for a long moment.

Finally, though it irritated her to back down, Isabel relented, folding the paper and sliding it across the table.

"What happened to Chase?" Reid asked, slipping the section back between the comics and the classifieds.

"He got in a fight with a boy at school."

"That's not like him. What happened?"

"Neither boy will tell. All the way home I tried to get him to talk, but all he did was sulk. They both got suspended for a day."

"Damn." Reid rubbed a hand over the back of her neck. "Listen, why don't you leave him here with me tomorrow? I was going to do some yard work anyway. It won't hurt him to have a rake in his hands for a while."

"I would really appreciate that. I wanted to try to get my office set up tomorrow, and it'll be good to have him occupied."

"I can see that—" Reid was interrupted by the ring of Isabel's cell.

Isabel pulled her BlackBerry from its holster and glanced at the display. "I'm sorry. I have to take this." She pressed a button on the device and stepped toward the kitchen.

As she walked out she saw Reid shake her head and return to her paper. Once again she'd allowed Reid to step in and take over. But just as she began to debate whether she should have accepted Reid's offer, she was forced to give her attention to the client on the phone.

❖

Isabel awoke the next morning to the insistent buzz of her alarm. She rolled back over and closed her eyes, determined to get just fifteen more minutes of sleep. But while she lay there she began to mentally review the list of things she hoped to accomplish that day. At some point, she would have to deal more in depth with Chase's fight at school. He had continued to be sullen and silent. Maybe she should ask Reid and Meredith for advice before trying to talk to him again. *Well, now that I'm awake, so much for going back to sleep.*

She rolled out of bed and padded toward the shower. Planning another day of dirty work, she dressed comfortably in sweats, tied a faded bandana over her hair, and didn't bother with makeup.

Waking Chase was a challenge, as usual. He buried his head under his pillow, but she persisted. When she was certain he wouldn't go back to sleep as soon as she left the room, she went downstairs to get breakfast.

"I don't even have to go to school today. Why couldn't I sleep in?" he pouted when he finally dragged himself downstairs and slumped in a chair at the kitchen table.

"It's not a vacation. You were suspended. You're going to spend the day working with Reid." She set a bowl of cereal in front of him.

Later when they entered the back door of Reid's house, Chase was still dragging his feet.

"Good morning." Meredith glanced up from her oatmeal.

"Can I have a doughnut?" Chase rested his chin on the table and looked up at her.

"Chase, you just had breakfast," Isabel said.

"But I want a doughnut."

As Meredith waited, Isabel merely waved her hand. "Go ahead."

Chase rushed to the counter and flipped open the box of doughnuts. He pulled one out and took a bite, leaving a ring of white powder around his mouth.

Smiling, Meredith handed him a napkin. "Do you want some juice?"

"Nope."

"Don't talk with your mouth full," Isabel admonished. She suspected Jimmy had been lax at times regarding Chase's manners. Judging from Chase's disregard for neatness at home, it seemed he and Jimmy had often lived like a couple of bachelors.

Chase swallowed before responding. "She asked me a question."

"He got you there." Reid laughed as she walked into the kitchen.

"Swallow what's in your mouth and then answer," Isabel said to Chase and turned toward Reid. "He's too smart for his own good."

Reid's hair was still wet from the shower and curled in shiny strands around her face. The white tank top that hugged her torso displayed her strong shoulders well, and worn blue jeans hung loosely around her narrow hips. She'd always been in good shape, but it seemed in recent weeks she'd grown leaner.

Isabel was astonished at her reaction as she watched those hips sway when Reid walked to the refrigerator. She'd never had a problem acknowledging an attractive woman. But never before had that awareness brought the slow heat that now curled in her stomach.

"Are you losing weight?" Without thinking, she grabbed the slack in Reid's waistband. When her knuckles brushed against a taut stomach she jerked her hand back. Reid's eyes flew to her face, and in them Isabel saw her own awareness mirrored and tinged with confusion.

"I don't know." Regaining her composure, Reid shrugged and grabbed the sweatshirt hanging over the back of a chair. She pulled it over her head. "How's the lip?" Reid grasped Chase's chin and lifted his face to inspect it.

Isabel stared at Reid. She hadn't expected the tiny shocks that had raced up her forearm when she touched Reid any more than she expected the warm feeling in her chest as she watched Reid tenderly examine Chase's injury.

"You'll live." Reid released his chin and ruffled his hair. "Go get your coat. We've got work to do."

As they left the room, Isabel exhaled the breath she'd been holding since Reid had appeared.

❖

"How much longer do we have to do this?" Chase complained for the fourth time.

"Until there aren't any leaves left." Reid finished bagging a pile of crisp leaves and picked up her rake. Chase really wasn't accomplishing much with his haphazard swipes, but Reid figured the point was that he felt he was being punished.

Raking Reid's backyard had taken the better part of two hours. Though it was only a moderately sized area, Meredith had planted a half dozen trees in it over the years. They shed their leaves among the cast-iron bistro set, matching bench, and flower beds, making them difficult to retrieve. Reid had given Chase a short break and then they moved on to Isabel's yard.

"I wish I was in school," he grumbled.

Reid laughed.

"It's not funny." He dropped his rake and kicked at the sparse mound in front of him. "I don't want to do this anymore."

Leaning on the handle of her own rake, Reid regarded him for a moment. *Maybe I'm being too hard on him. The kid has been through a lot.*

When he stomped across the yard and dropped down on the porch steps, Reid joined him.

"What did you expect would happen if you punched that boy?"

"I don't know." He rested his elbows on his knees and rested his chin in his hands. "I guess I didn't think about it."

"That's right. You didn't think. You could have hurt each other. You can't settle your problems with your fists or there will be consequences."

"Like raking leaves?"

"For starters." She draped her arm around his shoulders. He wasn't usually a hothead. "What happened to make you so mad?"

Chase was silent for several long moments. Reid waited for him.

"He called my dad a coward." He frowned in a struggle to contain the tears that filled his eyes.

"Chase, your dad wasn't a coward." Her heart breaking, Reid tightened her embrace. She had tried to shield him from the details of that night, but obviously someone had been filling his head with a distorted idea of what happened.

Hearing the creak of boards behind her, Reid glanced over her shoulder and saw Isabel standing just outside the door. Reid rubbed her hands soothingly over Chase's back. "Your father was the bravest man I've ever known. He's a hero. You know that, don't you?"

He nodded slowly.

"Don't ever forget it."

"Can I go inside?"

"Yes."

He didn't meet Reid's eyes. He was growing into that stage when he was embarrassed to show emotion. Soon, she realized, he would shy away from her hugs and kisses. She stood and turned to watch him go.

Isabel lightly touched Chase's head as he passed and waited until he disappeared inside before she spoke. "What the hell do you think you're doing?" Across the shadowed expanse of the porch, her eyes flashed in accusation.

"What?"

"Why would you fill his head with that crap? It's bad enough I have to listen to everyone talk about how honorable Jimmy's death was, without you forcing such lies on Chase, too." She crossed the porch in three quick strides, jerking to a stop in front of Reid.

Still standing two steps lower, Reid tilted her head back to glare at her. Isabel obviously didn't understand the importance of the honor that she was now trampling on. Reid held tightly to the idea that though people died every day, most would never know the higher purpose that Jimmy had in his profession. "It's not crap or lies."

"How do you do it? How do you go back into a burning building, knowing—"

"It's who I am. I don't know how to do anything else." She neglected to mention that she hadn't been anywhere near a burning building since Jimmy died, and she didn't know for certain how she would go back in.

"You could, if you wanted to."

What began as a spark of anger ignited, Isabel was attacking more than just her livelihood. She advanced, topping the stairs as Isabel retreated. "You don't get it. I couldn't *be* anything else. And more than that, I don't *want* to."

"I couldn't be that strong."

"It's not about strength. It's the job. Jimmy understood that as much as I do." Reid wasn't sure how else to explain what was simply instinct. She had never stopped to doubt whether she could do her job; she just did it. She had known it was her duty since her first day at the academy. And she happily embraced it. Firefighting was something to be proud of; surely Isabel could see that.

"It *is* about strength for the people who care about you, the families who have to send you off every third day, not knowing if you'll come back. Your mother and Chase. How can you ask that of them after what they've just gone through?"

In that moment Reid almost hated Isabel for making her feel selfish. But she hated herself even more for the guilty voice that whispered, *You* are *selfish and weak and you got your partner killed.*

She made one more attempt to defend herself. "If *we* didn't do it, somebody else would have to. Jimmy died a hero. Chase understands that."

"That's bullshit! He's a scared little boy. What he understands is that his father is gone. Everything else is just bravado because he thinks that's what you want from him."

"So this is my fault?" Reid didn't wait for Isabel to answer. She took several more steps, forcing Isabel to give ground until her back touched the door. Reid continued until they were separated by mere inches, their breasts and thighs nearly touching. "Why don't you just say it? Everything that has happened since Jimmy and I went into that hotel has been my fault. I ruined all of our lives."

Isabel was mute in the face of Reid's anguish. As Reid spoke, her voice had risen until she was shouting. Her eyes were impossibly dark, the pupils enlarged until they were barely ringed with irises the color of rich, undiluted coffee.

"You blame me. Say it!" Reid's open palm hit the doorjamb next to Isabel's head and she flinched.

"I do blame you," Isabel shot back. She was frightened, not by Reid's violence but by the pain swirling in her eyes. "Ever since we were kids you two were inseparable. And you had to be just like your father. You had to follow in his footsteps. Jimmy listened to every word as you pumped him up with talk of honor and traditions and *brotherhood.* My brother is *dead*, my nephew orphaned, and I blame you and your damn brotherhood."

Isabel's chest heaved with every breath, but she wasn't done and her next words escaped uncensored. Now that she'd started, she couldn't stop the torrent of accusations she'd been holding back for weeks. "You should have stayed with him. He *never* would have left you alone in there."

Though Reid expected the condemnation, the words still cut her. She absorbed them, believing that she deserved the censure. "Jesus." Her breath left her on a shaft of pain that pierced her chest and nearly doubled her over as she staggered backward. Isabel had put voice to Reid's nightmare, that Jimmy had died alone and afraid inside that building. She could have taken it from almost anyone—but Isabel. She was down the steps and striding across the lawn before the tears could fill her eyes.

"Reid, wait!" Isabel called, but she was too late. "Shit." She shoved a hand through her hair and sank down onto the steps. She'd reacted out of anger. Her outburst had been irrational and over the top, and Reid's reaction had only escalated the situation.

Part of her wanted to rush over to Reid and apologize. But she also recognized that she'd meant most of what she said. Despite the ease that had developed between them in recent weeks, Isabel realized that she obviously still harbored a good amount of anger. She was certain Reid had seen it and probably wouldn't accept her apology anyway.

CHAPTER NINE

Isabel studied her computer screen, trying to concentrate as she clicked quickly through several spreadsheets. She was meeting with one couple in the morning and needed to work them up a proposal, so she pulled the pen from behind her ear and scribbled a quick note on a legal pad.

After she reviewed the same figures for the third time, she scrubbed her hands over her face. God, her timing couldn't be worse. She did well enough in Knoxville, but there she was maintaining only a small apartment and supporting just herself. She needed to think long term now that she had to consider Chase's school tuition and eventually college. She needed to be serious about building a local client base, so she couldn't afford to be distracted.

Still, every time she imagined she heard a motorcycle outside, Reid's face filled her head. She'd replayed the scene on the porch a thousand times and was no closer to an answer. There had been a point in the conversation when she could have reined in her temper, but she and Reid had been building to that blowup for weeks.

An icon in the lower right corner of her screen flashed, indicating a new e-mail—from Alan Warner. As she read it, she almost wished he'd been one of the clients who had jumped ship. Sure, she made a fair amount of money from his portfolio, but he certainly aggravated her a lot. Now she needed to drive to Knoxville in the next few weeks to straighten some things out. Warner required a lot of reassurance, and their frequent e-mails and phone calls only soothed him for so long. He would need a face-to-face, though she hoped she could put it off until after Thanksgiving.

"Aunt Isabel," Chase said from the doorway.

"Yes?" she asked, distracted.

"Can I watch TV in here?"

She glanced at the television in the corner of the room. "Chase, that thing isn't even hooked up to the cable. Can you watch in the living room?"

"Yeah." He remained in the doorway, shifting from foot to foot. "Will you watch with me?"

"I can't right now, sweetie. I really need to finish up some things here." She wondered how she was supposed to balance everything. When she'd decided to move to Nashville she'd thought her schedule would settle down in a few weeks. She had actually imagined she would be able to get all of her work done while Chase was in school, leaving the rest of the time to spend with him.

But this wasn't the first time she'd had to tell him no, and she knew it wouldn't be the last. If she didn't build her business, she wouldn't be able to support them in the manner she wanted to. But lately, she worried that her preoccupation with work was contributing to his difficulties.

As Reid entered the living room, Meredith glanced up from her sudoku. "Hello, sweetheart."

"Hey, Mom." Reid sat on the couch beside her.

"How did you sleep?"

"Not so good." They hadn't had a very busy shift the night before, but even during their several hours of downtime Reid had found herself once more restlessly pacing the station. She'd tried to find something interesting among the early-morning television programs, but everything failed to hold her attention. Arriving home shortly after seven a.m. and wondering if she'd ever been happier to see a shift end, she had promptly taken a sleeping pill and fallen into bed. She managed a few solid hours before she got up, pulled on a T-shirt and a pair of sweats, and looked for her mother.

"Something wrong, dear?"

"Ah, I don't know. I'm just having trouble settling down lately."

"Everything okay at work?"

"As well as can be expected." She'd talked briefly with Meredith about the changes in her crew.

"How's the rookie working out?"

"She's okay."

"You're so talkative today," Meredith said sarcastically. Reid had been spreading herself thin lately. She was working too much and not getting enough sleep. Meredith couldn't remember the last time she'd seen Reid do something just for herself. She and Jimmy used to go out on the motorcycles or down to the Blue Line to shoot pool. "If it's not work, what's going on? Do you need to talk to someone about—well, about Jimmy?"

"No, Mom. I don't need to see a shrink."

Meredith could have predicted Reid's reaction. Having been married to a firefighter, Meredith was well aware that they believed they needed only the job and their brothers and they could get through anything. Reid was like her father in that way, too, which was one of the reasons she worried about her.

"Does this have anything to do with why you disappear every time Isabel comes over? Did you argue?" She'd witnessed several of Reid's quick escapes, and on the one occasion she'd seen them in the same room, the tension had been palpable. Reid had moved around the kitchen, seeming determined to keep a good amount of distance between them, and then she'd fled as soon as possible.

"I don't disappear." In the face of Meredith's disbelieving expression, Reid sighed. "It's complicated." She'd always been close to her mother and never had difficulty talking with her about *whatever* was on her mind. But this was Isabel. Jimmy's sister. Reid had feelings about her that she was still hesitant to voice; hiding was a difficult habit to break.

"Things will work themselves out." After squeezing Reid's shoulder again, Meredith went back to her puzzle. Though she could sense the myriad of emotions that haunted Reid, until she was ready to talk there was no point in pushing her. She was stubborn, and trying to coax her to discuss whatever was bothering her would only cause her to clam up further.

The morning sun made no attempt to break through the clouds. Instead, a light rain brought an icy bite to the already cool air. Having just returned from driving Chase to school, Isabel pulled into the driveway. Through the open door of the neighboring garage she heard the sound of Reid's bike starting up. *She's going to freeze to death on that damn thing.*

Isabel sat inside her car weighing her options. Reid had been avoiding her for almost two weeks, ever since their blowup. Isabel had finally worked out her schedule so that she got most of her work done while Chase was at school, so she hadn't been relying on Reid and Meredith as much lately. But Chase still visited the Webbs regularly. When Isabel would go over to retrieve him for dinner, she often found Meredith waiting with a cup of coffee or freshly baked cookies. Though she was curious, Isabel avoided inquiring about Reid, who was always suspiciously absent.

Not that she knew what she would say to Reid if she was there. Reid might not even listen. Isabel hadn't gone out of her way to see Reid, either, because she hadn't yet sorted out the confusion that twisted up her insides. She hadn't completely changed her mind and wasn't ready to take back her words, even if she could.

But before their confrontation it had been increasingly hard to ignore the vulnerable, caring side of Reid, and she did think she'd been somewhat harsh. They were both hurting over their loss, and she had placed all the blame squarely on Reid's shoulders. As time healed her wounds, Isabel began to realize that Reid didn't deserve *all* the blame. But being angry was easier than facing other emotions that had been teasing the edges of her consciousness.

As if prodding her into action the rain intensified, whipped against the window by an increasing wind. She jogged across the driveway, then darted inside the garage and shook the rain from her hair. Reid paused in the middle of donning a raincoat.

"You shouldn't be riding in this weather. It's not safe. I'm taking you to work," Isabel declared.

Reid bit back a sharp retort. A strand of damp hair clung to Isabel's cheek, and Reid fought the urge to cross the short distance between them and brush it aside. Isabel stood defiantly in the open doorway, the sky dark and turbulent behind her. There was an electricity in the air that Reid preferred to attribute to the storm that had been churning all day. She didn't want to admit that despite what had transpired between them, she only had to see Isabel and she was undone. She had to fight the urge to apologize.

She considered refusing Isabel's offer, but she really wasn't looking forward to riding in this rain. Her mother needed the Jeep for a doctor's appointment in the afternoon, but she could wake her and have her drop her off.

"Just get in the car," Isabel snapped.

Without a word Reid grabbed her keys from the bike and headed for Isabel's Honda, then settled silently in the passenger seat and stared out the window as Isabel backed into the street. The days since she'd been in such close proximity to Isabel had done nothing to diminish the impact. The humid air carried Isabel's familiar floral scent, and Reid drew it in, feeling the tug in her belly echo an ache in her chest.

Isabel endured the silence for several long moments. *Two can play at this game. It's not even that far to the station. I can go that long without talking to you.* She lasted another thirty seconds. "You've been avoiding me."

"I thought it was best."

"I didn't mean what I sai—"

"Yes, you did." Reid carefully set her features in a neutral expression before she turned to look at Isabel. "And it's okay."

"No, it's not."

"Do you think I haven't thought the same thing?" Reid averted her eyes. Their arms paralleled along the armrest between them, their hands resting so close that it would take only the barest movement for Reid to touch her. She sighed. How could she explain that she'd been blaming herself, too? "You asked for an explanation once and I didn't give it to you."

"You don't have to."

"Yes, I do," Reid insisted. Briefly, she outlined the events following their dispatch to the hotel fire. She spoke quickly and technically, as if giving a report. Isabel listened without interruption. When Reid talked about searching the hotel room, she stumbled for a second, then drew a deep breath and continued. "The chief gave the order to evacuate. Jimmy wanted to leave and I talked him into staying to find the kid."

Isabel pulled into the station's parking lot and shifted in her seat until they were face-to-face. A muscle jumped along Reid's jaw, and her knuckles protruded as her hand constricted into a fist.

"Reid—"

"If we'd left, he would still be alive."

"You can't know that." *He was being tough for you again.*

"But I do. That floor gave out while we were leaving. If we'd left earlier we might have still had the east stairwell, and we wouldn't have gone back down the hall. We might even have already been out of the building before the explosion. When I heard the floor giving way I lunged for him, but I couldn't hold him. I know we shouldn't have left him. I didn't want to." A hard lump formed in Reid's throat.

When Isabel's hand covered hers, Reid uncurled her fingers. She longed to turn her hand over and lace them into Isabel's. Instead she remained still.

"Reid, I went downtown earlier this week and read the fire marshal's report. You cracked two ribs trying to save him. You were under orders to evacuate, and you had to get that little girl out. She wouldn't be here today if it weren't for you. You are all heroes. I couldn't see that in my grief, but I know it now."

She waved off Reid's attempt to interrupt. "I'm not saying I like what you do. Or that I understand any better why you do it. But I do understand that it's not fair to hold you personally responsible when really I'm angry at Jimmy for choosing to put himself in harm's way. I'm angry at the circumstances of that night."

"You said it yourself. If it wasn't for me, he wouldn't have wanted to be a firefighter."

"Well, I guess I'll never know that for sure, will I?" Isabel drew her hand back, and Reid immediately missed the warmth. "What I'm trying to say is that regardless of my personal feelings, it wasn't right for me to attack you. Letting my reactions to the past get the best of me doesn't change what happened. It's more important to remember that Chase needs us—all of us—and that means we've got to find a way to coexist."

"Coexist," Reid repeated. Isabel's voice was impersonal. She might as well have been proposing a business arrangement. "You don't really have to have any contact with me at all if you don't want to, Iz. In fact, I've been trying to give you space. You're the one who insisted on driving me over here."

"Damn it, Reid. This isn't easy for me. I don't want to be at odds with you, but I can't just forget how I feel. Regardless, I can't afford to let it affect Chase." Isabel's voice caught. She cleared her throat and met Reid's eyes steadily. "He's lost so much already."

Isabel had found Reid's other weakness. Chase. And it wasn't fair. "I know. You're right. We'll work it out," Reid mumbled before she climbed out of the car. She wasn't certain how, but they *would* work it out. The only question that remained was, what would it cost her?

❖

An ambulance sat in front of the open truck bay door, and Nathan stood inside talking to two paramedics. Reid ran to the door, picking her way around several puddles. As she hurried inside and swiped the rain from her eyes, she noticed that one of the paramedics was watching her. The woman stepped close to Reid, tossing a mane of dark hair over her shoulder in a practiced motion. Her eyes raked over Reid and when she spoke, her voice dropped to an intimate level.

"Hello, Reid."

"Susannah, what are you doing here?" After the conversation she'd just had, Reid didn't have the energy to be polite. The last thing she needed was another confrontation with her ex, and nearly every conversation with Susannah Kenworth seemed to turn into a quarrel.

"We just left the hospital, and I told my partner we should stop by and say hi."

"Okay, well, hi." Reid turned abruptly away, but Susannah grabbed her arm.

"What's up your ass today, Webb?"

"I don't have time for this. Did you need something specific?"

"Who was the woman?"

"What woman?" Reid sighed and tugged her arm out of Susannah's grip.

"The woman who dropped you off. You two looked pretty intense in there."

"That was a private conversation, Susannah," Reid replied. Conscious of the two men standing nearby, she was careful to keep her voice low.

This was why she didn't like Susannah to stop by the station. With the exception of Jimmy, her crew didn't know anything about her personal life.

"I didn't ask what you were talking about, Reid. I just asked who she was." Susannah sulked. She was quick to affect a pout when she felt it would suit her cause.

"She's Jimmy's sister. She gave me a ride to work," Reid said because it was easier to tell Susannah than argue with her.

"She's cute."

Reid ignored this observation. "Thanks for stopping by, but I've got a lot of work to do."

Without giving her a chance to respond, Reid walked away. She'd recognized the look in Susannah's eyes. If the thought of Isabel dating men all these years had been hard to take, the possibility of her with another woman tied Reid's stomach in knots.

In the kitchen she was surprised to find Megan behind the stove instead of Joey. He was slouched comfortably in a chair nearby, his legs stretched out in front of him and his ankles crossed. When he saw her he grinned and nodded in greeting. Megan poured a medallion of batter on a griddle.

"What happened to my omelet?" Reid slanted Joey an accusatory look, pulled out the chair next to him, and sat down.

"I told you, Edge. The boss likes her routine," Joey drawled.

Megan expertly flipped a pancake on top of the stack already on a plate and slid it in front of Reid. "Don't knock it until you've tried it," she challenged.

"Where's the bacon? How am I supposed to get through my day without my protein? I'll be passed out by lunch."

"Bacon clogs your arteries," Megan quipped.

Reid paused, fork halfway to her mouth, not expecting the sarcastic reply. "My arteries are just fine," she muttered before she shoved the bite in her mouth.

Megan waited. When Reid took another bite, Megan failed to hide a cocky grin.

"Stop gloating, Edge. It's not attractive," Reid said, suppressing a smile of her own.

She'd barely begun her breakfast when the alert tones sounded over the station speaker. Their first traffic accident of the day marked the beginning of rush hour. Reid grabbed the dispatch information from the printer on her way to the engine. As she rushed through the station she glanced down at the paper that listed the address and patient specifics.

The rain continued through the day, and they barely had time to grab some burgers for lunch between runs. When they weren't checking out traffic accidents, they responded on medical calls. The number of engine companies in the city far outnumbered the ambulances. Since all firefighters were at least EMT certified and some were paramedics, on higher-priority medical incidents an engine crew went along as well. More often than not they arrived on scene before the medic unit and could administer care in the meantime.

They were headed back to the station for a much-needed break when the dispatcher called them. One of the large apartment complexes in the area was on fire, and they were sent along with a number of other engines, trucks, and district chiefs. When the first unit on scene reported that one building was fully involved and the fire was spreading, they knew it would be an extended operation.

Joey pulled up behind one of the other engines and Reid went to look for Chief Perez, who was again the incident commander. She found him standing a safe distance from the front of the building, the upper level of which was completely engulfed. Like a living being, flames consumed furniture and crawled up the walls. Seeking escape, it flowed out of windows and holes in the roof, fingers of orange and red that caressed the night sky.

A mass of firefighters manned hoses, and a master stream at the top of one of the aerials targeted the fire from above. Thick black smoke rolled from the building and mingled with the lighter clouds of steam. The hazy air reflected the glow of the fire and the flashing red of the apparatus lights. For the first time since she was a rookie, the scene inspired a tingle of apprehension along her spine.

The apartment complex consisted of six buildings with approximately a dozen apartments each. Real estate close to the city was becoming scarcer, and developers tried to maximize their profits. As a result buildings were placed far too close together, close enough for the fire to jump from one to the next. The buildings on either side were now involved as well.

"Webb," the chief called out. "Pull an attack line and start clearing the B building. Johnson, your guys give them a backup line."

"Edge, Brewer, pull a line," Reid shouted as she strode back to the engine. Her crew would be responsible for checking one of the adjacent buildings for occupants.

"You okay with this?" Joey asked Reid as he held an air pack for her.

"I'm okay." Reid slipped her arms through the straps and secured the one around her waist. She pulled the protective hood over her head, flipped up the collar of her coat, and put on her mask and helmet. The routine of preparation did nothing to calm the racing of her heart, but she was glad she was able to keep the tremor out of her voice.

Their engine was parked about fifty yards from the building. Joey had already laid a five-inch supply line to the nearest hydrant. Nathan and Megan were laying out one-and-three-quarter-inch hose, and Reid joined them as they approached the breezeway. She took the nozzle, with Megan right behind her. She told Nathan to stay outside and make sure the hose didn't snag or kink.

"Why does the rookie get the nozzle?"

"Because I said so," Reid returned without hesitation. Since this was Megan's first major fire and first interior attack, Reid wanted her along to test her skills. "Engine 9 portable to Engine 9, charge the line," she called into her radio seconds later as they paused outside the first apartment. The hose swelled as it filled to capacity and Reid cracked the nozzle, releasing any air before they went in. As she reached for the doorknob, she slammed her eyes shut against a flashback of the hotel bathroom door.

"Captain?" Megan called from over her right shoulder.

When she realized she was panting, Reid consciously slowed her breathing. *You can do this. God damn it, you're a firefighter. Get your ass in there.* The voice in her head wasn't her own. Though she would never tell another soul, she swore it was Jimmy's. She drew strength from the familiar baritone that rang clear and true through her mind, opened her eyes, and saw the green steel apartment door clearly.

She tried the knob and found the door unlocked. Hoping that meant that all the residents had already fled the apartment, she pushed the door open and did a quick visual sweep of the room that was just beginning to fill with smoke. When she crouched low and advanced inside, she did so with renewed confidence.

Reid and Megan methodically worked their way through the small one-bedroom apartment. It wasn't until they reached the far bedroom wall closest to the building of origin that they encountered flames. Reid flipped open the nozzle and applied several short bursts of solid stream to the base of the fire. Finding the apartment vacant, they backed out and checked the remaining three apartments on the ground floor in the same fashion.

Before they climbed the stairs, Reid paused to relay their status to the IC. "Engine 9 to Command, the ground floor of the B building is clear. We're advancing to the second floor."

After they cleared the rest of the building, they reported back to the IC for their next assignment. They were directed to the C side, the rear of the building, to assist in the defensive attack. They worked until their arms were heavy with fatigue, and even then the chief practically had to order them to rehab. The Fire Buffs, a volunteer group that supplied drinks and food for the firefighters, were set up a safe distance away, near the clubhouse.

Reid dropped her gear under a stand of trees and took four bottles of Gatorade from a cooler. Nathan, Joey, and Megan were gathering when she returned and she tossed them each a bottle.

Two buildings were still showing flames and heavy smoke. After all of the visible fire was under control, they would begin salvage and overhaul. They would remove or cover salvageable belongings, as well as removing any still-smoldering furniture. Then they needed to check the ceilings and walls for hidden fires.

"Drink up. It's going to be a long morning." She uncapped her own bottle and took several long swallows before she sat down to rest her back against a tree. She watched the group of firefighters around her talk and joke while they rested. They'd had a busy day and it wasn't over yet, but she knew she wouldn't hear any complaints.

This was why they did the job. They endured the less-exciting calls for the chance to work these calls, and Reid was no different. Adrenaline was a powerful hormone, and the challenge of fighting a force of nature far stronger than man induced an intense rush. Reid felt strength in knowing that she could save a life, or even a piece of someone's history that might otherwise be lost.

She had been worried that she wouldn't be able to go back inside. Despite the act she'd put on for the benefit of her chief and her crew, she had needed this incident to prove to herself that she was still good enough.

CHAPTER TEN

At six o'clock in the morning, one of the chiefs brought the next shift's crew to the scene to relieve them. Joey turned over the engine to the oncoming engineer, and they all piled into Perez's Tahoe to head back to the station.

"Gonna be a nice day," Joey said, squinting out the back passenger window. The previous day's rain had passed, and the sun was inching its way above the horizon.

"Good work, guys," Perez said as he dropped them off in front of the station. "Reid, can I talk to you for a second?"

As the others walked away, she propped herself against the open window of the passenger door. "Yeah, Chief?"

"I know you're tired, so I'll be brief. How is your crew adjusting?"

"Fine, sir," she answered quickly.

"Any problems?"

"No, sir."

He studied her through narrowed eyes, and Reid tried not to squirm under his gaze. Whatever her issues with her crew, she figured they were hers to sort out.

"Good. Get some rest, Reid."

"Yes, sir." Reid tapped her hand against the door and turned away.

In the parking lot, Isabel half stood and half leaned against her car. As Reid drew near, Isabel could see the exhaustion in her eyes. Reid had shed her turnout coat, and it and her helmet dangled heavily from her arms. The suspenders that looped over her shoulders did nothing to conceal the fitted T-shirt that was plastered to her body with what Isabel guessed was a combination of sweat and water. Her hair was wet and had run tiny rivers through the streaks of soot that covered her neck and face. All in all, she looked completely worn out and sexy as hell. *Where did that come from? When did I start noticing things like that?*

"Rough night, Captain?" Caught up in her previous thoughts, Isabel couldn't keep the hint of flirtation out of her voice.

Reid raised an eyebrow but didn't comment. "You could say that. Apartment fire. I don't want to get in your car like this. Do you have time for me to grab a quick shower?"

"Sure." Imagining Reid standing beneath the spray, soapy water cascading down her toned body and steam billowing around her, Isabel felt her mouth suddenly become dry.

"Do you want to wait inside?"

"It's actually shaping up to be a beautiful morning. I think I'll stay out here and enjoy it." *I need to clear my head. What the hell was that? Some kind of teenage boy porn fantasy?*

"I'll be quick," Reid said as she hurried toward the station.

She rushed through a shower and pulled on a clean uniform from her locker. After towel-drying her hair, she glanced in the mirror and shoved a few strands around with her fingers. Deciding it would do until she got home, she walked back through the kitchen.

"Hey, Reid." Megan sat at the table sipping a cup of coffee.

"Hey. You headed home soon?"

"Yeah, I just wanted to get a quick shot of caffeine before I headed out."

Reid paused, resting her hands on the back of an empty chair. "Listen, Megan, you did a great job today."

"Thanks."

Satisfied, Reid moved toward the door. "I'll see you Friday."

"Reid," Megan said.

"Yeah?"

"Do you bowl?"

"It's been a while. Why?" Reid held the door open for Nathan as he headed for the parking lot.

"I bowl in a league on Wednesday nights and we need a fourth."

Reid hesitated. *Is she asking me out?*

"My partner, Jasmine, usually bowls with us, but she's pregnant," Megan explained. "We tried for some time before we were successful, so she doesn't want to take any chances." She rinsed out her mug and hung it on a rack near the sink.

"Oh, okay. That sounds like fun. And congratulations." It had been some time since Reid had gone out with friends. In fact, for the past few years she'd spent most of her free time with her mother, Jimmy, and Chase. Maybe it would be good for her to get out of the house, perhaps meet someone new to help her get her mind off Isabel. *Yeah, right.*

❖

"Are you waiting for someone?"

Isabel turned at the voice from behind her. She remembered the beefy firefighter from Jimmy's funeral. "Hi. Nathan, isn't it?"

"Yeah."

He braced himself a little too casually against the hood of her car and folded his arms over a broad chest. A slow smile spread across features that were best described as a bit pretty. High cheekbones, a thin nose, and an elegant jawline all seemed at odds with his thick, muscular body.

"So how are you doing? Do you or Chase need anything?" He touched her shoulder lightly.

"We're okay. Thank you for asking."

"Good. Because you know, if you needed, say, a night out to get away from the kid, I'd be happy to take you to dinner."

He was good-looking, and despite the low opinion Reid seemed to have of him, Nathan was the kind of guy that, on first sight, Isabel would find attractive. And she didn't think she was mistaking the interest in his eyes. *So why do I feel absolutely nothing when I look at him, yet the sight of Reid dirty and sweaty has me imagining unmentionable things?*

❖

"You're on Montrose, aren't you?" Megan asked as they walked outside together. "We start bowling at eight. You can meet me or I can pick you up. You're actually on my way."

"That sounds good, if you're sure you don't mind."

Across the parking lot, Isabel and Nathan looked very cozy. He angled close to her and bent his head attentively when she spoke. Isabel smiled warmly in response to something he said.

"Nathan seems to think he's a player," Megan said, further stoking the jealousy that burned in Reid's stomach.

"Yeah, he does," Reid murmured.

"Call me if you need anything," Nathan was saying as they approached. "Captain." He offered a mock salute in her direction before he glanced at Megan. "Edge, see you around."

Reid tried not to glare as he sauntered away, but she was afraid she had a murderous look on her face. She was itching to commit murder, that was certain.

"Ready?" Isabel asked.

"Yeah." Reid tossed her backpack into the rear seat.

"I don't think we've met, I'm Megan Edge." Megan held out her hand.

"I'm sorry," Reid interjected, realizing she was distracted by Nathan and hadn't introduced the two women. "Isabel, Megan's on our crew now. Megan, this is Isabel Grant, Jimmy's sister."

"It's nice to meet you," Isabel responded politely, grasping Megan's hand.

"You, too. Well, I won't keep you." To Reid she said, "Pick you up around seven thirty?"

"Sure. See you then."

"So," Isabel said as she slid behind the wheel, "was it a big fire?" It wasn't what she wanted to ask. She was dying to ask why Megan was picking Reid up. Was it a date? *So what if it is? Reid is an attractive woman, surely she dates. Just because I haven't seen her go out doesn't mean there isn't a line of women wanting to spend time with her.*

"Yeah, three alarms," Reid said with a tired sigh. She shoved a hand through her still-damp hair. "They ended up losing about twenty-four units when all was said and done."

"Wow, that's tough for those families going into the holidays."

"Most of them probably don't have renter's insurance either. People just don't think something like that's going to happen to them. We called the Red Cross and they'll help out some, but for the ones with kids, Christmas won't be the same this year."

Isabel glanced at her. "Do you know what caused it?"

Reid shrugged. "The fire marshal narrowed it down to which apartment it started in, but they have to wait for some areas to cool before they can finish investigating."

Isabel pulled into her driveway, cut the engine, and reached for the door handle.

"Thanks for the ride." Reid got out and grabbed her bag from the backseat.

"No problem."

"Mom told me she invited you and Chase over for Thanksgiving dinner. Are you coming?"

"I don't know." While she was sure Chase wanted to spend the day with the Webbs, she hadn't known if Reid wanted her there.

"We'll have plenty."

Isabel studied her. "Are you taking pity on me?"

"You? No," Reid stated, a smile teasing her lips. They paused near the front of the car. "On Chase. You're forgetting I've been the victim of your culinary efforts."

Laughing at Reid's use of the word *victim,* Isabel swatted Reid's shoulder playfully. "Cute. Okay, what can I bring?"

Reid gave her an amused look. "Just bring Chase."

❖

Thanksgiving morning, Reid jerked awake as Chase launched himself onto her bed. Grunting as his flying knee jabbed her stomach, she gingerly set him aside and sat up.

Seconds later Isabel appeared in the doorway. "I'm sorry, I tried to stop him." She hesitated on the threshold.

"It's okay," Reid replied with a grin. "What are you doing up so early, little man?"

"We're having turkey and pie," he explained as if he made perfect sense. He bounced on the bed on his knees.

"And what does that have to do with anything?" Reid ruffled his hair and smiled at his unlimited energy.

"Can we eat the pie first?"

"I don't know if Mom will go for that."

Isabel watched them interact. The sheet had fallen down around Reid's waist, and her thin tank top did little to hide her trim torso and small, firm breasts. Only when Reid laughed at something Chase said did Isabel look away from Reid's body. The boy sitting in the middle of the bed smiling up at Reid clearly adored her.

When Isabel studied Reid's face, she caught her breath. Reid's smile was completely generous, touching off sparks in her eyes. And it struck Isabel that the few times she'd seen such openness in Reid's features had been when she was interacting with Chase. Reid held absolutely nothing back with him. And with everyone else, Isabel included, she kept herself carefully controlled.

"Okay, okay. I'm getting up," Reid protested when Chase jumped on her again. She shoved him playfully to the side and got out of bed.

"Come on, Chase. Let's give Reid some privacy. She'll meet us downstairs," Isabel said hurriedly when she felt her heartbeat accelerate at the sight of Reid in only a pair of flannel boxers and the tank top. The boxers hung off her waist and Isabel thought again that she had lost weight recently. But her thighs and calves were still firm and well muscled.

As Chase scrambled from the bed, Reid paused in the middle of pulling a pair of jeans from the bureau. Isabel's voice was unnaturally high and tight. She looked up to find Isabel's gaze sliding over her body, and when their eyes met she was surprised to find an unmistakable awareness there. Judging from the flush that rose up Isabel's neck and the heat in her gaze, Reid guessed Isabel was too surprised by her reaction to be able to hide it. Isabel jerked her eyes away and ushered Chase out of the room.

Left alone, Reid tugged on the jeans, her favorites, worn so thin that they were frayed at the cuffs and on the knees. She grabbed an olive green polo shirt from the top of a stack of folded laundry in the chair by the door. As she dressed she contemplated the look she'd seen in Isabel's eyes.

Her own body had tightened instinctively in response to the heat in Isabel's eyes. But beneath the simple appreciation had been a layer of confusion that worried Reid. She'd only recently begun to feel that they weren't on such shaky ground, and she didn't want anything to interfere with that improving situation.

The morning that Isabel had picked her up at the station, Reid had sensed some tension between them. But two days later when she'd stepped outside to go to work she found Isabel waiting in the car to drive her again. Despite Reid's protests, Isabel had insisted. And just as Reid expected, Isabel was waiting the next morning when she got off work.

In the days that followed, Isabel kept insisting until Reid stopped protesting. They carefully kept their conversations on safe ground. Isabel was easy to talk to, had a quick wit and a fun sense of humor, which was perhaps going to be Reid's downfall. She found it increasingly difficult to ignore the feelings Isabel inspired. And though Reid knew she should limit the amount of time she spent alone with her, she craved these moments. Every morning when the subtle scent of Isabel assailed her inside the close quarters of the sedan, Reid wondered at her apparent masochistic streak.

She needed a distraction from her seemingly constant thoughts of Isabel or she just might go crazy. After spending an evening with Megan at the bowling alley, Reid decided she and Megan could become friends, but she certainly didn't know her well enough to discuss Isabel. And what was there to say, really? Isabel was off-limits and had been for a very long time. Oddly enough, she seemed to be the one constant in Reid's life.

Reid slowly padded downstairs and found her mother and Chase on the couch watching the preparations for the Macy's Parade on television.

"Spongebob!" Chase exclaimed as he pointed at the screen.

Reid paused behind the sofa to look over their shoulders at the giant yellow balloon that floated amid tall buildings. Isabel came in from the kitchen. Wordlessly, she handed Reid a mug of hot, fresh coffee as she passed, then settled on the sofa next to Chase.

"Thank you," Reid murmured.

"You're welcome," Isabel said, glancing over her shoulder and smiling.

Warmed both by the intimate smile and the coffee with just the right amount of sugar, Reid didn't question the lifting of her heart.

❖

"I'm stuffed." Chase pushed his empty plate away.

"So, no room for pie, then?" Meredith asked.

Isabel watched his face take on the cutest look of confusion. He'd put away more turkey than a small boy should be able to, but he was obviously tempted by the offer of pie.

"Can I have some later?" he finally asked.

"Yes, dear. We'll do the dishes and then see if you feel like dessert. If you're finished you may be excused."

"Can I play video games?" Chase was already pushing away from the table.

"Sure—"

"No," Isabel interrupted. "You're grounded and that includes video games."

"Grounded? What did you do?" Reid asked.

"His teacher sent a letter home yesterday. He's failed his last two tests and he's being disruptive in class."

Reid and Meredith both looked at Chase, and Isabel watched him squirm under their expectant gazes.

"I don't care about stupid school," he declared, defiance hardening his young features.

"You might care some day. What if you decide to be a doctor or a lawyer? You need good grades to do that," Meredith argued.

"I already know what I want to be. I'm going to be a fireman, just like my dad."

"You have plenty of time to decide that," Isabel insisted. "The point is that you should do well in school so you can do whatever you want."

"I want to be a fireman."

"Well, you can't get in the academy if you don't pay attention in school," Reid said.

"I can't?"

"No. Before you can get in the academy you have to take a whole bunch of tests. And one of them has a lot of math and science on it. You have to do really well on that test before you can move on to the next ones."

"I guess." Chase shrugged. "Can I be excused now?"

"Yeah, go on," Isabel said. It was Thanksgiving and she didn't see any point in ruining the holiday for him. He slid out of his chair and headed for the living room. Isabel stood to help Meredith clear the dishes. "His principal offered to give me the name of a grief counselor. Do you think he needs to talk to someone?"

"I don't know if he would open up to someone like that," Meredith said.

They all carried stacks of dishes to the kitchen.

"But they're probably good at getting people to open up. That's what they do."

"What are we talking about here?" Reid interrupted. "He doesn't need a shrink."

"Just because you're a stubborn ass—"

"Come on, Iz, I'm just saying he doesn't need to talk to a shrink."

"He might benefit from talking to a *counselor.* He's only seven years old and just had a huge loss. I'm trying to do what's best for him."

"Okay, girls, calm down," Meredith interrupted. She could see where this was going and it wouldn't end well. "It hasn't been that long. Let's give him some time, and if he doesn't seem to be coping we'll revisit the counselor idea. Okay?"

Both Isabel and Reid nodded, but Meredith could tell neither was happy about it.

"You seemed upset by what Chase said earlier about his future." Meredith slid a slice of pumpkin pie onto a plate and handed it over. Isabel added a dollop of whipped cream and held out her hand for the next one.

"I was, at first," Isabel admitted. "But he's young. He'll probably change his mind ten times before he settles on a career."

"Reid never did."

"Weren't you worried?"

"Of course." Meredith sighed. "It's the fate of a mother to worry about her child. We never want them to have a moment's pain. But we can't keep them from experiencing life, so I just pray that she stays safe."

"Why didn't you try to talk her out of it?"

"You've obviously never tried to stop Reid from doing something she has her mind set on," Meredith said wryly. "She's stubborn—like her father. Besides, I can't remember her ever wanting to do anything else. It's hard to argue with that kind of determination."

"I guess. But if he really is set on being a firefighter, I'll certainly try to talk him out of it."

"By the time you need to worry about that, you may feel differently."

"No, I won't."

"Right now, he's just a boy. It's hard to think about him being in danger. But by the time he has to choose a career, he'll be nearly a man. Either way, there's no sense in worrying about it now. Time will tell."

"Maybe you're right," Isabel conceded, but she knew when the time came she would do everything possible to prevent Chase from fighting fires.

"Maybe this is none of my business, but I've sensed some tension between you and Reid lately," Meredith said after a moment of silence.

Isabel's first instinct was denial. There was really no reason to discuss their issues with Reid's mother, especially when she didn't fully understand them herself. She couldn't seem to help how on edge she felt when she was around Reid. Nor could she explain the slightly jittery feeling she got in her stomach sometimes when she looked at Reid.

"Does it have anything to do with Jimmy?"

Isabel paused with a plate in her hand. She and Meredith had never really talked about Jimmy. It was easy to discuss Chase and his future because it sometimes felt as if Meredith had as much stake in raising him as she did. But when it came to her conflicting emotions about her brother, Isabel preferred to keep them to herself.

"She told me once that she thought you blamed her for Jimmy's death," Meredith admitted.

"Well," Isabel began, searching for words. She was thrown off by Meredith's directness.

"You have to know how it tore her apart to leave that building without him."

"Meredith, I—"

"You need to hear this, Isabel. If it hadn't been for that little girl, Reid would have died alongside Jimmy. And it breaks my heart to say this…" Meredith's voice was barely more than a whisper but she continued, "but sometimes I think she wishes she had."

"Meredith, I'm sorry." And she was. She was sorry for the anguish she saw on Meredith's face. And she was sorry for her part in making Meredith face a difficult truth about Reid. But like Meredith, Isabel was coming to believe it *was* the truth. Reid would selflessly trade places with Jimmy if she could.

"We better get this out there." Shutting Isabel out, Meredith picked up two plates and headed for the dining room.

Isabel rubbed her hand over her face. As much as she still grieved for Jimmy, she couldn't imagine Reid dying as well. In just a matter of weeks the woman she'd seen only a handful of times over the years had become so important to her. Despite her conflicting emotions and what she'd said about them getting along for Chase's sake, it was more than that. Reid felt like a friend, more than a friend really, but she couldn't explain why.

Chapter Eleven

"Hard to believe it's Thanksgiving, isn't it?" Isabel pushed open the back door and stepped outside. Reid sat in a swing suspended from the far end of the porch with one leg tucked beneath her. She pushed the toes of her other foot against the floor, maintaining a gentle sway.

"It really is a beautiful day." It was warm for late November. The sixty-degree weather was even more unexpected after the cold snap they had experienced the week before. "Join me?" Reid stopped the swing so Isabel could sit.

"I thought you'd be watching the game." Reid and Jimmy had always watched the Thanksgiving Day football game together. Reid was a die-hard Cowboys fan and Jimmy—well, Jimmy was *not*. It was quite possibly the only thing Isabel had ever seen them disagree on. And, she now realized, she'd taken a degree of pleasure in seeing the chink in their otherwise perfect friendship.

At times she'd been jealous of them. She'd always assumed she envied Reid's closeness to her brother. Reid knew Jimmy in ways that she never would. Sitting companionably beside Reid on the swing, Isabel realized she was now equally jealous of Jimmy's knowledge of Reid. She was beginning to feel that she'd missed out on something by not really knowing Reid all these years.

"The game's not the same," Reid answered with a shrug.

She was quiet for a long time, and Isabel was lulled by the steady squeak of the chains and creak of wood as the swing moved.

She was almost startled when Reid spoke again. "I'm not trying to undermine your authority with Chase."

"I know you're not. But not everyone deals with things the way you do, Reid."

"He's more like me than you want to admit."

"I know. Because he's his father's son, and Jimmy was just as pigheaded as you are."

"You say that like it's a bad thing," Reid said and tapped her fingers against Isabel's knee. "Hey, let's not waste this weather. How about a ride on the bike?"

"Ah, motorcycles aren't really my thing," Isabel hedged.

"Have you ever tried it?"

"No."

"Then how do you know you don't like it?" Reid lifted an eyebrow.

Isabel's heart rate accelerated at the teasing glint in Reid's eyes. *Are we still talking about motorcycles?* "I guess I don't."

Reid grinned and headed for the garage. By the time Reid, astride the motorcycle, had pushed it into the driveway, Isabel was having second thoughts.

Reid dismounted and crossed to Isabel. Taking her by the shoulders, Reid gently guided her closer to the bike. "Come here."

"I don't know."

"Baby steps, Iz. Baby steps. Just swing your leg over there."

Isabel settled tentatively in the seat. She really didn't get what all the excitement was about. Reid helped her strap on the half-helmet and took her hands and wrapped them around the handlebars.

"Just imagine the rumble of the engine beneath you, the power of the bike eating up the road, and the wind in your face. It's like flying," Reid murmured over her shoulder.

The only rumble Isabel was feeling was the soft vibration of Reid's voice close to her ear. And it was sending shivers down her spine.

"I'm sorry, Reid. I guess I'm just not a biker chick."

"I don't know about that. I can totally see you in a leather vest and chaps," Reid quipped with a wink.

Isabel flushed, knowing Reid was teasing her, but she thought she saw a hint of sincerity in Reid's intense gaze. Seeking some distance and hoping to calm her racing heart, Isabel made a move to dismount.

"Uh-uh, you're not giving up that easily. Scoot back." Reid nudged her and climbed on the bike in front of her. Before Isabel could react, Reid heeled up the kickstand and started the engine. With a flick of her wrist she revved the engine, eliciting a throaty growl from the exhaust.

"Wait." Isabel grasped Reid's shoulders.

"We'll just take a short trip around the neighborhood. Hold on tight."

"Reid." As the bike surged forward, Isabel yelped and wrapped her arms around Reid.

Reid wheeled into the street with no real destination in mind. She kept to a reasonable speed in deference both to the residential streets and to the woman behind her, forcing herself to concentrate on driving rather than the length of Isabel's thighs squeezing the outside of hers. Her knuckles formed a sharp ridge with the force of keeping her left hand wrapped around the handlebar instead of dropping it down to cup the back of Isabel's knee.

Isabel felt as if they were going far too fast. She tightened her arms around Reid's ribs and pressed her face against the soft leather jacket covering Reid's back. *It* is *like flying.* The pavement passed beneath them in a blur and Isabel felt weightless as she leaned into Reid. The bike roared and vibrated as Reid accelerated around a curve. Isabel began to relax and she loosened her grip on Reid's torso.

As she did, her arms fell lower around Reid's waist, and her hands slipped beneath Reid's jacket and pressed against her stomach, with only the thin cotton barrier of a T-shirt between them. Sparks shot up her forearms. She felt Reid's abdomen tense beneath her fingers and pulled her hands back and placed them safely outside Reid's jacket.

"Sorry," she said over Reid's shoulder, unsure if she could be heard over the rushing of the wind.

Reid circled back toward their street and in moments they were pulling into the driveway.

"That was great!" Isabel exclaimed as she climbed off the bike.

"I knew you'd like it." Reid put down the kickstand and dismounted.

"Yeah, it was fun. But I wouldn't want to be the one driving."

"Well, anytime you want to go for a ride, just let me know," Reid said, smiling.

"I'll be sure to do that." Isabel held her gaze. *Are we flirting?*

Isabel reached up to remove her helmet at the same moment Reid made a move to help her, and their hands clashed beneath her chin. Isabel's body was still charged from the motorcycle ride, and her skin tingled where it touched Reid's. When Reid gently disentangled their fingers and pulled off Isabel's helmet, she detected the faintest tremor in Reid's hands.

Isabel sought her eyes and found them wide and depthless. Reid's dark brown irises held tiny flecks the color of rich toffee. For a moment they were completely unguarded, and so unlike Reid that Isabel ached with the vulnerability of them. She felt for a moment that she could see Reid's soul and it was gentle, in direct contradiction to the black leather jacket, the arrogant tilt of her hips, and her impenetrable strength.

She had to touch her. She needed that physical connection. And when she placed her hands on Reid's shoulders, it wasn't enough. *Not nearly enough.*

"Iz." Reid's voice was rough and filled with so much uncertainty that Isabel thought she might back away. But Reid didn't move.

Isabel slid her hands to the sides of Reid's neck and traced her fingertips over Reid's jaw. Her skin, still cool from the wind whipping across it, was as smooth as marble. *Not nearly enough.*

She stared at Reid's mouth, her slightly fuller lower lip. And before she could question what she was doing—standing in the driveway in broad daylight—Isabel kissed her. She felt Reid stiffen.

"Christ, Iz, wait." Reid pulled back.

Not ready to relinquish the light-headed pleasure rushing through her at that barest of touches, Isabel grabbed the lapels of Reid's jacket and tugged her close again. She lightly traced her tongue over Reid's lips, thrilling in their pliancy when Reid began to return her kiss. The hint of rejection she'd felt as Reid tried to pull away faded in the face of Reid's eventual response. Reid's tongue stroked boldly inside her mouth as if now that they'd begun she couldn't get enough. Reid eased her toward the bike and when her backside touched the seat, Reid pushed against her, bringing their bodies flush.

Isabel pressed her palms to Reid's chest and felt her heart hammering beneath them. Her own heart beat a staccato response. *It* is *like flying.* She was soaring and Reid's hands, squeezing the sides of her waist, were the only thing that anchored her to earth. Reid's fingers slipped beneath her shirt, touching skin, and fluttered upward to brush the underside of her breasts—and then they were gone. Reid jerked away and stumbled back two steps.

"This isn't a good idea," Reid whispered.

Out of touching distance, Isabel felt her head start to clear. She straightened and pulled at the hem of her shirt. "You're right. Of course, you're right." Her face flamed with embarrassment. *What was I thinking? I wasn't thinking, that's the problem. I just threw myself at her as if just because she's a lesbian she might welcome my attentions. I kissed a woman—what does that make me?* "I—uh—I'm going to go home. Please, thank your mother for the wonderful meal and for including me. And send Chase home in a bit," Isabel rambled as she began walking backward toward her house.

Still trembling and unable to catch her breath, Reid watched her go. *What just happened?* She'd just kissed Isabel Grant or, more accurately, Isabel Grant had just kissed her. Reid closed her eyes and allowed herself a moment to memorize the feel of her, the taste of her. It had been more than she'd ever imagined. Almost from the moment Isabel's lips touched hers Reid had been instantly and painfully aroused. She had been inches from dragging her inside the garage, closing the door, and taking her right there. She was certain she would have done it, right up until the point when her fingertips had touched Isabel's warm, soft skin.

The reality of what was happening had slammed into her, and her brain had screamed at her to stop. Because of Jimmy. Because of Chase. Because kissing her was such a rush that Reid had feared she might come right there, shoving her against the motorcycle. And because Isabel deserved more than a frantic groping in the driveway.

❖

"Are you sure you don't mind him staying here?" Isabel stood in Reid's kitchen glancing nervously at the doorway that led to the stairs. She wanted to be gone before Reid woke up. She didn't want to confront Reid any more than she wanted to face the highly erotic dreams that had caused her to wake extremely aroused and moaning that morning.

"Of course not, dear. He's always welcome." Meredith smiled at Chase.

"Thank you," Isabel said, then gave Chase a pointed look. "Behave."

"I will."

"Drive safely." Meredith handed Isabel a travel mug full of coffee.

"Are you going somewhere?" Reid asked, walking into the kitchen. She wore a navy T-shirt and sweats emblazoned with the fire department logo.

"Uh—yeah, I've got to run to Knoxville to see a client." Isabel couldn't meet Reid's eyes.

"It's a holiday weekend."

"I know. I just—I've been putting this off. I'll be back

tomorrow or Sunday." Isabel headed for the door and Reid followed.

"I'll walk you out," she said quietly, stepping into a pair of sneakers near the door.

"You don't have to do that."

"I don't mind." Reid's tone told her there was no sense in arguing, and the firm hand against Isabel's back guided her toward the door.

Outside, Isabel descended the steps of the porch quickly and headed straight for her car, hoping to escape.

"We need to talk about what happened." Reid stopped near the driver's door. She had spent the night before deciding how to approach Isabel. She was concerned that Isabel might be freaked out by the kiss or, worse, think that Reid had taken advantage of her. Regardless of who initiated the kiss, Reid believed it had been her responsibility to stop it. Eventually, Reid decided she should be straightforward. And now, faced with Isabel's obvious attempt at retreat, Reid felt an unexplained urgency to settle things before Isabel left.

Isabel sighed. "Can't this wait until I get back?"

"No." When Isabel tried to step around her, Reid blocked her entry into the vehicle.

"Well, it will have to." Irritated, Isabel made a show of glancing at her watch. "I've got to go and I don't have time for this."

"Make time," Reid insisted.

Isabel gave a harsh laugh. "All of a sudden you want to talk. Are you forgetting that you're the one who avoided *me* for two weeks because *talking* didn't suit you at the time? I think you can give me a couple of days."

Without waiting for a response, Isabel shoved past Reid and yanked the door open.

Reid made no move to stop her as she started the car and backed out of the driveway. As she watched her drive away, she admitted Isabel was probably right. She couldn't make her talk about the kiss, but the thought of waiting two days to discuss it left Reid frustrated. More than that, though, she was going to miss her. And, she suddenly realized, she'd never felt this way—as if a piece of her had disappeared from sight along with Isabel's car.

CHAPTER TWELVE

That afternoon, Isabel sat in Anna's living room in Knoxville trying to find the words to explain why she'd fled town on a whim. Confused by the events of the previous day, she needed to talk to her friend. If anyone could help her sort out her feelings, Anna could. Isabel had spent the entire drive alternating between berating herself for her actions and replaying the kiss in her mind. Finally, in an attempt to shut out her circuitous thoughts, she'd popped in a CD and tried to drown them out.

She'd shown up at Anna's looking as frazzled as she felt. After freshening up, she allowed Anna to settle her onto the couch and press a cold beer into her hand. She took a long pull from the bottle, ignoring Anna's expectant look as long as she could. Isabel spilled the whole story, since she knew she would end up doing so anyway.

"You kissed her?" Anna exclaimed.

"Anna—"

"I'm just surprised. I didn't know you were a les—"

"I'm not," Isabel interrupted. "I mean, I don't—aw, hell. I don't know what I was thinking, Anna. I just kissed her and then I couldn't think at all."

"Okay, okay. Calm down, Isabel."

Isabel took a deep breath. "It happened so fast and in slow motion at the same time. I know that doesn't make any sense. But one minute I was standing there looking at her and the next I was kissing her. I didn't do it intentionally."

"You accidentally kissed her?"

"Well, it sounds ridiculous when you say it like that."

"So, how was it?"

Isabel gave her a sharp look but found no judgment in her friend's eyes. "It was—so intense. I've never felt anything like it, Anna. Never."

"What did she do?"

"At first she kissed me back, but then she stopped and said it wasn't a good idea. Then I was so embarrassed that I got out of there as quickly as I could. And this morning I took off and, well, you know the rest."

"Why do you think she said it wasn't a good idea?"

"I don't know. She's so closed off sometimes. Sometimes I'm sure that she's hurting, but she'd never purposely let her pain show."

Anna shrugged. "Maybe she's not into you. I mean, she probably thinks of you as just Jimmy's little sister."

Isabel studied her friend, sure she was playing devil's advocate but uncertain why. "She *did* kiss me back, you know."

"Well, you probably caught her off guard."

"So when she recovered her senses she realized she didn't like it?" Isabel said sarcastically. She flushed as she recalled the length of Reid's body against hers, Reid's hips pressing insistently against hers right before she pulled away. "No. She was into it."

Anna laughed. "Oh, Lord, I wish I could see the pictures in your head right now."

Isabel felt even warmer and shoved Anna's shoulder. "It doesn't matter. It won't happen again. I don't want it to be uncomfortable when I get back there. Things are going to be hard enough as it is."

"So that's it. The kiss is just forgotten?"

Isabel considered the question. She could admit she'd felt something, couldn't she? She had to. There was no denying the steady pulse of her body as she'd stumbled back to her house or the images that had crept into her dreams last night that were too hot to tell Anna. But what exactly did that mean? She'd never considered that she could be attracted to another woman, let alone initiate a kiss with one. And Reid Webb, of all people. Even if she wanted to, Reid was not a woman she could simply experiment with. "It's forgotten. When I get back if she still insists on talking, I'll simply explain that I don't think it's a good idea either. After a while any awkwardness will go away."

Anna looked skeptical. "How long are you staying?"

"A day or two. I've got to meet with Warner. He was a convenient excuse, but I really do need to see him."

"You'll stay with me. The girls are with their father for the holiday, so I could use the company."

It was not a question. And Isabel knew better than to argue with Anna. Besides, she needed to save all of her energy to sort out her feelings about Reid.

Two hours and twice as many bottles of Dos Equis later, Isabel lay stretched out on Anna's sofa. Anna lay at the other end, mirroring her pose. They had opted to order in dinner and chased Chinese takeout with cold beer. Isabel was now cruising through a pleasant buzz.

"I'm sorry I missed the girls. How do they like the new place?"

Anna had separated from her husband nine months earlier, and the divorce had been final for only three months. She and her ex-husband planned to share custody of their twelve-year-old twin daughters.

As part of the settlement they had sold the house they lived in for eight years. Anna used as little of her share as she could to secure the small two-bedroom apartment in the same school district. The rest she was saving until she had enough for a house.

"They're making the best of it, but I can tell they miss home."

"They're smart girls. I'm sure they know you're doing the best you can."

"Sometimes it seems they're handling it better than I am. It's been so hard having them gone this weekend."

"You get Christmas, don't you?"

"Yes. They'll go see him during their winter break. But they'll be with me first for Christmas."

"Well, you know if you get lonely while they're gone you can always take a few days off and come visit me."

"I might just do that. It would certainly be worth the trip to meet your firefighter." Anna nudged Isabel's thigh with her foot.

"She's not *my* firefighter. She's not *my* anything," Isabel protested.

"So, now that you have a few beers in you, tell me honestly, how was that kiss?"

"Anna."

"Come on. I haven't had a date since the separation, let alone a kiss. Let me live vicariously through your lesbian experimentation."

"It wasn't like that." Stalling, Isabel took a long draw from her beer. "It was—"

"Incredible? Amazing? Sexy?"

Isabel's face flushed hot. "Yes."

"And you can't stop thinking about her?"

"Yes," she admitted reluctantly. "But what the hell am I supposed to do about it?"

"Let's look at this logically," Anna began, sitting up.

"Jesus, can we be logical when I'm not half-drunk?" Isabel protested, but she took Anna's outstretched hand and allowed herself to be pulled into a sitting position.

"We're talking about some pretty big changes here. Are you even willing to consider a relationship with her?"

"Anna, a relationship with a woman, any woman, isn't exactly in my life plan."

"Neither was moving back to Nashville and raising Chase,"

Anna said bluntly. Her words were softened by her sympathetic tone. "Sometimes life doesn't follow our plans and we have to adjust. Yesterday a woman kissed you. And you felt something. So now I'm asking you what you want to do about it. Are we talking about a casual fuck, just to see how it feels? Or a relationship?"

Isabel set her beer bottle on the coffee table, leaned forward, and cradled her head in her hands. "Neither one seems like a good idea. I don't know if I could be in a relationship with a woman. What if it didn't work out? It's not like I could never see her again. *She lives next door.* And Chase needs her too much." But Reid was already so much a part of her life, it didn't feel like that much of a stretch to imagine them being even closer.

"And she's a firefighter," Anna added, understanding what Isabel wasn't saying.

"Yes," Isabel agreed. "Do you think it's weird that her being a firefighter bothers me more than her being a woman?"

"No, sweetie, I don't."

"If anything happened to her…"

Anna rubbed Isabel's back in a soothing gesture.

"I can't lose anyone else in my life."

Chase was sprawled on his back on the weight bench tucked in a corner of Jimmy's garage. Jimmy's truck and motorcycle took up the rest of the space. Chase held his arms in the air, reaching for the bar suspended above his head. Reid stood at the end of the bench and spotted him. Neither of them had noticed Isabel when she paused in the open door, so she continued to watch unobserved.

"Ready?" Reid asked before lowering the bar. She paused to let him wrap his fingers around it, then continued to hold it as he let it drop toward his chest. He carefully counted out five reps before Reid replaced the bar.

"Hey, guys." Isabel stepped inside.

"Hi, Aunt Isabel. I'm working out." Chase scrambled off the

bench and posed for her, pressing his fists together in front of him and flexing like a bodybuilder. "Pretty soon I'll be able to lift more than Reid."

"It'll be sooner than we think," Reid added.

"Me and my dad used to work out together." He climbed back onto the bench.

Sitting down next to him, Reid said, "I know. I used to work out with him, too, at the station. Your dad was a strong guy."

"He said he could lift more than me and you put together." Chase grinned, but tears shone in his eyes.

"I think he probably could." The tenderness in Reid's tone made Isabel's chest ache.

"My dad could do anything." He stared at his hands.

"You miss him a lot, huh?"

"Yeah."

"Me, too." Reid put her arm around his shoulders.

Chase's chin quivered but the tears clung stubbornly to his lashes. He wrung his hands together in his lap.

Isabel crossed the room and knelt in front of him. "It's okay to miss him. And it's okay to cry about it, you know?"

"Men don't cry."

Isabel took his hands in hers. "Yes, they do."

"My dad didn't cry."

Reid's heart broke at his attempt at bravado and the tremor in his voice. The pain that slid across Isabel's face mirrored her own. The two of them had lost so much, and Reid would do anything to make it better. She would give them anything.

"Oh, honey, yes, he did," Isabel said.

"No, he didn't." Chase yanked his hands out of hers.

"He did, Chase," Reid said. "I saw him."

"No. My dad was brave and strong. You said he was." Chase bit his lower lip. And then when he couldn't contain himself any longer, he sobbed.

"He was." Isabel gathered him close even as he struggled against her. "He was the bravest and the strongest. But he cried when he lost your mother. He loved her so much and it hurt him to let her go."

"I cried, too," Reid said.

"*You*?" He seemed even more shocked by this revelation than by the recounting of his father's tears.

"Yes. I cried with him."

"So it's okay if I do sometimes." He drew out of Isabel's arms and studied Reid, seeming to search her face for the truth.

"Yes. It's okay."

He nodded, satisfied, and swiped at his eyes with the back of his hands. "Can I go play outside?"

Sensing he wanted to be alone, Reid nodded.

"Did you just get back?" she asked when Isabel began to follow him.

"Yes."

"Listen, Iz, about the other day, you caught me off guard."

Isabel suspected that was an understatement, if Reid was feeling anything close to the confusion swirling inside her.

"I didn't think you were a lesbian," Reid said.

"I'm not." *Why does everyone keep saying that?*

"Well, you sure kiss like one," Reid quipped. "Are you bi?"

"Do I have to put a label on it?" Isabel sighed. Suddenly feeling claustrophobic, she took a step back to put some distance between them. She debated whether to deny her feelings, but after the way she'd responded to that kiss, she doubted Reid would believe her. "I've always enjoyed my relationships with men. But I *am* attracted to you. I don't know what that means. I've never wanted to kiss another woman." Even now, Isabel couldn't keep her eyes off Reid's mouth. "But you—"

"I can't be the one to help you figure out who you are," Reid interrupted. "Iz, you're Jimmy's sister. And Chase—"

"Say no more. I understand, Reid." Isabel rushed to give them both an excuse to back away from the conversation. *You're not a lesbian.* The voice in her head sounded suspiciously like her father's.

"You do?"

"Yes. The last thing you need right now is some confused straight woman coming on to you. And you have to see me every day, so you want to let me down easy."

I'm trying to let me *down easy. It would tear me up when it was over.*

"It's okay, Reid. I mean, you're not exactly my ideal mate either."

"I'm not?"

"A firefighter? No, I can't be involved with a firefighter."

Remembering Isabel's outburst that night on the porch, Reid believed her. She stared into slate gray eyes hard with conviction, the same eyes that had been liquid silver with desire only days ago. The recollection of that desire made her weak.

Isabel took another step back. The heat that leapt into Reid's eyes was like a caress, urgent against her skin. She shivered. "Look, Reid, there doesn't need to be any awkwardness between us. We're both adults and we both agree it's a bad idea. So, I—I kissed you. It's not a big deal."

"Right. Not a big deal," Reid repeated. She'd been fighting her attraction to Isabel for years; she could do it with her eyes closed. At that moment, Isabel brushed her hair back, exposing the tempting column of her throat, and Reid was overcome with the urge to kiss the soft skin there. *Christ, closing my eyes would probably help.*

Joey maneuvered the engine into the narrow driveway of the ranch home and parked near the garage, next to the ambulance, leaving room for it to get out past them. They'd been called to the location to check on an unconscious female.

Reid and Megan approached the open back doors of the ambulance, where a female paramedic inside passed a large duffel to the man standing outside, who in turn handed it to Reid. As she shouldered the strap, the man also gave Megan a small box, and then he and his partner removed the yellow and black Stryker stretcher from the back of the rig. As a group they moved toward the house where a brunette stood next to a green Volvo.

"My friend, Sharon, she never showed up for lunch so I came over and found her in there," the brunette called out, near tears.

They followed her into the house and found a woman lying unresponsive on the sofa, one arm hanging off the edge. Her dark hair obscured her face. The two medics rushed over and checked her vital signs.

"She's breathing, but just barely," the female paramedic said and reached into the duffel without looking up. She pulled out an oxygen mask and a coil of tubing. "Check out her skin. Carbon monoxide." The woman's face was bright cherry red.

"Okay. Everybody out. Let's go," Reid ordered.

Joey moved forward and helped transfer the patient to the stretcher while the paramedics worked. They attached the sensor of the pulse oximeter to the woman's finger and placed the mask over her face.

Reid stepped quickly out of the way as Joey and Nathan wheeled the unconscious woman toward the door. As she did so, she glimpsed a baby's car seat by the front door. "Ma'am, does she have a baby?" she asked the patient's friend.

"His father has him this weekend."

The hair on the back of Reid's neck stood on end. "Check the rest of the house, quickly," Reid told Megan. They all needed to get clear of the house until they could determine the level of the toxic gas inside. She directed the visiting woman to wait outside.

When Megan didn't return right away, Reid hurried down the hall in search of her. The first two bedrooms were empty, but then she entered the nursery, a study in baby blue and teddy bears, and found Megan standing next to a crib.

"Megan."

Her back was to Reid, who moved quickly to her side. Reid's heart lurched when she saw the infant lying in the crib, unmoving. She checked for a pulse and didn't find one.

"He's gone," Megan rasped.

Reid glanced at her sharply. Megan's eyes were distant and her skin remarkably pale. A fine sheen of sweat covered her face. Reid scooped up the baby, not because she believed he could be saved but because she couldn't bear to leave him there alone. She tucked the tiny body against her chest.

"Out. Now," she ordered and shoved Megan in front of her.

They were outside the house in seconds. On their way, Reid passed Joey going inside the house with a sniffer, the device used to check the saturation level of the carbon monoxide. She handed the baby to the medics and led Megan out of view behind the open passenger door of the engine.

"Megan." She received no response. She shook the other woman's shoulders until dark eyes met hers. "Megan, are you all right?"

Megan shook her head numbly and her jaw bunched, tight. "I'm fine."

Reid understood exactly how Megan felt.

❖

"Do you need me to drive you home?" Reid asked Megan later as they walked out of the station together. She was still concerned about her.

"I told you I'm fine, Captain."

Ignoring the deliberate use of her title, Reid grasped her shoulder. "Kids are tough, but you'll get through it. Please, call me if you need to talk."

Megan nodded. Pausing just outside the door, Reid watched Megan walk to her car. She guessed it had been Megan's first bad call, and children were always the worst. Despite her efforts to hide her reaction, Megan had been shaken up.

Reid was still standing there when Joey and Nathan came out. Joey said good-bye and kept walking, but Nathan lingered.

"I guess your rookie showed her true colors today."

Reid wanted to slap the smug look off his face. "What's your problem, Nathan?"

"She doesn't belong here," he said. "Where's your chauffeur today?"

As if summoned by his snide comment, Isabel's car came around the corner and into the parking lot. She steered into a space and waited for Reid.

"Ah, there she is. Come on, Cap. I've seen the way you look at her. You can tell me. Are you hittin' that?" Nathan leered in Isabel's direction.

Reid curled her hands tightly at her side. It took a good amount of effort to keep from slamming him against the brick wall. She didn't say a word, but the look she gave him had been known to shut down greater men than he.

He wasn't quite smart enough to let it go. "All I'm saying is she's got a hot—"

"Shut up, Brewer," Reid ground out. She stepped close, bringing them eye to eye. "You need to remember your place. Regardless of how you feel about it, I am your captain. If you don't like it, then you better ask for a transfer because I'm not going anywhere. You *will* treat me and the rest of my crew with respect. And if I *ever* hear you say anything even slightly disrespectful about Isabel Grant again, I'll lay you out faster than you can blink. Believe that." She walked away and toward the parking lot. If he said another word she would likely smash her fist into his face.

When she reached the car, she tossed her duffel into the backseat and climbed in the front. Isabel looked as if she was just out of bed. A strand of hair fell from her ponytail and brushed her jaw, and her face was free of any makeup. She had obviously thrown on her jeans and T-shirt in order to come and pick Reid up. That just-rolled-out-of-bed look had Reid imagining how it would feel to wake up next to her.

"What was that all about?" Isabel asked as she put the car in gear.

"Nothing," Reid mumbled, her blood still boiling.

"You looked like you wanted to hit him."

"It's nothing. You know, you don't have to drive me every day," Reid said, and her lingering anger made her voice sound harder than she'd intended. Since the day they had settled the business about the kiss, Isabel had resumed her practice of driving Reid to and from work. Though a week had passed, Reid still found the close proximity to Isabel disconcerting. When she spoke again she softened her tone. "I appreciate it. But I don't want to impose on your schedule."

"Don't worry about my schedule. I don't mind driving you." The truth was she looked forward to these few minutes alone with Reid. Just because they had agreed to forget about that kiss didn't mean she couldn't enjoy Reid's company. She had seen the slow perusal Reid gave her as she got in the car. And while she certainly didn't intend to act on the obvious attraction, what did it hurt to enjoy it?

"Megan looked upset," Isabel said after a long silence. She had seen Megan getting into her car as she pulled in the lot.

"We had a rough night. She'll be okay."

"Are you and she…dating?"

"No."

"She's very attractive," Isabel said matter-of-factly.

"Yes, she is." Reid paused and glanced at Isabel's profile, wondering at the casual tone that sounded forced. "And I'm sure that her pregnant girlfriend thinks so, too."

CHAPTER THIRTEEN

"You and Isabel seem to be getting along better."

With her upper body half under the sink Reid couldn't see her mother's face, but she did detect something in her tone. She paused, her hands stilling on the wrench she'd been using to loosen the pipe. "What do you mean?"

"Just that some of the tension between the two of you has eased." The rhythm of Meredith's knife against the cutting board never slowed. The pungent odor of the onions she chopped for a stir-fry stung Reid's eyes.

"Mom." Reid pulled the trap free and water drained into the bucket she had shoved underneath. She flipped over the U-shaped pipe in her hand and the item she sought fell into the bucket. "These past months have been hard for all of us. Things are just settling down, that's all."

"I was worried for a time that they wouldn't."

"Well, they have." Reid finished replacing the trap and crawled from beneath the sink.

"Good. Because for Chase's sake—"

"I'm well aware of what I have to do for Chase's sake," Reid snapped. She fished into the bucket, pulled out the small gold band simply adorned with a brilliant sapphire, and placed it carefully on the counter. Aware that her mother wasn't to blame for her frustration, she softened her tone. "You might want to clean it before you put it back on."

Reid watched her mother tuck the ring into her pocket and held back the question that had crossed her mind countless times. *How can you still wear his ring?*

Her father had chosen the perfect engagement ring for her mother. Meredith would want not something as common as a diamond, but rather a sapphire that danced with blue fire. After their divorce Meredith had removed her wedding band but continued to wear this ring. For Reid it seemed to tether Meredith to him, and she wondered if her mother saw it the same way.

"Is something wrong?"

"Nothing I can't handle." Reid gave her standard response.

Meredith laid down the knife and turned to Reid. Confronted with the frank appraisal of eyes so like her own, Reid looked away.

"Did something happen between the two of you?"

She'd never been able to lie to her mother. They had always been close, but after the divorce that bond had deepened. When she answered she did so honestly, because she knew Meredith would keep her confidence. "She kissed me."

A look of surprise passed quickly over Meredith's face, but she covered it well. "And what did you do?"

"Well, I kissed her back. And then, I—uh—"

"You panicked and ran away?"

"No," Reid said defensively. "I didn't have a chance to. She ran away first."

Meredith just shook her head and rolled her eyes.

"She's Jimmy's sister."

"So you think that's more important than the fact that you've been in love with her since ninth grade?" She covered Reid's hand with her own.

"I—you—what?"

"Reid, you're my daughter. I know you. I watched you fall in love and then bury it all those years ago. And I understood why. But since Jimmy died," Meredith tightened her hand around Reid's, "since Isabel moved back I've watched you fall in love all over again. Am I going to watch you smother it again, too?"

"There are a million reasons why I should. If it didn't work out—" Pain knifed through her chest at her mother's recounting of her stifled love.

She remembered clearly the moment, at sixteen, that she'd realized her feelings for Isabel were more than just friendly. Jimmy had invited her over to watch a movie and they were sprawled over opposite ends of the couch when Isabel had skipped downstairs. At fourteen, Isabel was excited that her parents had finally agreed to let her go on a date. She was going to a school dance with an older boy and, after spending over an hour getting ready, she came bounding down the stairs wearing a teal skirt and white off-the-shoulder top. She'd teased her long red hair, put on makeup, and smelled faintly of summer flowers.

For the first time, Reid had felt that flutter in her stomach that had always been lacking when she looked at the boys to whom she was expected to be attracted. She felt jealousy rise, and she wished more than anything that she could be the person Isabel had primped for. When Isabel opened the door to the gangly pimple-faced boy in a dress shirt and his daddy's tie, Reid longed to be the person who inspired the shy smile that transformed Isabel's face. She'd silently tortured herself for the rest of the evening, wondering whether Isabel would let him kiss her good night.

Reid hadn't felt a longing so acute as she had that night, until Isabel had kissed her. *I don't know if I could survive losing her.* She shook free of the memory and focused once more on her mother. "Well, Chase doesn't need any more disruptions in his life. And I feel like I'm going behind Jimmy's back."

"Reid, he would want you both to be happy. If being together—"

"This isn't open for discussion." Reid pulled her hand away and was through the back door before Meredith could argue. She had to get away.

❖

As Reid fled the house she didn't know where she was going. She hadn't stopped to grab her keys or a jacket, and the December dusk was too cold for a walk. Pacing across her driveway, she glanced at the garage next to hers. Jimmy used to leave the keys in his truck. She doubted Isabel had bothered to do anything with them. Without giving herself a chance to change her mind, she hurried inside and saw the keys dangling from the ignition of the old green Chevy.

The truck had been frozen in time. Jimmy's sunglasses lay on the dash. A battalion of Chase's little green plastic army men was scattered across the tan vinyl seat, creating a battlefield of tiny casualties. Using the remote clipped to the visor she raised the garage door, pulled the truck out, and closed the door behind her. She drove aimlessly for several miles, then found herself in front of the cemetery. As she entered she felt only a moment's trepidation. She slowed to a stop and parked alongside the road. She hadn't been here since the funeral, but she was desperate to feel Jimmy's presence, missed his stability in her life. He had always been the one to curtail her tendency to run headlong into things.

She had left the house wearing only a T-shirt and jeans, and as she got out of the truck an icy wind whipped her. It had been raining on and off since the day before, and the sky was still dark with angry clouds. One of Jimmy's sweatshirts lay on the passenger seat and she pulled it on, choking back a sob at the familiar scent of his aftershave.

She crossed the grass and knelt in front of the stone bearing Jimmy's name, situated between Amanda's and his parents'. The ground was still wet from that morning's rain, and moisture immediately soaked through her jeans. *Beloved Brother, Father, and Friend.* Seeing the words etched in stone hit Reid like a punch in the stomach. The breath wheezed out of her and she doubled over. Pressing her palms against the cool grass, she let go of the grief she had been holding back for so long. Tears fell unimpeded from her lashes to the ground.

"Jimmy, I miss you so much. It hurts every day—not having

you here," she whispered when she could speak again. "Man, I don't know what I'm doing here without you."

Reid didn't move from her tucked position, even when the rain started. As it ran down her face, she swiped her soaked hair off her forehead. Thunder rolled in the distance.

"I'm sorry—so sorry. I should have left when the chief gave the order. I just—that little girl, Jimmy. I wanted to get her. But I didn't know what it was going to cost. I wish I could go back." She sucked in a deep breath, having difficulty speaking between sobs. "If I could do it over, I'd make you go down that hallway in front of me. Chase needs his father. You had so much more to lose. It's just not fair."

She stayed there, talking to him about Chase and everything that had been happening since he'd gone. The only topic she avoided was her feelings for Isabel. She was still amazed that her mother had known all along. And she now wondered if her emotions had been more obvious than she knew. Had Jimmy suspected? Wouldn't he have said something? If only he was still alive, she might even find the courage to ask him what she should do about Isabel.

Night had fallen by the time Reid pulled back into Isabel's driveway. She could barely make out the silhouette of a figure sitting in the rocking chair on the porch. *Damn.* Reid returned the truck to the garage and was considering how rude it would be to slip back to her house without saying hello. She was freezing and emotionally drained. In the end, manners won out over exhaustion, so she reluctantly headed for Isabel's house. Her muscles were tight from the cold and her legs felt heavy.

"I hope you don't mind that I borrowed the truck." While it still felt like Jimmy's, she was aware it now belonged to Isabel and she'd taken it without asking.

"Of course not. You can use it anytime."

"What are you doing out here?" Reid paused at the bottom of the stairs, intent on lingering only long enough to exchange pleasantries.

"Watching the storm." Lightning flashed, and in the stark light, Isabel glimpsed Reid's pale face. Her clothes were plastered to her. "You're soaking wet, you should get inside."

"I'm fine."

Something was wrong. Reid's eyes looked vacant and she didn't seem to notice the rain that pounded her. Her clothes were soaked and her lips were tinged blue. She hugged her arms around herself in a failed attempt to stop shivering.

"Come here, Reid," Isabel ordered, standing and crossing to the top step. "You're going to get sick. Come up here."

After Reid stumbled up the steps, Isabel grabbed her hand, pulled her into the house, and led her directly to the master bathroom. "You need to get out of these clothes. I'll find something for you to wear."

Minutes later, when Isabel returned with a towel and some dry clothes, Reid still stood in the same place, dripping water onto the tile. She stared at the vanity mirror, but her expression was so haunted that Isabel doubted she was seeing her own reflection. Pushing aside her fear, Isabel turned on the shower, then tugged the waterlogged sweatshirt over Reid's head and dropped it to the floor. Reid's T-shirt followed. Isabel barely stifled a gasp when she realized that Reid wasn't wearing a bra. Her skin was pale and goose bumps covered her torso. Isabel couldn't tear her eyes away from firm breasts tipped with tight nipples until Reid shivered.

"Jesus, Reid, you're freezing." When Isabel reached for her fly, Reid stopped her.

"I better do this part." Reid's hands were shaking, which wasn't entirely the result of being cold. Isabel's fingers against her skin had penetrated the fog; the warm brush of them had reached through the icy shell. When Reid had looked up and found Isabel's eyes riveted on her chest, she'd felt the gaze as surely as a caress.

"Okay. I'll be out here if you need anything." Isabel slipped from the room.

Forcing from her mind the image of Reid stripping off her pants and stepping into a hot shower, Isabel went to the kitchen to make tea. Reid needed warming up. *And I need cooling down.* She knew Reid was in shape, so it stood to reason she would have a nice body. What Isabel hadn't expected was the intensity of her own reaction to seeing it. She'd grown used to unexpected twinges of awareness when she was around Reid and could rationalize them as the result of an overemotional couple of months. She had even managed to delude herself into believing that the kiss was a fluke as well.

But the rapid beat of her pulse and the tightening of her nipples when she looked at Reid's naked torso were harder to explain away. *I would have stepped into that shower with her without a second thought.* She was shaken by the realization that all of her talk about not getting involved with a firefighter was apparently just that, talk. Could she really just forget her fears in exchange for a night in Reid's arms? And *now* she was picturing Reid in the shower again. *Shit, Isabel, control yourself.*

Reid stepped out of the shower and quickly toweled dry. The hot spray had effectively warmed her skin, and the memory of Isabel's esurient gaze on her breasts had overheated her insides. She pulled on the flannel pajama pants and long-sleeved T-shirt Isabel had left out for her, then headed for the kitchen.

Resting her shoulder against the archway leading from the living room, she watched as Isabel pulled two mugs from the cabinet and dropped tea bags into them. She had felt empty when she left the cemetery, as if she was leaving a piece of herself there. But now, in Jimmy's home, wearing Isabel's clothes, she felt a corner of her heart begin to fill again. Her mother was right; she would most likely do everything she could to bury her feelings.

But it would be harder than she had originally planned. Isabel was no longer the girl she had lusted after from afar. She was the sweet, caring woman who had come to mean a great deal more to Reid than she ever had before.

Reid was in the doorway when Isabel looked up and noticed her. Her face held the strangest expression of awe and regret, and Isabel found she very much wanted to know the cause of it.

"Is chamomile okay?"

"It's great, thank you." Reid took the offered mug.

"I thought you might want something to help you relax and warm you up." Isabel heard Reid's sharply indrawn breath as she squeezed past Reid and into the living room. "Come sit down. Are you still cold? Do you need a blanket?" Isabel sat in the chair nearby.

Reid sipped her tea, then smiled at Isabel. "I'm warming up." The teasing note and the flicker of heat in Reid's gaze gave Isabel hope that she was returning to herself. Her eyes seemed more focused and aware. "You've already gone to enough trouble."

"I wasn't just watching the storm," Isabel admitted. "After you didn't return for dinner, Meredith came over here looking for you. She said you'd been gone for hours."

"I just needed to clear my head."

"She was worried you might be upset about something you and she talked about. But she wouldn't say what it was."

"And you're hoping that by plying me with a hot shower and some tea, I might," Reid teased.

"I can assure you if I were plying you with a hot shower, conversation wouldn't be my goal," Isabel said without thinking. *Did I just say that?*

"Iz, I—"

"You know if you need someone to talk to, I'm here. Don't you?" Isabel rushed on before Reid could say anything. She hoped Reid would take the hint and ignore her impulsive words.

"There's nothing I need to talk about."

Isabel nodded, aware Reid was shutting her out and unsure

why it surprised her. Obviously, the bond she had felt growing between them was one-sided. She carefully avoided Reid's eyes.

"Oh, Iz, don't look like that." Reid couldn't handle the withdrawal in Isabel's eyes. It hurt to know that she had put it there. She sighed and set her mug on a coaster on the coffee table. She didn't want to talk about this. She didn't. But she would because she had to erase the look of dejection from Isabel's face. "I went to the cemetery. I—I needed to talk to Jimmy."

"Did it help?"

"Maybe. And if I don't catch pneumonia it will have been worth it."

"How long did you sit out in the rain?"

Reid shrugged. "An hour or so. Once I started, I didn't want to stop. I didn't realize how much I missed just talking to him."

"I know what you mean. I took for granted that he would always be there when I needed him."

Seeing the tears shining in Isabel's eyes, Reid lightly touched her knee. Isabel covered her hand with her own. Reid couldn't ignore the warm comfort of Isabel's thumb idly stroking the back of her hand.

Chapter Fourteen

Reid opened her eyes and rolled her head to the side, then groaned and pressed her face into the sofa cushion.

"I have *got* to stop falling asleep on you," she said softly. "Your couch is very comfortable."

"That's your excuse?"

Reid's only response was a slow smile, and Isabel wondered if she had any idea how sexy that smile was. She doubted it was deliberate.

"You don't get enough sleep as it is. I'll try not to take it personally," Isabel said.

While Reid had slept, Isabel had rinsed their mugs and straightened the kitchen. Then she'd lit some candles and turned on some soft music, careful not to wake Reid, who slept fitfully. Her twitching muscles and fluttering eyelids made Isabel wonder what she dreamt about. At one point, Reid moaned and flailed her arm above her head. Isabel returned to the sofa and rubbed a hand soothingly over her shoulder. She'd murmured quietly until Reid calmed. Isabel had still been there, watching Reid sleep, when she had shifted and opened her eyes.

"It's by no means a reflection on your company." Reid stood and stretched. "What time is it?"

"Ten o'clock."

She had been asleep for only an hour. She had dreamt she was back at the cemetery staring at Jimmy's headstone, and he appeared next to her. He stood tall and had a glow about him that Reid couldn't describe except to say it seemed to emanate from inside. Sadness etched on his face, he studied the stone and then his eyes drifted to the one next to his. He whispered his wife's name. Then eyes so familiar they felt like her own focused on Reid. A tear ran over Jimmy's clean-shaven cheek. Neither of them said a word, but Reid felt his emotions touch her. Sorrow. Love. Then peace. And as his image faded away she felt him hand his family over to her care.

Shaking off lingering traces of the vision, Reid crossed to the mantel and studied the pictures of Jimmy's family. Isabel had added a few of her own from their childhood. In one of them Reid recognized a much younger version of herself and picked it up to get a closer look.

"This was that day at Percy Priest Lake." Their two families had gone there for a day of swimming and fishing. Meredith had packed a picnic lunch of fried chicken and potato salad, and Isabel's father had rented a couple of canoes. The photo showed the three of them in a faded maroon one. Isabel sat in the front, Reid in the middle, and Jimmy in the back. Reid and Jimmy both held oars, and all three wore wide grins and squinted in the bright sunlight.

"Yes."

"We must have been about thirteen, and you eleven," Reid guessed. Isabel's hair had been touched by the summer sun and the rich color was highlighted by shades of copper as shiny as a new penny. Her cheeks and the bridge of her nose were tinged pink. Isabel's fair complexion didn't tan, rather it burned.

"That's about right. Jimmy used to hate that I always had to tag along with you guys."

"He did not."

"*Sometimes* he did."

It was probably true, and since Reid didn't hear any bitterness in Isabel's words, she didn't argue. Reid traced her finger over the photo. She could remember that day like it was yesterday, and she longed for the careless summers of her youth. "You sat in the front of the boat saying you were a princess and made us paddle you all over that cove. It wasn't too long after that you lost interest in hanging out with us."

Isabel's expression took on a strange sadness. "Once I was a teenager I was too interested in makeup and boys."

"I remember." Reid would never forget the teenage boys who used to chase after Isabel. She had been jealous more than once, when Isabel seemed to be interested in one of them.

"Those were the days, huh?"

"Yeah." Reid carefully replaced the frame. "I knew it would never be like that again after the day Jimmy told your parents I was gay."

"They didn't handle it very well, did they?"

Reid laughed. "Didn't handle it well? Your dad forbade Jimmy to hang out with me."

"He was raised in a different time, Reid. *His* father was a Southern Baptist preacher."

Reid ignored Isabel's attempt to rationalize her father's behavior. It was in the past and there was no point in starting an argument about using ignorance as an excuse for intolerance. "Jimmy wasn't having it, though. He told him we were friends and nothing was going to change that. God, we couldn't have been more than seventeen and he stood up to him."

"That was the first time he really went against Dad. Remember how red Dad's face got?"

Jimmy had told his parents one night when Reid was over for dinner. She sat at the table with their whole family and stared at her plate while their father ranted about perversion and hellfire.

"Do I ever. I was sitting there wishing I could crawl under the table."

"I was surprised when Jimmy spoke up."

"Why?"

"That was the only time he ever went against my father's beliefs, that I can remember. He always pretty much fell in line."

That wasn't the way Reid remembered it. For some reason she had the image of Jimmy as a conquering hero fighting the evil prejudice. Was it possible that her love for Jimmy colored her memory? Certainly it was possible. That day, she'd been too busy wondering if she should indeed feel ashamed about who she was. After that she'd insisted that Jimmy come over to *her* house if they were going to hang out. Though Jimmy had stood up for her, she never again felt totally comfortable around his parents.

"Your mom didn't take sides. But I always worried that you guys wouldn't like me anymore after all the stuff your dad said," Reid admitted.

"I don't think I even understood what it meant to be gay. I mean, it's not like I really knew anyone else who was."

For the first time since she awakened, Reid noticed the soft music, and she latched onto a reason to change the subject. "What are you listening to?"

"You don't like it?"

"Well, this music isn't really my style." Reid tried for diplomacy, but her tone didn't quite carry it off.

"Norah Jones? It's soothing."

From across the room Reid watched as Isabel leaned her head back and closed her eyes. When Isabel stretched her arms over her head, the hem of her T-shirt rode up, exposing a pale strip of her abdomen. Reid was anything but soothed.

Isabel opened her eyes to find Reid's hot gaze on her. In the flickering candlelight Reid's dark eyes appeared bottomless. The now-familiar curl of arousal low in her belly erased any apprehension she might have had. "Dance with me?" Isabel stood and slowly crossed to her. "I'll even let you lead."

"I don't really know how."

"Come on, I rode a motorcycle. Shouldn't you be at least as open-minded? Besides, I don't believe *you've* never danced with a woman." Isabel had gotten the impression that Reid did okay with women. And while she certainly didn't have the reputation of being a player, Isabel suspected that was due more to preference than to opportunity.

Reid shrugged. "The women I've been with weren't really into—dancing."

"They didn't need to be romanced?" Isabel guessed, lightly touching Reid's collar, then her shoulder.

Reid shook her head. The women she had been with were nice enough. But none had inspired romance in her, and they didn't seem to expect it either. Until that moment she'd never considered it strange that she hadn't really courted anyone before. Suddenly she found herself wondering what it might be like to take flowers to a woman, to treat her to a romantic dinner or to surprise her with a candlelit bath.

"Well, it's not difficult. I'll show you." Isabel took Reid's hands and drew them to her hips. She linked her hands behind Reid's neck.

"I—"

Isabel pressed a finger against her lips. "Shh. Just enjoy it."

Reid *was* enjoying it. That was the problem. She was enjoying it entirely too much. She slid her hands from Isabel's waist to the small of her back, closed her eyes, and allowed Isabel to guide them around the floor. Their sock-clad feet slid over the hardwood with the barest whisper. The mood was seductive—the candles, the music, and the singer's voice, flowing and slightly breathy. And unlike the sharp edge that Reid usually experienced when she was near Isabel, this was a languid climb to arousal. The scent of Isabel's perfume was a drug, and Reid floated on a high so smooth and sweet that it made her want more. She was definitely acquiring a new appreciation for Norah Jones.

"I thought you were going to let me lead," she whispered close to Isabel's ear.

Isabel's hand sifted through the hair at the back of Reid's neck. "I lied." Her fingertips were hypnotic and light as they swept Reid's skin.

Isabel pressed closer and her swaying hips moved against Reid's. Holding Isabel was absolute torture, incredibly exquisite torture. Reid slipped her hands up Isabel's back, fighting the urge to push beneath her T-shirt. She bit back a groan and gently restored some distance between them.

"What's wrong?" Concern evident in her eyes, Isabel touched

Reid's cheek. Reid trembled against her. She wondered if she would forever have to fight her attraction to Isabel and found it ironic that she was the one who kept pulling them back from the edge of intimacy.

"Isabel, I'm only human." The entire evening had been like foreplay. She had already been beyond primed by the time Isabel had talked her into dancing, and Isabel's fingers on her skin made her throb with need.

"What are you talking about?"

Reid tried to move away, but Isabel's hands on her shoulders kept her within touching distance. "It's no secret that I find you attractive. I can deal with it. But I can only stand so much of this." She pulled Isabel's hands away from where they had wandered back into her hair.

"I'm sorry. I'm not being fair to you." Isabel dropped her arms to her sides.

Reid should have left it at that. She'd made her point and should have found some way to escape. But the question that echoed in her head slipped out unbidden. "Why?"

"I don't know what's going on, Reid. I think about you—about things that I shouldn't be thinking about."

"Oh, hell," Reid groaned. It took every ounce of her willpower to keep from dragging Isabel against her and kissing her senseless.

"I guess I just don't want to think about all the reasons why this wouldn't be a good idea." Isabel gently pushed a strand of hair off Reid's forehead. "I don't want to think about what it would do to Chase if things ended badly between us. Or how hard it would be living next door to you after that."

Reid captured her hand. The feather-light caress against her skin threatened to snap the last taut string of her self-control. She couldn't help herself, she kissed Isabel's fingertips. "Would it be harder than going to bed every night, just next door, and thinking about how it would be between us?"

Isabel sucked in a breath as much from the feel of Reid's lips against her skin and the raw edge to her voice as the words. Her body flushed hot as she conjured up images of those lips on other parts of her body. "If I could forget who we are, what you do—"

"You want to forget that you hold me responsible for Jimmy's life." With a sad smile, Reid released Isabel's hand, then stroked her cheek. "But you can't. You see it every time you look at me."

"No, I—"

"I know you do, Isabel. Because it's all I see when I look in the mirror."

"Oh, Reid, I don't." Isabel's heart broke at the defeat in Reid's voice. She *had* blamed Reid and hadn't given her injustice a second thought. It was so easy to hold Reid responsible if she defined her only as a firefighter. The problem was that she was no longer able to think of her as *only* a firefighter.

"I'm sorry, Isabel. I'm tired and not thinking clearly. I'll talk to you tomorrow." Reid stepped back and was gone.

The emptiness left by Reid's absence startled Isabel. She sank back down on the couch and rested her head in her hands. *I've lost my mind. Soft music, candles. Hell, I practically set a seduction scene while she slept. Certainly I didn't want to seduce* Reid. *Did I?*

No wonder Reid was confused. First Isabel had blamed her, then she had kissed her. And now Isabel, presumably a straight woman, had practically forced Reid to dance with her and nearly thrown herself at her in the process. It was no wonder neither of them had a clue what they were doing.

Reid stepped inside her back door and closed it quietly, then slipped off her shoes and crossed the dark kitchen without turning on any lights. She was halfway through the living room when her mother's voice startled her.

"You don't need to worry about waking me." Meredith sat in the corner of the sofa with a mug cradled in her hands.

"What are you doing sitting here in the dark?" Reid sat down at the opposite end of the sofa.

"I couldn't sleep. I made some cocoa."

"Mom, I'm sorry I took off on you." Reid rushed to assuage her guilt. She hadn't meant to make her mother worry, but she'd needed some space.

"You are so much like your father."

It was the type of comment that Reid would normally let go. But so soon after the exchange with Isabel, Reid's emotions were raw and more difficult to control than usual. "You know, Mom, just once I wish you would say that without regret in your voice."

"Honey—"

"There must have been a time when you thought he was a good guy. You married him."

Meredith sighed. "Reid, my issues with your father don't have anything to do with you."

"They do," Reid argued. "Just because I was already grown up when you guys divorced doesn't mean it didn't affect me."

"I never wanted to talk badly about your father in front of you. I didn't want my problems with him to affect your relationship."

"What relationship? We barely had one by then. I'm not blind. I saw what happened to him—to both of you after he retired." A district chief, her father had been responding to a fire when another driver, ignoring the lights and sirens, ran through an intersection and hit his Tahoe. He had sustained a back injury in the crash that eventually forced him to retire. By the time her parents divorced, Reid had witnessed her father stumble home from the bar on more than one occasion.

"I figured when he retired we would spend more time together. Travel. Do all of the things we always talked about but didn't have time for." Meredith sipped her cocoa.

Reid sensed her mother's reluctance to continue, but this conversation had been coming for a long time. And Reid was tired of stifling the questions she really wanted to ask. "What happened, Mom?"

"He would never talk to me about what was going on. He didn't know what to do when he couldn't work. He started spending more time at the bar with his old buddies. Sometimes it seemed like the only time he was happy was when he was down there reliving the old days. Finally we couldn't even relate anymore. He just wasn't there, even when I told him I was leaving. He didn't try to talk me out of it."

"So me being a firefighter is just a reminder of his failure," Reid guessed.

"No, sweetheart. You have your father's stubbornness. And sometimes you keep your emotions so closed off that I get concerned about you. But your father's failure is his alone."

Reid thought about her father's inability to find value for himself beyond firefighting. *Am I the same as him?* She knew that her job was where she went when she was uncertain because it was where she was most confident. She knew her abilities and her limits while working.

Meredith set her mug on the coffee table, then moved closer and touched Reid's forearm. "Your father lost his job and he fell apart. You lost—you've lost much more than just a job, and you're holding together. I know it hasn't been easy for you, and I wish you would let us help you more than you do. But you've been there for Chase and Isabel. You're not your father, Reid."

"Thank you, Mom." Reid squeezed her mother's hand.

Meredith smiled and squeezed back before releasing her hand. "I don't know about you, but I've had a long day. How about we go to bed?"

"You go ahead. I'll go up in a minute," Reid replied. And when Meredith reached for her empty mug, Reid said, "I'll take care of that."

After her mother went upstairs, Reid sat in the dark replaying their conversation. Her mother had lived with her for nearly ten years, and they had always tiptoed around the topic of the divorce. At first when she brought it up, her mother would avoid her questions until Reid learned not to ask them. Of course she had known about her father's drinking, and the fact he wasn't there for Reid had led her to conclude he hadn't been any more present for her mother. But hearing it from her made it all the more real.

I am *here for Chase. Someday when I have kids of my own I won't let them down like he has me.* For just a moment she allowed herself to imagine a little girl with red hair and a boy with expressive gray eyes. *I am* not *my father.*

❖

The next morning, Isabel sat in her car waiting for Reid to come out of her house. After their exchange the previous evening, she wasn't sure if Reid would still welcome a ride to work. Isabel had spent a good amount of time the night before thinking about the way she'd behaved. She finally decided that it wasn't fair to Reid for her to send mixed messages. Further, these past weeks had been very emotional, and it was only natural that she would feel closer to Reid since she had been so close to Jimmy. Her attraction to Reid would pass as their lives settled down again. She just needed to get her life back to normal.

She felt relieved when Reid came out and didn't hesitate to get in the car.

"Good morning," Isabel said, determined to act as though everything was completely normal.

"Good morning. Did you sleep well?"

Isabel glanced quickly at Reid but found her staring out the passenger window. It was silly to think that Reid could somehow know that she'd haunted Isabel's dreams the previous night. Deciding Reid's words were just an attempt at small talk, she lied, "I did. Did you?"

"I guess."

Reid didn't turn from the window and she didn't say anything more. She seemed content to ride in silence, and Isabel wasn't in the mood to force small talk, so she focused on driving.

After Isabel pulled into the parking lot and stopped near the station, she said, "Have a good shift. I'll pick you up tomorrow."

"Okay." Reid headed for the station without looking back.

Isabel sat there for a moment longer and watched her go. She hardened her resolve to keep things level with Reid until their emotions settled.

As Isabel reached for the gearshift, an ambulance pulled up, parked on the concrete apron in front of the engine, and two paramedics climbed out. The tall, dark-haired man walked inside and the brunette woman started to follow, but she glanced over at Isabel's car and changed direction. Curious, Isabel rolled down her window as the woman drew close.

"Aren't you Jimmy's sister?"

"Yes," Isabel answered cautiously. The woman's blue eyes were friendly enough, but she seemed reserved.

"I'm Susannah, a…friend of Reid's." She allowed just enough pause for Isabel to draw the conclusion she undoubtedly intended. And already Isabel didn't like her.

"It's nice to meet you."

"You've been driving her to work?"

"Yes."

"Well, that's so nice of you." Susannah folded her arms over her chest.

"It's the least I can do. She's really been a big help with Chase."

"Yes, and from what I understand, Reid has been helping *you* out a lot as well." Susannah smirked.

"Is that what you understand?" Isabel was careful to keep her expression neutral. "Well, I doubt very much Reid would be happy to hear that she's been the topic of gossip, especially the inaccurate gossip of petty people who obviously don't have anything better to do with their time."

Susannah laughed. "You know, I'm familiar with Reid's—talents. So I can understand why you're enjoying your little experiment now. But will you be so eager when the whole department is talking about how the sainted Jimmy's sister is a dyke who took up with his partner?"

Isabel was so stunned that she didn't correct Susannah's assumption that she was sleeping with Reid. Before she could regain her composure, Susannah walked away. For all of her talk about keeping an emotional distance from Reid, Isabel couldn't ignore the twist of jealousy she'd felt when Susannah referred to Reid's talents.

Jimmy's sister is a dyke who took up with his partner. Susannah's parting shot inspired a different kind of feeling in Isabel's stomach. Her father's face flashed in her head, and she remembered his reaction to discovering Reid's sexuality. If he were still alive he would likely disown her if he even heard rumor of a relationship with Reid.

In her rearview mirror she saw Nathan climbing out of his pickup. He approached her car and bent to look in the window.

"Hey, Isabel."

"Hi, Nathan." He wore a faded denim jacket over a navy T-shirt, accentuating his broad shoulders. Isabel thought again that he was the type of guy she would normally go for.

As if reading her mind, he asked, "Listen, have you given any more thought to having dinner with me?"

Isabel glanced toward the station, as if she could see Reid through the walls. Maybe her going out with Nathan would help them both move past whatever was hanging them up. "I'd love to."

"Great. Is tomorrow night too soon? Or we could wait until the weekend." He seemed surprised by her acceptance, but recovered quickly and flashed a charming smile.

"Tomorrow night is fine." She handed him one of her business cards. "Give me a call."

"Okay." He pointed apologetically toward the station. "I've got to get in there."

She nodded and shifted into reverse. She spent her entire drive home trying to convince herself she hadn't just made a mistake. Knowing that Reid wasn't Nathan's biggest fan, she realized Reid wouldn't like her to go out with him. And she resented her feeling of guilt. She and Reid had no claim on each other, so she had no reason to feel guilty. Reid was free to go out with whomever she wanted as well.

Chapter Fifteen

Reid glanced up from her magazine and found Nathan watching her. She shifted in the armchair and returned her attention to the page in front of her but could still feel his eyes on her. He'd been giving her smug looks all shift, but every time she asked him what they were about he simply said, "Nothing."

They'd been busy most of the afternoon, but the early evening was slow. Megan and Joey had taken advantage of the lull and were making dinner. The spicy scent of Joey's chili made Reid's stomach growl.

"Dinner's ready," Megan called from the kitchen.

Reid intercepted another arrogant grin from Nathan as she stood. "Nathan, for the last time, what's your deal today?"

"Nothing."

Reid smothered a curse and stepped in front of him to enter the kitchen first. Joey set the pot of chili on the table and Megan put a plate of cornbread next to it.

After they'd all been served, Reid asked, "Joey, didn't you say tomorrow was your wife's birthday? Did you make any plans?"

"We're going to a movie. She says with all of the grandkids around, we never take any time for ourselves."

"How many grandkids do you have?" Megan asked.

"Seven."

"Well, I can see how that would make it tough." Megan took

another piece of cornbread, then passed the plate to Joey. "What about you, Nathan, do you have any plans for your days off?"

"As a matter of fact, I have a date," he replied with a smug smile. He met Reid's eyes before he continued. "With Isabel Grant."

No one said anything and Reid noticed Megan and Joey's eyes drop to their plates. She cleared her throat and laid her spoon down. She had just lost her appetite, but Nathan hadn't stopped talking.

"Yeah, I'm taking her to dinner and after that"—he let his words hang in the air for a moment and winked at Joey—"maybe back to my place for drinks."

Reid knew the arrogant tone in his words was meant to rile her, but that didn't keep her hands from fisting in her lap below the tabletop. *Isabel is going out with Nathan?* Anger swamped her, forcing her away from the table. She shoved her chair back and stormed outside with no explanation to her silent crew.

At two o'clock in the morning, Reid was awake and restless. The inactivity of their evening had stretched into the night, and her crew had gone to bed hours ago. Reid had tried to entertain herself in front of the television, but the inane infomercials didn't hold her attention. Then she'd gotten a radio so she wouldn't miss any calls and had gone to sit on a bench under the tree in the front yard.

The clear night sky was filled with stars, but Reid was unable to appreciate their wonder because her mind was elsewhere. Her thoughts kept returning to Isabel and Nathan. She imagined what their date might be like. Nathan wouldn't open the car door or pull out her chair at dinner; he didn't have the manners. Judging from his earlier comments, he had one goal in mind. The idea of Nathan touching Isabel made Reid sick with fury. Her stomach clenched and her veins ran hot.

"Are you going to sleep tonight, Captain?"

Reid didn't turn at Megan's words.

"Mind if I sit with you?"

Reid gave a dismissive wave to indicate she didn't care.

"Nathan's an ass," Megan said, as if she didn't know what else to say.

Reid laughed bitterly. "Yes, he is."

"Listen, it's none of my business, but if you want to talk—"

"There's really nothing to talk about. He has every right to go out with her. If he's what she's looking for, then I don't know why that should bother me."

"Did you two—"

"No." It wasn't that she necessarily thought Megan would say anything, but Reid didn't want the other firefighters gossiping about Isabel. Instead she took responsibility. "It's strictly my problem."

Megan nodded. "Ah, unrequited love."

Reid didn't respond and they continued to sit in silence. *Unrequited love.* She'd been dealing with that for so many years. If Isabel was going to be dating Nathan, Reid would have to find a way to put her feelings aside or she might just go crazy.

Isabel stood in front of the mirror and stared at her image. She wore her favorite Calvin Klein cocktail dress, and the slate gray silk matched her eyes perfectly. But it wasn't Nathan's reaction she was trying to picture.

She could try all day to convince herself that this date with Nathan was a good idea. But she couldn't deny the fact that she was not dressing for him. It was not the response in *his* eyes she was trying to imagine as she smoothed her hands over her waist and hips.

"Chase, are you ready to go over to Meredith's?" she called down the hallway as she swept her hair up and pinned it at the back of her head.

"I can't find my new PlayStation game."

"You have a ton of toys over there. And you're going to bed in an hour anyway. Do you really need it?"

"I want to show it to Reid."

Isabel added pearl earrings and declared her outfit complete. She went to the living room in search of Chase. "Did you find it?"

"Got it." He held up the video game.

"Okay. Let's go."

She walked him across the yard, and as they approached the back porch Isabel heard the creak of the swing. She hoped she would find Meredith sitting in the darkened corner, but somehow she knew it was Reid. Certain that Nathan would have told Reid of their plans, Isabel didn't want to face her.

"Hey, Reid. I got a new game." Chase ran over to the swing. Isabel paused halfway up the steps, but Reid wasn't clearly visible across the porch.

She took the game he offered and glanced at the back cover. "Cool. Why don't you go get it ready and we'll play for a while before bed," she suggested and handed it back to him.

He headed inside to turn on the video-game system. Isabel heard him greet Meredith as he passed through the kitchen, and she stood in awkward silence, staring at the wooden slats of the porch floor.

"You look very pretty."

Reid's softly spoken words were so unexpected and sounded so sincere that for a moment Isabel longed to curl up on the swing next to her and forget that she had accepted a date with Nathan. When she finally did meet Reid's eyes, she found them soft and filled with something close to pain.

"Reid, I—"

She was interrupted by the sound of a car door slamming nearby and realized that even if she knew what to say, she didn't have time to resolve things with Reid. She backed up enough to see around the corner of the house. Nathan stood in her driveway next to a black pickup.

"I'm over here," she called when he started toward her house.

She wished she could have reached home before he arrived, but before she could get around the corner to head him off, Nathan was beside her. He wore blue jeans and a light blue button-down shirt that stretched across his broad chest. The air, which had been previously filled with emotion, went suddenly cold. Reid's withdrawal was tangible.

"Hey, are you ready to go?" Nathan put his arm around her shoulders. He nodded at Reid as if he'd just noticed her sitting there. "Captain."

"Yeah, I'm ready." Isabel looked at Reid, whose expression was closed. But there was nothing Isabel could say in front of Nathan.

Nathan grinned at Reid. "Don't wait up."

Isabel swore she could hear Reid's teeth grind. She tried to catch her eye, to convey some type of apology, but Reid avoided her gaze. Nathan steered her toward the driveway.

Isabel sat across the intimate table from Nathan and wondered, not for the first time, what she was doing here. He was attractive, there was no denying that, but he lacked something. On the short drive to the restaurant, after a few cursory questions about her, he'd talked nonstop about his truck, not even seeming to notice if she was paying attention. When they'd arrived he hadn't held the door or pulled out her chair. Not that she required him to, but it was nice when someone did.

As they waited for the server to return with their drinks, he seemed more interested in their surroundings than in her. He constantly scanned the dining room, and more than once she watched his eyes track another woman across the room. *I'm just looking for reasons not to like him. How about keeping an open mind?*

Their young waiter returned and placed their drinks in front of them, then retreated discreetly after they ordered. Having renewed her determination to have a good time with Nathan, she smiled at him.

"So, how are you settling in here in Nashville?" he asked.

"Chase and I have both had to adjust, but we're doing better. Meredith and Reid have been so helpful."

He bent forward as if he were about to share a secret. "Doesn't it bother you that Reid's always hanging around?"

"I don't know what you mean."

"Well, she has no life of her own. I mean, for years she's been butting into Jimmy's."

Isabel was surprised that Nathan would speak so openly and negatively about Reid to someone he barely knew. She didn't think for a second that Jimmy viewed Reid's presence in his life as an intrusion, and she was overcome with the desire to defend Reid.

"She hasn't been butting in. Reid has always been a good friend to him, and to me, too, for that matter."

"Yeah, but just because she can't have kids of her own, she acts like Chase is hers."

"Who says she can't have kids?" Isabel realized she'd never actually asked Reid whether she wanted children. She hadn't given it much thought, but having seen her with Chase, she knew Reid would be a great parent.

"Well, you know, because she's gay."

"That doesn't mean she can't have children. Gay parents have kids all the time."

"Well, they shouldn't. It's not natural."

"It's not—" Isabel realized she was raising her voice and bit off her words. Nathan's words infuriated her, but she shouldn't have expected anything different. Everything from his truck with its oversized tires to his good-ol'-boy attitude screamed Southern intolerance. But Reid's lifestyle wasn't Isabel's battle, so she let the subject drop. "Let's not spend the whole night talking about Reid. Tell me about yourself." *Since I'm sure it's your favorite topic.*

"Sure. What would you like to know?"

Isabel waited while their meals were set in front of them. "Did you grow up around here?"

"I'm from Alabama, originally. I moved up here when I got accepted to the academy." He lifted his fork and knife to cut his steak.

"Is your family still down there?"

"Yeah. Daddy owns a pig farm about an hour outside of Birmingham."

"And you had no interest in farming?" Isabel guessed.

"My two older brothers still work down there. But no, farming wasn't for me. I couldn't wait to get out."

"Have you always wanted to be a firefighter?" As she asked the question Isabel was struck by the irony of her situation. She'd told Reid that she couldn't be with a firefighter and here she was on a date with one. But it wasn't like she was going to get seriously involved with Nathan. Honestly, this dinner was just an attempt to prove she could move past her attraction to Reid. And who better to prove that with than someone who was the total opposite of Reid?

"Not really. After high school I didn't know what I wanted to be. But I thought it was cool the way everyone looked up to firefighters. And the ladies sure seem to like them," he said with what he probably assumed was a charming smile. "So I figured, why not."

Isabel forced a smile in response.

"What about you? Did you always know what you wanted to be when you grew up?" Isabel could tell from the way he phrased the question that he had no idea what she did for a living, even though she was certain she'd told him earlier in the truck. She was used to that reaction, though; most people's eyes started to glaze over when she began talking about investments and stock options.

As Isabel explained how she chose her profession, she was once again struck by his inattention. The entire time his eyes wandered between the plate in front of him and the tables surrounding them. She couldn't help but compare that to the way Reid looked at her as they spoke. Her attention never seemed to waver, as if Isabel was the most important thing in the room no matter what she was talking about.

❖

Reid paced the length of her living room and paused to look out the front window. *No headlights yet. How long does it take to eat dinner?* Ten o'clock wasn't really very late, but the past three hours had felt like an eternity. For a time she was able to distract herself with Chase's video game, but he'd gone to bed over an hour ago. Now she paced back and forth behind the couch, ignoring the curious looks her mother kept giving her.

"Reid, is there something you need to talk about?" Meredith picked up the remote and turned off the movie she'd been watching.

"No."

"Does it bother you that much that she's on a date?"

Reid stopped in the middle of the room. She recalled the burning in her stomach as she'd watched Nathan put his arm around Isabel. The thought of any man touching Isabel had always bothered her, but over the years she'd gotten used to ignoring her jealousy. But *Nathan* couldn't touch her; Reid wouldn't allow it. She had to find a way to prevent them from going out again.

She moved around the sofa and sat down. "Yeah, I guess it does."

"But you're not angry at her?"

"I don't know."

Was she angry? Certainly she was hurt. Part of her wanted to just let Isabel go, for good. If only she could figure out how. For once, she wished she was the type who got angry and got drunk. After a few drinks, it would be much easier to close her emotions off. She wasn't against a beer now and then, but watching her father drown himself in Scotch had made her leery of dealing with her problems that way.

"Honey, you have got to get Isabel off that pedestal."

Meredith's gentle tone didn't soothe the defensiveness that rose up in Reid.

"I don't have her on a pedestal."

"Yes, you do. She told you Jimmy's death was your fault, and you forgave her the second she came around saying she was sorry."

"She'd just lost her brother and we needed to think of Chase—"

"And even now you're defending her."

"I am not."

"You just did." Meredith's tone was calm but firm.

Reid stared at her mother, attempting to figure out why she would try to rile her. "What do you want me to say? I can't make myself be angry."

"Honey," Meredith covered Reid's hand with her own, "I'm not telling you what to feel. You're not a pushover, Reid. I've seen you stand your ground plenty of times, but with Jimmy, and now with Isabel, it's as if you feel the need to protect them"—she hesitated—"to save them."

"Well, what's wrong with wanting to protect someone?" Reid burst out, frustrated.

"Nothing. But you also need to see that Isabel isn't perfect. She has faults, just like the rest of us."

Headlights tracked across the far wall, and Reid stood and strode to the window. Nathan's truck was parked in Isabel's driveway but she couldn't see past its bulk to the front porch. She pictured Nathan and Isabel standing there under the porch light. Would he kiss her good night? It was all she could do not to storm across their driveways.

"I'm going to bed," she said and headed for the stairs without bothering to excuse herself properly. Maybe sleep would shut out the fear that Isabel had invited Nathan inside.

Chapter Sixteen

"I wish we never had to go back to school."

Reid jerked her head up at the sound of Jimmy's voice. He smiled down at her from the tree limb above her, only he wasn't Jimmy as she had last seen him. He was the preteen version. His face was boyishly round and devoid of the constant five o'clock shadow she'd teased him about as an adult. His hair fell in his eyes and he compulsively pushed it off his forehead, only to have it flop forward again.

"What's wrong? Why are you looking at me like that?" he asked.

"Um—nothing. No reason." She forced herself not to stare.

"This is a great tree. Next summer we should build a tree house up here. Maybe your dad could come help us."

My dad? Not likely. Reid's eyes welled up as she remembered that her father used to do stuff like that with them. She and Jimmy used to think her dad could do anything, and that was the man Jimmy was referring to.

"Reid? Do you think he would?"

"Yeah." Reid's chest hurt. "I'm sure he would."

Jimmy looked past her to the ground. "Iz, go away."

Isabel stood at the base of the tree staring up at them. Reid knew before she even glanced down that Isabel would have a purple Popsicle stain on her shirt.

"I want to come up there, too."

"No, Iz. I said go away." Jimmy rolled his eyes at Reid.

"Fine. I'll go find my own tree."

Isabel stomped her feet as she walked to a tree about ten feet away. She awkwardly grabbed hold of the trunk, but the soles of her sandals kept slipping on the bark. Jimmy laughed at her.

Over her shoulder, she stuck her tongue out at him. "Shut up."

She finally found a foothold and pushed herself up enough to grab a low-hanging branch. Reid watched as she pulled her wiry body up. She was nearly high enough to perch on a substantial limb when, as if in slow motion, her foot slipped.

"Isabel." Reid lurched forward, but she couldn't get out of their tree. Isabel was falling, suspended in air for what seemed like a lifetime. Frantic, Reid jerked her head around and found the back of her shirt snagged on a branch. She searched for Jimmy but he sat frozen in the tree, staring as Isabel fell.

"Jimmy, I can't get out of the tree. Do something," she yelled, but he didn't move. She tugged on her shirt but she couldn't get it free.

Isabel hit the ground with a sickening thud and lay still. Reid called to her but she didn't move. Reid tried once more to free herself, throwing all of her weight forward. She heard the sound of tearing fabric, but she had already overbalanced herself and tumbled off the limb.

Reid woke up, gasping, seconds before she hit the ground. She stared around the semidark room, hardly believing it had been a dream. The fear that still seized her heart and the fact that her racing pulse had yet to slow surprised her.

She hadn't thought about that day in years and wondered why she was dreaming about it now. She and Jimmy hadn't witnessed Isabel's fall, but it had been so vivid that she almost believed it had happened exactly as she had seen it. She told herself the urge to go next door and check on Isabel was irrational, and Isabel would probably call her crazy if she showed up there at four o'clock in the morning. Nathan's smug smile flashed in her head, and Reid leapt out of bed and rushed to the window. She was relieved to discover that his truck wasn't in the driveway.

❖

"This was a great idea, Meredith," Isabel said as they trailed Reid and Chase through a Christmas-tree lot. Rows of trees leaned against makeshift rails and a string of lights was stretched overhead. The weather had cooperated, giving them a cold, clear December day. When Meredith had called that morning with the idea of finding a Christmas tree, Isabel had been nervous about spending time with Reid. She hadn't talked to Reid since her date with Nathan three days earlier. Though Reid had kept her distance, today she acted as if things were fine between them.

"I thought we needed to get out and do something as a family. Besides, we've been using that artificial tree for the past few years. I've missed having a real tree."

"When we were kids Christmas seemed magical."

"It was."

"Remember the hot chocolate and sugar cookies you used to make us, Meredith?"

"And she would let us decorate them. Jimmy and I used to put fire helmets on our snowmen," Reid chimed in. She waited for them to catch up, then fell in step beside Isabel. Aside from the car ride, this was the closest they had been in several days, and Isabel caught a clean citrus scent. Reid's shoulder brushed hers as they walked.

"Hey, Chase, any luck finding us a tree yet?" Isabel called.

"Not yet, Aunt Isabel. I gotta find the perfect one." Chase was running from tree to tree, and to Isabel's dismay he seemed to be searching for the tallest one.

"You were around Chase's age that year that you asked for a reindeer for Christmas," Reid teased.

"Yeah, and I cried for an hour on Christmas morning when I didn't get one." Isabel recalled that, like Chase, her favorite Christmas movie had been *Rudolph, the Red-Nosed Reindeer.* That year she had gotten it in her head that she wanted a pet reindeer, one that could fly.

She had dutifully written her letter to Santa, confident that if he couldn't spare one of his own reindeer he would find her one somewhere. She spent hours planning what she would feed hers and how he would be waiting by the fence for her when she came home from school. Isabel met Reid's gaze. "Luckily I've grown out of asking for things I can't possibly have."

Reid's eyes became serious and she looked like she was about to say something, but Chase's triumphant shout interrupted her.

"This one!"

"It'll never fit," Isabel muttered, preparing to talk Chase into picking another.

"It's perfect, Chase," Reid said. When Isabel cast her a disbelieving look she simply said, "We'll make it work."

And to Isabel it felt like she was talking about more than just the tree.

"Great tree, Chase." Isabel stood in the middle of her living room and studied the tree that occupied a good portion of one corner. They had opted to put the tree up at Isabel's for Chase's benefit. Reid would be working Christmas Eve anyway, so Isabel offered to have Christmas dinner at her house. That way Reid could go home and sleep undisturbed for a few hours while Meredith and Isabel prepared the meal at her place.

"I told you this was the one." Chase stood next to her, staring with pride at his tree. She put her arm around his shoulders.

"I hope we have enough ornaments." Meredith emerged from the kitchen. "Chase, let's go up to the attic and you can help me bring them down."

Reid came in right behind her. "I'll get them, Mom. I remember where Jimmy keeps them. And if there aren't enough, we'll get some from our house. You can find some music to listen to while we decorate."

"We'll help you," Isabel said as Reid approached. She reached up and brushed her hand through the front of Reid's hair, next to her temple. "You've got some sawdust—"

Reid glanced over Isabel's shoulder at the tree. "I had to cut at least a foot off the bottom. Let's go get those decorations."

Isabel followed Reid and Chase to the attic, still mulling over the quick flash she'd seen in Reid's eyes. The buzz of attraction between them only seemed to be getting stronger. This back-and-forth they were engaging in just wasn't working out. They would get so close to giving in, then one of them would run away. Most recently she was the one doing the running.

Her disastrous date with Nathan came to mind. After it she and Reid had spent the next few days trying to act like nothing had happened. Meanwhile, Isabel was finding it harder to ignore these flashes of awareness. And from the darkening of Reid's eyes when Isabel had touched her hair, she guessed she wasn't the only one.

They carried boxes full of decorations down and began to unpack them. Meredith had put on a CD of traditional Christmas music and she brought mugs of hot chocolate into the living room.

"Reid, will you do the lights? I think the ladder is in the garage." Isabel pulled a knotted string of Christmas lights out of one of the boxes.

By the time Reid returned with the ladder, she had them untangled. Reid climbed the ladder and Isabel handed her one end of the string. Working together, they managed to get the lights on the tree.

Chase rummaged through the boxes, pulling out ornaments he had made over the years. He ran excitedly around the tree and covered the bottom third of the branches with the colorful decorations. Isabel carefully unearthed a set of glass ornaments that had belonged to her grandmother, directed Reid onto the ladder, and instructed her where to hang them. Meredith and Reid added a few they had brought over from their collection.

"I like it," Chase said when they stood back and studied the finished product.

"It looks good," Meredith agreed. She started to collect the empty boxes, but Isabel waved her off.

"I'll take care of that, Meredith."

"I don't mind helping."

"Really. It's okay."

"All right. It's getting late, I'd better head home."

"Can I stay over? I haven't stayed in a long, long time," Chase asked.

When Meredith looked at her, Isabel nodded.

"Sure you can, sweetie. *Rudolph* is on tonight." Meredith knew it was his favorite holiday movie. "We'll make some popcorn."

"I'm going to help Isabel clean up and then I'll be home," Reid said. She collected the mugs and carried them to the kitchen. When she returned to the living room, Isabel was gathering the empty ornament boxes and putting them in one of the larger cartons.

"I guess he's missing his sleepovers," Reid said.

"It hadn't occurred to me that he might miss them since I'm here every night and he hasn't needed to stay with you. Do you think he's improved?"

"Yeah. He seems to be handling things a bit better since that day in the garage."

"His teacher says his grades are improving. And I haven't heard about any more fights."

"It'll take some time. But he doesn't clam up automatically when we talk about Jimmy now. Where do you want these?" Reid picked up the largest of the boxes.

"Let's just put them in the hall closet for now."

While Reid stowed the boxes, Isabel went to the fridge. "Do you want a beer?"

"Sure."

Isabel returned carrying two bottles of Heineken. She passed one to Reid and gestured to the sofa, waiting until they had settled next to each other to speak. "I wanted to talk to you about Nathan."

"Iz, I don't think talking is going to do any good."

"I'm not going out with him again." She remembered the events of their date once more. She'd spent the entire night comparing him to Reid, and he was completely oblivious to the fact that she wasn't having a good time. At the end of the night when he had tried to kiss her, she had turned her head to the side so that his lips brushed her cheek, then retreated inside as quickly as she could politely do so.

"It's none of my business who you go out with."

"What if I want it to be your business?"

Reid sighed. The dream about Isabel's fall had shaken her, and her resolve to prevent Isabel from dating Nathan had crumbled.

She couldn't do this again. Every time Isabel pulled her closer she allowed herself to hope, only to be disappointed. Suddenly, she understood what her mother had been trying to tell her. If Isabel smiled at her, Reid would reassure her and act like everything was okay. She was tired of acting like she could handle everything.

"I don't want it to be my business. You can go out with every member of my crew if you want to. I don't care."

"You really don't?"

I don't want to care. "You want us to be friends when it's convenient for you." All of Reid's frustration bubbled to the surface. "But you also want to blame me for Jimmy's death and that's supposed to be okay. You tell me in one breath that you don't want to be involved with a firefighter, and then you go out with the biggest ass on my crew."

"Reid—"

When Isabel moved to touch Reid's arm, Reid jerked off the couch and out of reach. She couldn't bear for Isabel to touch her. "No. No. I can't think about Chase and what's best for him *and* keep my sanity, if you're going to act like you did that night we danced." Reid stopped, afraid if she said any more she would go too far.

After a long silence, Isabel said, "There's so much baggage between us, isn't there?"

Reid didn't answer. Emotionally, she was nearing an edge and she wasn't about to let Isabel see her in that condition, so it was better to let Isabel direct the conversation.

"Well, let's get one thing out of the way." Isabel took a deep breath and exhaled. "I blamed you for Jimmy's death. I was wrong. Jimmy was a grown man and his decisions were his own. Reid, I was grieving and scared."

Reid sighed and returned to the sofa. "You don't have to—"

"Just listen, please," Isabel insisted. "Losing Jimmy turned my life upside down. I had to relocate and assume responsibility for a seven-year-old. I don't know anything about raising kids, Reid, and I'm so afraid I'm going to do it wrong. And I miss Jimmy terribly. I was looking for someone to blame and you were there. I'm sorry."

"Why are you saying this?" Reid had been steeling herself against her reaction to Isabel all day. The restless agony of not knowing what was going on with her and Nathan had worn on her. She had promised herself not to let Isabel get to her anymore, only to find it futile when Isabel was near once again.

"Because it's not fair to let you believe I blame you. Because I know you blame yourself. And because you're right. We can't keep doing this roller-coaster thing. We're constantly running away from each other and never resolving whatever this is between us."

"So what's the solution?" Reid knew frustration colored her voice.

"I don't know, Reid. I just don't—"

Isabel broke off as an idea formed in her mind. *It might work.* It was insane. *It could backfire in your face.* It was perfectly insane. *You don't even know if she would go for it.*

"Iz, what is it?"

She looked at Reid, really looked at her. Her hair had been flattened by the knit cap she wore earlier, but it curled out at the edges, around her face and over her ears. And Isabel knew that a fringe of curls rested against the back of her neck. The sleek line of her jaw tapered and then squared off at her chin. Her lower lip was slightly fuller than the upper. Isabel could recall the feel of them as if they were imprinted on her own. There was concern in her beautiful brown eyes.

She'd been having this crazy reaction to Reid for weeks, and she was nearing the breaking point. Something had to change. She hadn't chased Reid from her head with Nathan, but possibly she could do it with the woman herself.

"I need to get you out of my system," Isabel whispered, uncertain if she'd actually spoken aloud.

CHAPTER SEVENTEEN

"What?" Reid asked, sure she had misheard.

"I need to get you out of my system." This time she spoke louder. "We keep going back and forth and I—I can't get you out of my head, even when I'm out with someone else. But maybe—"

"What are you suggesting?" Reid was afraid she knew what Isabel was thinking. If she was right, she wasn't sure Isabel would accomplish what she hoped, but Reid knew for certain it wouldn't do the same for her. Still, she wasn't sure she was strong enough to say no. She didn't know if she had the integrity to refuse the one thing she'd always wanted if Isabel offered it.

"Reid, we're both adults." Isabel slid closer to Reid. "I'm attracted to you. You're attracted to me."

Reid swallowed, her mind screaming at her to move away. But when Isabel touched her thigh, she was paralyzed.

"I'm saying, if we go into this with our eyes open, then no one gets hurt. And maybe it'll ease some of the tension."

"So, what? You just need to get laid, and I'm convenient?" *She doesn't know. She doesn't know how I feel. She thinks it's just a physical thing. And this silly plan of hers might work if that were the case.*

"You know that's not what I meant. You are much more than just convenient."

"Oh, yeah. What else?"

Isabel studied her, trying to judge the tone in her voice. She'd felt Reid's thigh tremble beneath her hand, but other than that Reid hadn't moved. Testing, she touched Reid's temple and stroked down the side of her face. Reid's eyes drifted closed.

"You are strong…caring…sexy." Reid opened her eyes on Isabel's last word, and Isabel tumbled into eyes so expressive that they were sometimes the only place she could get a hint of what was going on. Though Reid tried so hard to hold herself apart, she couldn't hide what was in her eyes. *But surely I'm not seeing what I think I'm seeing.*

"I don't think—"

"You know what I think, Reid? I think"—Isabel slipped her fingers inside Reid's collar—"that you should stop thinking."

Reid's muttered protest was smothered by Isabel's mouth against hers, Isabel's tongue stroking hers. The hunger that had been haunting Reid for months surged in response, like a ravenous animal consuming her willpower. She slid her hands beneath the hem of Isabel's shirt and caressed the warm skin of her back.

She had one shred of chivalry left and she drew on it to ask, "Isabel, are you sure? Because if you're not we need to stop right now." She had left Isabel's house turned on and aching more than once already, and she didn't know how she would do it again.

"Reid."

"Yes."

"Take me to bed."

"Oh, yes." Reid made a move to scoop her up, and Isabel stopped her with a hand on her arm.

"You won't find me nearly as easy to carry up the stairs as Chase."

"Wanna bet?" Reid trailed her eyes down Isabel's body, judging her weight. She'd carried more out of a burning building. Confident in her abilities, she took her time as she visually devoured Isabel on the way back up. She traced the subtle curve of Isabel's hip into a trim waist and over the swell of her breasts. The smooth skin of Isabel's neck would be warm beneath her mouth, and Reid briefly allowed herself to imagine how it would feel to nip the tender flesh between her teeth.

When she finally gazed on Isabel's face she found Isabel watching her. Trembling, and knowing her intentions were laid bare in her expression, Reid forced herself not to look away.

Isabel had felt this kind of interest flare in more than one person's eyes before. But nothing compared to the palpable longing she found in Reid's dark gaze. Despite the layers of clothing that separated them, Isabel could practically feel the flames of Reid's desire licking at her skin.

When Reid bent and picked her up, Isabel wrapped her arms around Reid's neck. Reid held her as if she weighed nothing, one arm hooked under Isabel's bent legs and the other around her back. As Reid began to mount the stairs, Isabel trailed her fingers over her neck, the prominence of her collarbone, and down her chest.

Reid paused when Isabel's hand wandered close to her breast. "Isabel," she warned through gritted teeth.

"Yes?"

"Unless you want me to drop you, I suggest you stop."

"Stop what?" Isabel hummed and let her fingers graze an erect nipple through the thin cotton of Reid's shirt.

"Jesus. Isabel."

Reid ground out her name with a degree of desperation that excited Isabel. But since she had no desire to be dropped on the stairs, she returned her hand to Reid's shoulder.

After they reached the top, Reid carried her into the bedroom. She set Isabel on her feet next to the bed and sought her eyes. Isabel reached for her and their mouths sealed hungrily.

Eager to feel skin, Isabel unbuttoned Reid's shirt and pushed it off her shoulders, then tugged her own T-shirt over her head. She wore no bra beneath it.

"Beautiful," Reid whispered as her eyes roamed over Isabel's neck and chest. Her hands followed, brushing lightly over a nipple, then slipping lower. She opened the fly of Isabel's jeans and pushed them over her hips and thighs, then knelt in front of her. She pressed a kiss reverently to Isabel's stomach and to the triangle of silk between her thighs. Isabel claimed a handful of her hair as Reid slid the silk panties down her legs.

"Come here. I want to feel you." Isabel tugged lightly and Reid got to her feet.

Isabel smoothed her hands over broad shoulders, then walked around to stand behind Reid and outlined the angle of her shoulder blade. When her fingers discovered the strap of Reid's navy cotton bra she opened the clasp, then followed the line of Reid's spine, and felt Reid tremble as she caressed her lower back. Reveling in the answering tightness in her own body at Reid's response, she circled her fingers on her back.

She took her time, gazing at Reid's body and marveling in the contradictions she found there. Reid was strong, her job demanded it. But her body held traces of softness in the curve of her breasts and the flare of her hips.

Reid stood still, letting Isabel explore her body. She fought her own urgent need, ignoring the throbbing low in her belly. She trembled with the effort, but she wanted to let Isabel set the pace, at least as long as she could stand it. When Isabel curled her hands around Reid's biceps and pressed against her back, Reid felt the soft swell of Isabel's breasts and the prominence of her nipples. She was only half able to stifle a groan.

"You have an incredible body." Isabel's arms circled Reid and her hands brushed across Reid's chest and over her rib cage. When they touched her stomach, the sensitive skin there jumped beneath them. Finally Isabel pushed inside the waistband of her jeans.

Reid grabbed her wrists. "I need to touch you." Her body was screaming for release, and she would never last if Isabel touched her. She drew Isabel around until she stood in front of her once more. "Please, let me." She pushed back the bed linens and guided Isabel into bed.

Carefully holding her body inches from Isabel's, Reid moved over her, then kissed along Isabel's jaw to her neck. And then lower still, she trailed her tongue around an already tight nipple without quite touching it. When Isabel slid her hands into her hair, Reid took the nipple in her mouth, gently at first, then harder, closing her teeth with just the right amount of pressure.

"Oh, that feels good," Isabel said with a groan.

Reid smiled against her skin and edged lower to press her mouth against Isabel's flat stomach. She took her time, stroking nearly every inch of Isabel, worshiping her as she had longed to do for what seemed like her entire life. Her own needs took a backseat to the awe of touching Isabel.

When Reid's hands or mouth drifted close to sensitive areas, Isabel moaned and arched beneath her. Otherwise, she granted Reid unrestricted access. Reid was filled with the wonder of Isabel's freely offered body, and her every nerve was alive with the feel of Isabel against her skin. She let her fingers glide over Isabel's hip, then across the top of her thighs.

"Reid, please. More." Through a haze of arousal, Isabel pled for a more ardent caress. The continued feather-light touches were driving her half mad with desire.

"Here?" Reid brushed her hand over the inside of Isabel's thigh, then higher. She eased her fingers into warm, wet folds.

"Yes, there," Isabel moaned as Reid's fingers skimmed her clitoris. Reid's sure strokes over the already sensitive nerves had her clutching at Reid's bicep. "I need you inside me."

Reid pressed her mouth to Isabel's ear as she complied. "You're beautiful," she whispered as she eased two fingers inside. She wanted to be gentle, but Isabel's hand was insistent on the back of her arm, forcing her deeper. Still she let Isabel set the pace, matching the thrust of Isabel's hips.

"Oh, yes." Isabel was consumed by Reid, burning from the inside out. When Reid shifted her thigh against the back of her own hand, each thrust reached deeper. Isabel wrapped her hand around the back of Reid's head and pulled her down. She grazed her teeth lightly against Reid's throat.

Reid claimed Isabel's mouth, smothering the cry that rose in her throat as Reid pressed her thumb against the prominence of

Isabel's clit, her fingers still stroking inside. Isabel convulsed, and she barely whimpered Reid's name as the inferno within flared with scorching intensity.

When the almost painful pleasure eased, Isabel's body throbbed pleasantly. Reid kissed her tenderly and moved to her side. Through a haze of fulfillment, Isabel gradually felt Reid's body against hers. Reid still wore her jeans but was bare from the waist up.

Isabel rolled onto her side and propped her head on her hand. She wanted to touch Reid. God, she wanted to do so much more, but suddenly she was overwhelmed with doubt.

"Reid, I don't—I've never—"

Though slightly disappointed, Reid wasn't surprised by Isabel's hesitance. She'd been with straight women before, and their interest was often somewhat one-sided.

"Don't worry about it. I can take care of myself." She rolled onto her back, opened the fly of her jeans, and pushed her hand inside.

Reid had obviously misunderstood her nervousness. "No," Isabel insisted, brushing her hand down Reid's chest and stomach. "Much as I might like to watch you do that, right now I want to touch you." She slipped her hand in front of Reid's, her fingers alongside Reid's. "Show me what you like." Reid's hips jerked when their joined fingers brushed her clitoris. "I just want to please you."

"You do," Reid groaned. She cupped Isabel's hand against her, guiding her fingers. "Oh, God, you do." She was so close already. *So close.* She'd almost come simply from touching Isabel. Even now, the recollection of Isabel pulsing around her was nearly enough.

"Do you know? Do you know how you make me feel?" Isabel whispered against her lips before kissing her deeply.

"How?" Reid managed, aware that her voice sounded strangled. Their hands moving together inside her jeans threatened any remaining concentration.

"I can still feel you, inside me."

"Like this?" Reid guided two of Isabel's fingers inside, one of her own sliding along with it. Only the sensation of their fingers filling her eclipsed the impact of Isabel's words. And as she rolled her hips against Isabel's hand one final time, she cried out and clamped her hand over her crotch, holding Isabel's hand tightly to her as she shuddered.

When she finally relaxed, she eased their hands out of her jeans, but she kept their fingers entwined, needing the continued contact to reassure herself that their lovemaking hadn't been only a beautiful dream.

❖

"So, am I out of your system?" They lay side by side in the center of the bed. Reid still held Isabel's hand because she couldn't bear not to touch her.

Isabel rolled on top of her, and Reid moaned when Isabel pressed her thigh against the apex of Reid's. "Not just yet."

"Oh, Iz," Reid moaned as Isabel rocked against her. The delicious pressure of Isabel's body moving over hers had her ready again in seconds. Lifting her own thigh, she thrust her hips, immediately finding the rhythm of Isabel's and then increasing it, driving them both faster toward climax. They came together, rocking in unison, each clutching the other's thigh tightly between hers.

Isabel collapsed on top of Reid and shifted slightly to the side. Reid circled her arm around her and held her close. Isabel's leg was thrown over Reid's and she rubbed her foot lightly against the inside of Reid's calf.

"I've never, I mean with men—"

Reid silenced her with a kiss. "Darling, now isn't the best time for you to talk about past lovers, especially men."

"Oh, you have nothing to worry about. I have *never* felt this way."

Reid smiled and kissed her again, and this time she lingered.

"I should get home." Reid sighed.

Isabel pressed a kiss to Reid's neck, tasting the saltiness of her skin. "Mmm, you don't have to go yet. Do you?"

"I don't even know if I can move. You've worn me out."

"So stay." Isabel surprised herself with her own words. Swamped with emotions she hadn't expected to feel, she didn't want to let Reid go. She didn't want to break the spell around them, because then she would have to examine why what was supposed to have been a purely physical experience seemed to have touched something deeper in her.

Reid was tempted to stay, which was precisely why she sat up and slid to the edge of the bed. Isabel went with her, moving behind her. Because she couldn't help it, Reid turned and kissed her, fighting the urge to crawl back in bed with her.

Though she hadn't told Isabel, she knew what she wanted out of this relationship, had always known. But it was likely not what Isabel wanted. Despite her feelings, she was aware of what Isabel hoped to accomplish with this little experiment, and she had tacitly agreed to it.

The realization of what she had just done almost crushed her.

CHAPTER EIGHTEEN

The next morning, when Reid entered her kitchen Chase was eating cereal at the table. Isabel sat at the bar sipping a cup of coffee.

"Good morning, Chase wanted to have breakfast over here." Isabel greeted her with a shy smile. "Did you sleep well?"

"Surprisingly well," Reid replied as she headed directly for the coffeemaker. Despite having only gotten a couple of hours of sleep, Reid felt incredibly well rested. She poured a cup of coffee and turned back to Isabel. She looked gorgeous, with her hair in loose waves around her face. Reid longed to cross the room and kiss her, but she was very conscious of Chase's presence. "I must have been exhausted. How are you?"

Isabel's gray eyes were clear but her gaze was tentative, as if she was unsure about the morning after. Reid had no idea what to expect from her. She hoped that last night hadn't been just a one-night thing because she wanted Isabel more than ever. But she didn't know how Isabel felt, and she hadn't wanted to bring it up the night before. She wanted the memory of that night untarnished.

"I'm okay." Isabel looked like she wanted to say more, but her eyes flickered to Chase. Whatever it was would have to wait.

Reid took her coffee to the table and sat next to Chase, ruffling his hair. "How was the sleepover?"

"We watched *Rudolph*. I might get to stay again next weekend."

"That's good news. I don't have to work today and I thought about doing some Christmas shopping. Do you want to go?"

"Yeah."

"Well, you're not going in your pajamas. So go get dressed."

"Don't forget to brush your teeth," Isabel called after him as he raced from the room. She went to the doorway and watched him until he disappeared up the stairs. Then she crossed to Reid and kissed her soundly on the mouth. "I've wanted to do that since you walked into the room."

"I wanted to talk to you, to make sure you're okay with—everything. But we don't have much time. He won't brush nearly as long as he should."

Isabel smiled and rested her hand on the center of Reid's chest because she needed to touch her. "I am more than okay. Last night was amazing. But I have a lot to think about. And I'd like to keep this between us for now."

"Of course. I understand."

"If it helps, I've been plotting all morning how to get you alone again." Isabel ran her hand down Reid's body and hooked her fingers in the waistband of her jeans. She tugged her close to kiss her again, this time lingering in the pleasure of Reid's mouth. Reid's arms came around her and held her close.

"And what have you come up with?" Reid asked and kissed Isabel's neck.

"Well, Chase did just mention another sleepover next weekend." Reid sucked Isabel's earlobe into her mouth. "But if you keep doing that, I don't know how I'll wait that long."

"That's really only six days away," Reid said between kisses, thinking she definitely wouldn't be able to wait that long. "What are you doing today?"

"I want to finish up some work, and then I've got a lunch meeting with a potential client."

"It's Sunday, the day of rest. Come shopping with us."

"Look who's lecturing me about working too much."

Reid glanced down, annoyed as the device clipped to Isabel's belt chirped. Isabel looked at the display. Before she could answer it, Reid took it from her and moved away.

"Do you always have this thing with you?"

Isabel tried to snatch it back, but Reid held it just out of her grasp.

"I'm self-employed. I don't have the luxury of being out of contact with my clients."

"What's going to happen if you don't answer this call?"

"Reid, give it back," Isabel warned. But when she reached for it her body slid against Reid's and their eyes met. Reid wrapped her other arm around Isabel's waist and for a moment the phone was forgotten.

Hearing footsteps on the stairs, Reid stepped back. She handed over the phone and picked up her coffee mug to take a sip.

"I'm ready." Chase came in, pulling on his jacket. "Are you coming with us?" he asked Isabel.

"No, sweetie." She gave Reid a pointed look. "I've got to return a phone call. You guys go have fun."

"Okay, buddy, let's go," Reid said, steering Chase toward the door. Just before she stepped through it she looked back at Isabel. "Bye."

Isabel was struck by the intimacy of that glance. There was a promise in Reid's eyes meant only for her. And as unexpected as that look was, Isabel found that she welcomed it. Heat suffused her face and her stomach tightened pleasantly. Apparently the previous night had done nothing to diminish her craving; if anything it had actually intensified it. Knowing how it felt to touch and be touched made her want more. *I might be in trouble here.*

Reid carried a tray of burgers and fries through the food court as she looked for an empty table that was also at least marginally clean. In her other hand she held several large shopping bags. Chase was taking his Christmas shopping very seriously, insisting on searching through every store and, after much deliberation, picking out his gifts.

She had also managed to pick up a few things. She'd found a sale on those very soft socks her mother liked to wear around the house and picked up several pairs. She also bought her a DVD of *A Streetcar Named Desire*, the Brando and Leigh version because, according to Meredith, it really was the best one.

Reid finally found a table, and after she got Chase settled, she unwrapped a burger and set it and some fries in front of him. As she ate her own lunch she pondered the gifts she still had to purchase.

She knew what she was giving Chase; she had picked up the pirate-themed Lego set a month ago when he first mentioned it. But she still wasn't sure what to get Isabel. They were in such a weird place in their relationship that if she got something that meant too much she would be embarrassed. But a trivial gift didn't feel quite right either after what they had shared the previous night.

"What are you thinking so hard about?" she asked, noticing Chase's serious expression. He was picking apart his burger.

"Is my dad in heaven?" Chase asked.

"What do you think, sweetie?"

"That he's with my mom in heaven and they can see me."

"I think you're right. So what brought this up?"

"I'm sad that he won't be here for Christmas this year." He took a sip from his soda.

"Me, too."

"Aunt Isabel is sad sometimes, too."

"Well, your dad was her brother. She misses him."

"I don't have any brothers."

"Did you want brothers?" Jimmy and Amanda had wanted three children. Amanda said a boy and two girls, but Jimmy would have been thrilled with three sons.

Chase shrugged. "If Aunt Isabel had a baby then I would have a cousin."

Reid nearly choked on a french fry.

"Do you think she wants kids?" he asked.

"Maybe, someday." Reid gathered her napkins and burger wrapper onto her tray. She forced the image of a pregnant and glowing Isabel from her mind. "Are you ready to finish shopping?"

"Yep."

Reid carried their trash to the nearest bin, then led Chase toward the wing of the mall they had yet to visit. They had almost passed the jewelry store when something in the display case caught Reid's attention. She stopped.

The little crystal reindeer couldn't have been more than two inches tall. Its tail curled and its head was thrown back as if it was sculpted amid a fanciful moment of play. Touches of gold glinted on its antlers and the harness around its neck. It was precisely cut and the angles reflected tiny rainbows.

"They certainly are beautiful pieces, aren't they?" A salesman approached and gazed into the case as if Reid would believe he was looking at the display for the very first time.

She'd been so intent on the reindeer that she hadn't noticed the other pieces. There was a snowman, a Christmas tree, and a bear on a sleigh.

"Swarovski crystal. They're collectors' items."

Chase stepped in front of her, stood on his tiptoes, and peered inside. "Reid, I like the reindeer one best. But he doesn't have a red nose like Rudolph. Maybe it's Dasher."

"That's the one I was looking at." She turned to the salesman. "I'll take it."

"Would you like me to gift wrap it?" he asked as he unlocked the compartment below the case and removed a boxed version of the reindeer.

"Yes, please." She handed over her credit card.

"Who is that for?" Chase asked, slipping his hand in hers.

She crouched down to look him in the eye, fixing a serious expression on her face. "Can you keep a secret?"

He nodded solemnly.

"Promise?"

"I can, Reid. I can," he insisted.

"It's for Isabel." She stood and signed the receipt. "Do you think she'll like it?"

"Yep."

Reid smiled at the look of pleasure on his face. He delighted in their shared secret.

❖

Tuesday morning, Isabel parked in an empty slot near the front of the fire station and saw Reid standing with Nathan inside the open truck bay. Reid held a sheaf of papers and was going over them with him.

Isabel rolled down the window and rested her arm along the edge, content to observe Reid until she was ready to go. Too late she caught sight of Susannah approaching.

"Hello, Isabel."

"Susannah." Isabel forced politeness.

"Still doing Reid's bidding, I see. Well, she can be—persuasive, can't she?"

There was no mistaking Susannah's meaning. *Does she know? Would Reid have told her?* No, Isabel decided, Susannah hadn't known, but the guilty expression Isabel knew she had failed to hide had confirmed her suspicions.

"You don't even appreciate it, do you?" Susannah said snidely.

"I'm sorry?"

"That beautiful butch over there is absolute putty in your hands." Susannah gestured toward Reid. "She doesn't let anyone in. Except apparently you," she sneered. "And you don't even appreciate it."

Stunned as much by what she said as the way she said it, Isabel regarded Reid curiously. *Butch.* It had never occurred to her to apply that label to Reid. Trying to study her objectively, Isabel admitted Reid wasn't exactly feminine. But butch? In

Isabel's limited experience with the word, Reid didn't quite fit. Looking at her now, she was willing to admit Reid was butch, but she simultaneously altered her definition of the word to take a more positive spin.

Reid's raw power made her a captivating woman. She stood confidently next to the man beside her. They both looked strong and capable. Their fitted T-shirts showed off tightly muscled arms, and neither trim waist seemed to have an extra inch on it. But that was where the similarities ended. With her smaller build, high firm breasts, and shapely ass, Reid was most definitely a woman.

At that moment, Reid glanced up and her eyes found Isabel's. She grinned, held up a finger indicating she would be only a moment longer, and returned her attention to the papers in her hands. Isabel's heart skipped as the warm smile lit up Reid's face, adding to the attractive visage. *Beautiful butch.* Isabel mentally caressed the words, having no difficulty now attributing the description to Reid.

Isabel looked back at Susannah and took a bit of pleasure in knowing she had seen Reid's smile directed at her. "As a matter of fact, I do appreciate it," Isabel said, allowing a generous amount of gloating to enter her tone.

"Susannah," Reid greeted her coolly as she walked over to the Honda and tossed her bag in the backseat.

"Reid, so nice to see you again."

"If you'll excuse us, I've already made us late." She got in the passenger seat. As Isabel drove out of the parking lot, Reid said, "What did she say to you?"

Isabel's attention never wavered from the road. "Why are you worried about what she said?"

"Susannah has a tendency to overstate things."

Isabel smiled and touched Reid's thigh. "Reid, you don't owe me any explanations."

"Why?"

"Why what?"

"Why don't I owe you any explanations? You're sleeping

with me, Isabel. If this means nothing else, there's still that. So my personal life should at least concern you in those terms."

If this means nothing else. Isabel glanced at Reid's profile. Her jaw was set and the muscle beneath Isabel's hand was tight. Isabel had asked for time to think, and despite the tension she now sensed within Reid, Reid seemed willing to give it. Just looking at Reid made Isabel want her, but there was more than that. She loved the way Reid was with Chase, so caring and attentive. And when Reid focused on her, Isabel's heart warmed. No one had ever made Isabel feel so special with just a look.

"Reid, I only meant that I got the impression that anything that happened between you and Susannah was over before you and I…and therefore not something that I need to worry about."

"Well, you're right about that."

Isabel hesitated. They had yet to talk about what all of this meant. And she wasn't even sure she knew. She enjoyed Reid's company and found her completely compelling. Reid was strong and confident, but she had moments of sweetness when Isabel least expected them.

"Reid, I don't know what this is. I honestly thought if we slept together, then I wouldn't feel this mysterious attraction every time I looked at you."

"And?"

"And now all I can think about is what else I want to do to you."

Reid sucked in a breath as Isabel's hand slid higher on her thigh. She knew she was in dangerous territory and would most likely end up getting hurt when it was all over. But when Isabel said things like that, Reid couldn't find the strength to stop.

"Would you like to come over? I'm going to make some coffee." Isabel gestured toward her house as she parked in the driveway.

Reid got out of the car and waited while Isabel walked around to her side. "I can't drink coffee if I have any hope of getting some sleep this morning."

"Hmm." Isabel stepped closer and dropped her eyes to Reid's

mouth. "Chase is gone to school. I could make you some warm milk and then tuck you in."

Reid didn't like milk. "That sounds great."

She followed Isabel into the house. They had no more than stepped into the kitchen when Isabel framed Reid's face in her hands. She pulled Reid close and kissed her languorously.

"How is it possible that I've missed you in just two days," Isabel said when they finally parted. She rested her forehead against Reid's shoulder and her fingers feathered against Reid's neck. After a moment she drew back. "I'm sorry, I promised you warm milk." She went to the cabinet and pulled out a mug.

Reid stepped close behind her and slipped one arm around to touch her stomach. She took the mug from Isabel's hand and set it on the counter. "We can skip the milk. I know another way you can put me to sleep."

Isabel turned her head and Reid nuzzled her neck. She eased Isabel back until she pressed against the length of her. A heaviness swelled between her thighs and her nipples tightened against Isabel's back. Her body's urgent reaction to Isabel's nearness surprised her. She had intended to seduce Isabel, but the mere flicker of the memory of making love to her accelerated Reid's arousal.

"Follow me," Isabel said, taking Reid's hand and leading her from the room.

Anywhere.

I love her. Isabel lay beside Reid listening to the slow rhythm of her breathing. Nothing about this moment was as Isabel had imagined it. All of her life she had thought a day would come when love would blindside her. Yet she had never felt anything remotely close, until now. And it wasn't at all like she had expected it would be.

This was no lightning bolt of revelation, no grand dramatic moment. She simply realized it quietly while she looked at the sleeping woman she loved. Love was a soft, warm feeling in her heart and the knowledge that this was the person she wanted beside her.

Then Reid opened her eyes and Isabel found herself the subject of that sexy, sleepy gaze. And the warmth grew and heated until a rush of passion followed.

Chapter Nineteen

"Engine 9 to dispatch, we're on scene." Reid spoke quickly into her radio before she jumped out of the engine behind her crew. They were the first ones there, but she could hear the sirens of the approaching rescue and medic units in the distance.

They had been dispatched to a motor-vehicle accident, with a reported car over an embankment. Witnesses stated that the sedan had flipped twice before it landed upright. The four of them worked their way down the slope, and at the bottom they could see a blue Nissan Altima with the roof crushed and the windows broken out.

Outside of the vehicle about ten yards away, they found a passenger who had apparently been ejected. Reid checked her neck for a pulse and found nothing. Another passenger, a teenage boy, lay a few feet in front of the car. He was semiconscious and moaning. From the odd angle of his legs, Reid guessed at least one, if not both of them, was broken.

"Nathan, Joey, take care of him," Reid said as she carefully walked farther down the embankment to the car. "Megan, with me."

The driver was unconscious and still inside. Reid scanned her quickly, assessing her injuries. She had a cut on her head and several superficial ones on her face and neck, but the real concern was the blood rapidly soaking the right shoulder of her denim jacket.

"She's bleeding pretty badly," Megan said from over Reid's shoulder.

Reid tried the doors but they didn't open. "Rescue just got here."

Several men were looking down at them, while others gathered the heavy pieces of equipment they would need.

"They'll have to cut her out."

"She might not make it that long." Reid tried to reach through the window, but the roof was so compressed that she couldn't quite get to the woman's injured side. She walked around the car assessing their options. Finally, she stripped off her jacket and removed her helmet.

"What are you doing?" Megan asked.

"We need to get in there and stop the bleeding. And the way that roof is crushed in, I won't fit through the window with all of this gear on."

She selected the window that appeared to have the largest opening and was halfway through when she felt her T-shirt catch and rip. Ignoring a sharp stinging in her side, she pushed herself the rest of the way through.

Two paramedics reached the window as Reid landed in the backseat. She leaned between the front seats and rested her hip against the center console. The rescue crew laid out equipment and pushed cribbing under the frame to stabilize the vehicle.

"Can somebody get me some scissors?" Reid yelled through the window, and one of the medics handed them over. She sliced through the seat belt, then cut away the woman's jacket and shirt. For the next five minutes she worked quickly, applying pressure until the bleeding slowed, then bandaged the wound. She put a cervical collar on the woman to protect her neck. Shouting over the sound of the equipment being used to remove the door, she relayed the patient's vitals to the paramedics outside.

Finally the rescue crew pulled away the door and slid a backboard up to the driver's seat. Working carefully, Reid stabilized the woman's neck and shoulders while they eased her onto the board and carried her toward the waiting ambulance. Reid climbed out through the open driver's side.

"Reid, you're hurt," Megan said as she helped her out of the car.

Reid glanced down. Through the tear in her shirt she could see a laceration just below her ribs and the dark stain of blood that spread across the fabric.

"I felt a piece of metal or something when I went through the window." She shrugged and started gathering up her gear. They climbed toward the road.

"Joey, hand me that bag," Megan called as the two guys met them at the top of the embankment. She dug into the medical bag for some tape and gauze pads. "Come here, let me look at that."

She tugged Reid over and sat on the back bumper of the engine, putting Reid's injury at eye level. She spread her knees, grasped Reid's hips, and pulled her between them.

"It's fine," Reid protested, but Megan was already jerking up her T-shirt.

"Hold this," she ordered, pressing the hem of the shirt into Reid's hand. "Hold it, or I'm cutting it open."

Reid complied, though she wasn't sure why, since her shirt already had a sizeable tear in it.

"You're going to need stitches."

"I don't need—" Reid hissed as Megan applied pressure to the wound.

"You need stitches. Now, are you going to the hospital or do I have to call the chief?" Megan stood and didn't back down even when Reid glared at her.

Reid slouched against the wall in the waiting area of the emergency department. The pale peach walls were probably meant to be soothing, but they just left her wondering who on earth would choose that color. The chairs weren't built for comfort, and Reid had given up on them after shifting in one for the first fifteen minutes. The throbbing in her side intensified every time she moved, so she tried to remain as still as possible. But Megan had done a good job dressing it, and the bleeding had stopped.

"Are you sure you don't want to sit?" Nearby, Megan was leafing through a magazine, about four months old judging by the headline on the cover about the race to the World Series. Nathan and Joey were outside with the engine.

"I can't get comfortable in those chairs." When they had arrived they were told there had been a shooting in addition to the car accident. The doctors were tied up on those emergencies and Reid would have to wait.

"That lady in the car could have bled out," Megan said.

Reid shrugged. "One of the paramedics would have gone in there if I hadn't." Reid noticed a trace of worry in Megan's expression that she suspected didn't have anything to do with this call. "What's wrong?"

"You don't even think. You just act. It's instinct. And I'm worried that I don't have those instincts. I froze that day."

Now Reid did sit, settling carefully next to Megan and putting her hand on her shoulder. "Acting without thinking isn't always a good thing. I've made my share of mistakes. I can't tell you how many times Joey had to jerk me up and tell me not to rush in. It's only with years of experience that I've learned to temper some of that instinct. But I'm still a bit too impulsive." She swallowed the lump in her throat and schooled her features into a neutral expression, but something in them must have given her away.

"I've heard all the accounts, and they say Jimmy's death wasn't your fault." Megan touched Reid's knee.

"*They* weren't there," Reid responded vehemently. "I'm the one who has to live with the images of what happened in that building. Just like you have to live with what you saw in that baby's bedroom. He was beyond help, Megan. But you learned something about yourself that day. And you have to be conscious of that knowledge and grow from it."

Megan nodded, a pensive expression on her face.

"You're smart and you work hard. And with a few years under your belt you'll make an excellent firefighter. In the meantime, pay attention and absorb everything you can from the people around you. Being conscious that you still have more to learn is half the battle. I can't even guess where I'd be today without guys like Joey to show me the way."

"Okay. Thanks, Reid."

"You're welcome. Listen, I'm going to be here for a while. There's no sense in you guys hanging out with me."

"Ms. Webb, we need you to fill out your insurance information and then we'll get you back there." The receptionist handed a clipboard across the desk. Reid took it and picked up the pen attached to the board.

"Just do me a favor," she said as she began to complete the form. "Call my house and tell my mother what's going on and have her come pick me up. Ask her to bring me a clean T-shirt."

"Okay, boss," Megan said with a grin.

"Make sure you tell her it's nothing serious," Reid called as Megan left. She returned to her paperwork muttering, "The last thing I need is for her to get in a wreck driving down here."

After she finished her paperwork she was led down the wide hallway. They passed several crowded trauma rooms where medical personnel worked frantically. In the first was the woman from the car accident. Across the hall a young man who didn't appear to be more than fifteen years old was being treated. He was unconscious, his chest was covered in blood, and someone was trying to put a tube down his throat. Two uniformed police officers stood outside the room watching the activity inside.

Reid entered a large open area that could be cordoned off by curtains pulled around gurneys to create separate examining areas and was directed to one along the far wall. Once she was settled on the gurney, the nurse helped her remove her T-shirt, covered her with the sheet, and said the doctor would be right with her.

Fifteen minutes later, still waiting, she was reclining on the gurney, one arm tucked beneath her head. When the curtain jerked back she expected to see the doctor; instead she saw

Isabel's worried face. Isabel clutched a gray T-shirt and frantically scrutinized Reid as if trying to reassure herself that Reid was okay.

"I'm surprised they let you back here," Reid said.

"They almost didn't. But I can be pretty persuasive when I want to."

"I remember." Reid smiled and Isabel flushed. "I asked Megan to call Mom."

"Chase and I were having dinner with your mother. When the phone rang she asked me to get it." Isabel's voice shook with relief and she covered Reid's hand with hers, unable to keep from touching her.

"I told her to make it clear that it wasn't serious."

"Yes, she did mention that. But I'm not sure I heard much past *hospital*." She barely remembered speaking to Megan on the phone. She had tried not to freak out, but she hadn't succeeded. She could vaguely recall Megan reassuring her it was a minor injury and that Reid just needed a ride. Isabel couldn't get past the fear that had gripped her throat and choked the breath from her when she thought of Reid being injured.

She trailed her fingers along Reid's strong forearm, tracing the slightly spongy line of a prominent vein that snaked across her wrist. Isabel imagined that if she increased the pressure of her fingertips only a fraction, she would be able to feel the reassuringly steady pulse of life.

Isabel was torn between wanting to wrap Reid in her arms and the need to protect herself from the pain of another loss. She'd just realized she loved her. She hadn't told her and now she couldn't. She couldn't say "I love you" in one breath and "I don't think I can handle being with you" in the next. "I don't know if I can do this."

Reid remained silent, Isabel's words playing back in her head. Turning her hand over, she captured and held Isabel's fingers. "Do what?" she asked as calmly as she could.

"Worry about you."

"Sweetheart, there are no guarantees no matter what my profession."

Isabel dismissed Reid's attempt to make light of things. "I can't be the one who kisses you good-bye, praying you'll return to me."

"You're overreacting. I cut myself climbing into a wrecked car."

"That's how you reassure me? By telling me that I'm overreacting?"

"Isabel, firefighters get hurt. Most of the time it's not serious. Jimmy once twisted his ankle running down a set of stairs. I know another guy who got some debris in his eye when we were pulling down a ceiling. Of course, if he'd had his shield down that might not have happened. The point is, this is the nature of our work, knowing we can get hurt at times. We do everything we can to protect ourselves, but sometimes…" *Sometimes we can't save each other.* Reid shook her head to try to erase the image of Jimmy falling through the floor. *That's not where I was going with that.*

"Making light of my concerns isn't making me feel better."

"None of us know how much time we have. We take the risk every day that it might be our last." Reid really didn't understand why Isabel was making such a big deal out of her cut. If she hadn't needed the damn stitches, Isabel never even would have found out about her going into that car. She should have called Megan's bluff. She doubted she would have had the nerve to call the chief.

"No, Reid. We're not talking about the unpredictability of life here. I accept that. In case you've forgotten, I know very well how much our lives can change in an instant."

The pain in Isabel's eyes reflected loss that hadn't diminished much over the last seven years. "But *you* put yourself in harm's way every day. And you do it on purpose. *That's* what I'm talking about."

"Damn it, Isabel, what do you want from me? I'm not changing careers anytime soon."

Before Isabel could reply someone pushed the curtain back once again. A tall African American man stepped inside and pulled it closed behind him. He glanced at Isabel, then turned his attention to Reid.

As he pulled on a pair of gloves, Isabel moved around to the other side, allowing the doctor room to work.

"Let's see what we've got here." He folded back the sheet to reveal her torso clad only in a white sports bra. "Have you had a tetanus shot recently?"

"I had one last year."

Isabel tried not to watch when the doctor lifted a syringe and numbed the area around the laceration. He spoke quietly to Reid, explaining what he was doing, but Isabel didn't hear anything he said. She focused solely on Reid's face, her strong features and her beautiful mouth. It physically hurt to think about not being with her, but a vestige of panic remained. The fear that she might someday get another call from the chaplain weighed heavy on her heart.

Reid and Isabel drove home from the hospital in strained silence. Reid stared out the window, her thoughts firmly on Isabel. There was really nothing left to say; the only thing that stood between them was Isabel's fear. And only Isabel could break through that barrier. Being a firefighter was so ingrained in Reid that it was impossible for her to even imagine being anything else.

Perhaps it was better that their relationship ended this way. They hadn't yet defined what was between them anyway. Despite the moments of tenderness Reid had felt in Isabel's arms, a part of her still expected that Isabel would tire of experimenting and things would return to the way they were. Although they wouldn't be exactly as they were. *How can they? After touching her, I'll never be the same.*

Reid was so caught up in her thoughts that she didn't notice the car in her driveway until it was too late. "Shit," she mumbled under her breath.

"What?" Isabel glanced at Reid, then spotted the newer model Charger parked in front of Reid's garage.

"My father."

As Reid got out of Isabel's car, the driver of the Charger stepped out. Isabel hadn't seen him since Reid's parents divorced. *God, that had to be nearly ten years ago.* Even given the time that had passed, Isabel was shocked by his appearance. He had lost the solid physique she remembered. In addition to the fact that his shoulders stooped and his stomach was distended, his complexion was sallow and his eyes glassy.

Reid's demeanor had changed. On the drive home she'd been distracted and quiet. But now, tension was evident in her rigid posture and her fists clenched at her sides.

"What do you want?" Reid asked when he approached.

"Can't I bring my angel a Christmas present?"

"Christmas isn't until next week. But I guess you're not planning to be around for that, are you?" She walked past him, ignoring the gift he held out to her, and shoved through the gate into her backyard.

His shoulders slumped as he walked back to the car. He didn't look at Isabel as he got in and backed out of the driveway.

Isabel followed Reid and found her on the back porch in the swing. Unsure of what to say or do, Isabel hesitated on the top step. And when Reid didn't slow the swing for her to sit, Isabel remained there.

"Reid, your dad—"

"He's an alcoholic, has been for years."

Isabel had never heard Reid's voice turn so cold. "I'm—"

"Sorry?" Reid finished with a harsh laugh. "Yeah, me, too. He never drank on the job, though. He wouldn't. He lived for that job. But when he hurt his back and had to take an early retirement, there was nothing to stop him from drinking more and more."

Isabel took a step forward, but the emptiness in Reid's eyes stopped her.

"I'm not my father, Isabel. If for some reason I woke up tomorrow and couldn't be a firefighter I would be okay. But it's not something I would choose to have happen."

"I can't let myself care about you and worry about something happening to you all the time. So where does that leave us?"

"Right where we were a week ago—two women that Chase needs in his life." Reid knew it wasn't true. She might have to pretend, because she would do anything to keep from disrupting Chase's life again, but she would never really return to the way things were.

"Reid..." *I love you, and I don't know how to set that feeling aside.*

"We didn't make each other any promises, Iz." Something inside her tore as she said the words, and she knew something as simple as the row of stitches in her side wouldn't repair the wound.

CHAPTER TWENTY

Reid very nearly stumbled to a stop as she walked into the kitchen two mornings later and found Isabel sitting at the bar having coffee with Meredith. Accustomed as she was to a visceral reaction to Isabel, she wasn't prepared for the intensity that the sight of her inspired today. Instead of the usual twist in her stomach, this reaction was like a sledgehammer to the gut.

She had been avoiding Isabel, finding she was actually pretty adept at it, considering that they lived next door and their lives naturally intertwined. The pain that threatened to double her over now was exactly why she had made herself scarce.

"Good morning." Meredith handed Reid a cup of coffee. She didn't miss the tense glances between Isabel and Reid when each knew the other wasn't looking. Reid gulped her coffee faster than Meredith thought possible without burning her mouth. "How's your side feeling?"

"Fine." Reid rinsed her mug and placed it in the dishwasher. At the sound of a horn honking outside she grabbed her bag and headed for the door. "That's my ride."

When the door closed behind her, Isabel still hadn't said anything.

"Are you okay, dear?" Meredith asked.

"I—um, I've been driving her to work. I thought she would still need a ride."

Meredith studied Isabel, vacillating between her loyalty to

her daughter and her concern for both of them. In the end, the fact that Isabel looked as shell-shocked as Reid made her decide to intervene. "She hasn't needed a ride in weeks."

"What?"

"I told her at least a dozen times last month that she could take the Jeep. With you working from home and Jimmy's truck sitting in the garage, I would have been fine if there was an emergency. Plenty of days I could have managed without it. I've also offered to drive her just as many times."

"I don't understand."

"She didn't need you to drive her. She *wanted* you to. I suspect she enjoyed those mornings as much as you did." Meredith folded her arms over her chest and watched her words sink in.

"Did she say—"

"She hasn't said anything, Isabel. But it's obvious there's something between you."

Stalling, Isabel sipped from her now-lukewarm coffee. "No…no, there's not."

Meredith remained silent, letting the lie stand.

"What are your plans for today?" Reid asked as she climbed into the passenger seat of Megan's Silverado after their shift Christmas morning.

Megan slid behind the wheel and put on her seat belt. "Dinner at Jasmine's parents' house and then a quiet evening in." After starting the truck she drove out of the station parking lot.

"She's due anytime now, isn't she?"

"Next week. He might be a New Year's baby." Though they knew the baby's gender, Megan had said they hadn't agreed on a name yet. "What about you? Got big plans for Christmas?"

"Chase will probably be awake when I get home. He'll want to open presents. It's a good thing we had a quiet night." Christmas Eve had been slow, and they'd gotten several hours of uninterrupted sleep. "Then I guess dinner with all of us."

"Are things any better with Isabel?" Megan had been driving Reid to work since her confrontation with Isabel, so they'd had time to talk without the guys around. Reid had confided some of what had happened.

"We haven't really said much to each other. But either way, Mom and Chase will expect us all to eat together."

A few minutes later Megan dropped Reid off in front of her house. Reid headed immediately for her front door, but Chase flew out of the open door of the house next door, so she stopped. Isabel stood in the doorway watching as he raced toward her.

"Reid, Santa came!" he exclaimed as he reached her. He grabbed her hand. "Come on. I want to open presents."

"Sorry, Chase, it's not time yet," she teased, resisting as he tugged her toward his house. She couldn't help glancing at Isabel, and when she found a smile on her face, Reid smiled, too. "I think Mom is still sleep. So we'll have to wait until she wakes up."

"When will that be?"

"Gosh, I don't know, buddy. It might be a few hours—"

"A few hours? I'll wake her up." He released her hand.

"Take this and drop it in the kitchen for me." She gave him her backpack and he took off.

"That was mean," Isabel said with a small laugh as Reid approached her porch.

"She's probably already up anyway." *God, you look gorgeous.* Isabel's hair fell to her shoulders in varying shades as rich as the autumn leaves. The front of her white terry-cloth robe had loosened to reveal a brown silk nightshirt that complemented her pale skin. Her slate eyes were still sleepy, and faint impressions from her pillowcase ran across her cheek.

Reid ascended the steps with an unmistakable spark in her eyes. Isabel saw Reid's gaze drop and glanced down to find her robe open. She hastily pulled it shut. Isabel could argue the practicality of getting involved with Reid all she wanted, but that did little to decrease the awareness that simmered between them.

"I'm sorry." Reid looked away.

"It's really not any better, is it?" Isabel asked quietly.

"No." Reid didn't pretend not to know what she was talking about.

They were saved from having to say anything further when Chase ran across the driveway toward them. Meredith followed at a slower pace.

"Come *on*," Chase said impatiently as he pushed between them and rushed into the house.

By the time they joined him, he was seated on the floor near the tree. His entire body seemed to vibrate with barely contained excitement. Reid and Isabel sorted the gifts, heaping a large pile in front of him and smaller ones for the three of them. When they were all settled around him, he tore the paper off the first box. It was the set of Legos from Reid, exactly what he wanted, he proclaimed. Then he set it aside and ripped into the next, a video game from Meredith.

After he had opened each one, Isabel, Reid, and Meredith began on their gifts. Not quite as interested in theirs and overwhelmed by his, Chase sifted through his assortment and started to grapple with some of the stubborn packaging that held his toys.

Isabel politely thanked Meredith for the monogrammed leather portfolio, then picked up a small square box from Reid.

Chase finally dropped his presents and stood next to her, his hand on her shoulder as he waited for her to open it. "I helped pick it out."

"You did?" She smiled when he nodded seriously.

Isabel removed the paper to reveal a plain white box. The lid came off easily and she carefully lifted the delicate piece of crystal. Remembering her unfulfilled Christmas wish from so long ago, Isabel understood the significance of the gift immediately. And when she looked at Reid she made no effort to hide the tears shining in her eyes. She had once thought she couldn't handle being with Reid. She now realized that though it wouldn't be easy, she couldn't be without her. Fate had cast them together as Chase's caretakers, and they had become so much more to each other.

"Do you like it?" Chase seemed concerned by her tears.

"Yes, sweetie. I love it." She hugged him, but over his head, she met Reid's eyes.

"Iz, I—"

"Open mine," Isabel interrupted. Reid too looked uncertain about Isabel's reaction. There was so much Isabel wanted to say, but she would have to wait until they could be alone.

Reid located the brightly wrapped box, found a loose edge, and tore off the paper. She flipped open the top of the square jewelry box to reveal a gold medal in the shape of a Maltese cross shining against a black velvet background.

"Saint Florian, the patron saint of firefighters," Isabel supplied as Reid studied the medal. "He was said to have stopped a town from burning with a single bucket of water."

"It's beautiful," Meredith said.

"Yeah," Chase added, once again distracted by his gifts. He went back to trying to open one of the packages. "This one takes batteries."

"I've got some in the kitchen."

Isabel started to get up but Meredith stopped her. "I'll get them, dear."

"Okay, thank you. They're in the drawer by the pantry."

Meredith went into the kitchen with Chase trailing her, carrying a radio-controlled car.

Reid lifted the medal from the box by the twisted gold chain. "It's perfect. Thank you. Will you help me put it on?"

They stood, and Isabel took the necklace and felt a tingle of electricity when their fingers touched. She circled behind Reid. "I figured if I can't protect you, maybe he can."

Isabel's breath blew across the back of Reid's neck as she fastened the clasp, and Reid stiffened as Isabel's fingers brushed against her skin. She wondered if she imagined that Isabel's hand was lingering there.

"I was scared, Reid," Isabel said quietly. "I still am. This place hasn't felt like home to me since I lost my parents. As much as I loved Jimmy, I hated coming back here because it reminded me of what was missing. And after Jimmy died—"

Reid turned. "Iz, you don't have to—"

"I need to say this. I was dreading coming back here. I thought I would feel so alone. But I haven't. You've made this home. You and Meredith and Chase." Distantly she registered voices in the next room and guessed she had only a minute or so more until they were no longer alone.

Isabel took Reid's hands in hers, then stepped back, pulling Reid with her, until they stood beneath the archway between the living room and the dining room. She glanced up at the tiny green sprig above them. "We're standing under the mistletoe."

"If we weren't before, we certainly are now." Reid's eyes sparkled.

"Well, it's tradition, you know." Isabel slid her arms around Reid's neck.

"Iz." *Jesus, I'm not this strong, I can't...* She never finished that thought because in the next instant Isabel's lips were pressed against hers.

"Hey, Reid, I—" Chase skidded to a stop as he came around the corner. Meredith was right behind him.

Reid and Isabel jerked apart. Reid pressed the back of her hand to her mouth as she tried to keep from looking guiltily at her mother. She did look at Isabel, who was averting her eyes as well.

"How come you were kissing Aunt Isabel?" Chase stood between them, addressing Reid.

"Um—mistletoe," Reid stuttered, pointing up.

"Yeah, but you were kissing like my dad kissed my mom."

"What?" Isabel spoke up. She looked more than a bit stunned.

"I saw. In the video, I saw them."

Isabel still looked confused. Reid dropped to one knee in front of Chase. "Jimmy used to show him their wedding video and tell him about Amanda," she explained. "Chase, did it upset you that I was kissing Aunt Isabel?"

He considered the question, his face scrunched up in concentration. "Do you love her?"

"Yes," Reid answered without hesitation.

"Like Dad loved Mom?"

"Yes." This time she looked at Isabel when she said it, but Isabel's expression was unreadable.

"But I thought that girls were supposed to love boys."

"Sweetheart, sometimes girls do love boys," Meredith said. Taking his shoulder she drew him over to a chair, sat down, and pulled him into her lap. "And sometimes girls love girls or boys love boys. What's important is that two people love and take care of each other. Do you understand?"

He nodded. "My friend Richie has two dads."

"That's exactly what I mean." Meredith looked at Reid, whose jaw was tight and whose body quivered with tension like a bowstring pulled tight. "Now, didn't I see some doughnuts in the kitchen? Why don't we go get you some breakfast and then you can get back to those presents?"

Reid glanced at her mother with gratitude as she led Chase back to the kitchen. Her back to Isabel, she walked to the window. She fumbled for the words to explain what had just happened. She might have only one shot at it.

"Reid—"

"I'm in love with you," Reid blurted without turning around.

"I know."

"You—what?"

"I've known since the first night we made love. I saw something in your eyes, but I just didn't want to believe it then."

"Isabel." Reid hesitated. Isabel thought her love was a recent occurrence. She could continue to let her believe that. After all, Isabel certainly hadn't said that she returned Reid's affections. It would be much less embarrassing to be rejected based only on newfound love.

But she might never have another chance, because if Isabel rejected her now, she would never confess her feelings again. "I've been in love with you for as long as I can remember."

"You...you never said—"

"How could I? Your dad would have killed me."

"Yes, that might have been too much for him."

"Besides, you were my best friend's little sister. It's like an unwritten rule. And then, of course, by all appearances you were straight. What kind of jerk would I have been to try to mess with my best friend's *straight* little sister?" Reid stared out the window.

Isabel stood behind Reid and slipped her arms around her waist. Undeterred, though she felt Reid stiffen, Isabel rested her chin on Reid's shoulder. "No more of a jerk than I am for falling for my brother's best friend."

"What?" Reid turned.

"I'm in love with you, too."

"But you said—"

"I know what I said, and I was wrong." Isabel stroked Reid's shoulders and up her neck to frame her face. "All the logic and all the fear in the world can't keep me from loving you."

"Are you sure?"

"Am I sure I love you? Reid, what—"

"I don't want to hurt Chase. He's lost so much. Hearing him talk about that video made me realize that not only did he lose his father, but he also lost his strongest link to his mother. I don't want him torn between us."

"I'm sure. Reid, no one has ever made me feel the way you do. I only have to look at you." Isabel paused to kiss her tenderly. "We both love Chase. And whatever happens, we'll see that he's taken care of. So what is this really about?"

"I don't want to hurt you." Reid drew her close and rested her forehead against Isabel's.

"I've been in love with you for as long as I can remember." After hearing Reid's confession, Isabel could understand Reid's sudden doubts. She knew Reid well enough to guess she'd probably convinced herself that this would never happen and that she didn't deserve love. But Isabel found herself wondering what she had ever done to deserve Reid's love.

"Then don't ever leave me," Isabel said with a smile.

"I'll do my very best," Reid promised.

As Reid drew her close and kissed her, Isabel knew that would be more than enough.

About the Author

Born and raised in Upstate New York, Erin Dutton now resides in Nashville, Tennessee. No longer a Yankee, and yet not a true Southerner, she remains somewhere between the two, and is happy to claim both places as home.

She is the author of *Sequestered Hearts* and her story "Two Under Par" is included in the anthology *Erotic Interludes 5: Road Games*. Watch for her newest romance, *A Place to Rest*, coming up in 2008.

For more information visit www.boldstrokesbooks, www.erindutton.com, or e-mail erin@erindutton.com.

Books Available From Bold Strokes Books

Place of Exile by Rose Beecham. Sheriff's detective Jude Devine struggles with ghosts of her past and an ex-lover who still haunts her dreams. (978-1-933110-98-1)

Fully Involved by Erin Dutton. A love that has smoldered for years ignites when two women and one little boy come together in the aftermath of tragedy. (978-1-933110-99-8)

Heart 2 Heart by Julie Cannon. Suffering from a devastating personal loss, Kyle Bain meets Lane Connor, and the chance for happiness suddenly seems possible. (978-1-60282-000-5)

Queens of Tristaine by Cate Culpepper. When a deadly plague stalks the Amazons of Tristaine, two warrior lovers must return to the place of their nightmares to find a cure. (978-1-933110-97-4)

The Crown of Valencia by Catherine Friend. Ex-lovers can really mess up your life…even, as Kate discovers, if they've traveled back to the eleventh century! (978-1-933110-96-7)

Mine by Georgia Beers. What happens when you've already given your heart and love finds you again? Courtney McAllister is about to find out. (978-1-933110-95-0)

House of Clouds by KI Thompson. A sweeping saga of an impassioned romance between a Northern spy and a Southern sympathizer, set amidst the upheaval of a nation under siege. (978-1-933110-94-3)

Winds of Fortune by Radclyffe. Provincetown local Deo Camara agrees to rehab Dr. Bonita Burgoyne's historic home, but she never said anything about mending her heart. (978-1-933110-93-6)

Focus of Desire by Kim Baldwin. Isabel Sterling is surprised when she wins a photography contest, but no more than photographer Natasha Kashnikova. Their promo tour becomes a ticket to romance. (978-1-933110-92-9)

Blind Leap by Diane and Jacob Anderson-Minshall. A Golden Gate Bridge suicide becomes suspect when a filmmaker's camera shows a different story. Yoshi Yakamota and the Blind Eye Detective Agency uncover evidence that could be worth killing for. (978-1-933110-91-2)

Wall of Silence, 2nd ed. by Gabrielle Goldsby. Life takes a dangerous turn when jaded police detective Foster Everett meets Riley Medeiros, a woman who isn't afraid to discover the truth no matter the cost. (978-1-933110-90-5)

Mistress of the Runes by Andrews & Austin. Passion ignites between two women with ties to ancient secrets, contemporary mysteries, and a shared quest for the meaning of life. (978-1-933110-89-9)

Sheridan's Fate by Gun Brooke. A dynamic, erotic romance between physiotherapist Lark Mitchell and businesswoman Sheridan Ward set in the scorching hot days and humid, steamy nights of San Antonio. (978-1-933110-88-2)

Vulture's Kiss by Justine Saracen. Archeologist Valerie Foret, heir to a terrifying task, returns in a powerful desert adventure set in Egypt and Jerusalem. (978-1-933110-87-5)

Rising Storm by JLee Meyer. The sequel to *First Instinct* takes our heroines on a dangerous journey instead of the honeymoon they'd planned. (978-1-933110-86-8)

Not Single Enough by Grace Lennox. A funny, sexy modern romance about two lonely women who bond over the unexpected and fall in love along the way. (978-1-933110-85-1)

Such a Pretty Face by Gabrielle Goldsby. A sexy, sometimes humorous, sometimes biting contemporary romance that gently exposes the damage to heart and soul when we fail to look beneath the surface for what truly matters. (978-1-933110-84-4)

Second Season by Ali Vali. A romance set in New Orleans amidst betrayal, Hurricane Katrina, and the new beginnings hardship and heartbreak sometimes make possible. (978-1-933110-83-7)

Hearts Aflame by Ronica Black. A poignant, erotic romance between a hard-driving businesswoman and a solitary vet. Packed with adventure and set in the harsh beauty of the Arizona countryside. (978-1-933110-82-0)

Red Light by JD Glass. Tori forges her path as an EMT in the New York City 911 system while discovering what matters most to herself and the woman she loves. (978-1-933110-81-3)

Honor Under Siege by Radclyffe. Secret Service agent Cameron Roberts struggles to protect her lover while searching for a traitor who just may be another woman with a claim on her heart. (978-1-933110-80-6)

Dark Valentine by Jennifer Fulton. Danger and desire fuel a high-stakes cat-and-mouse game when an attorney and an endangered witness team up to thwart a killer. (978-1-933110-79-0)

Sequestered Hearts by Erin Dutton. A popular artist suddenly goes into seclusion, a reluctant reporter wants to know why, and a heart locked away yearns to be set free. (978-1-933110-78-3)

Erotic Interludes 5: Road Games, ed. by Radclyffe and Stacia Seaman. Adventure, "sport," and sex on the road—hot stories of travel adventures and games of seduction. (978-1-933110-77-6)

The Spanish Pearl by Catherine Friend. On a trip to Spain, Kate Vincent is accidentally transported back in time—an epic saga spiced with humor, lust, and danger. (978-1-933110-76-9)

Lady Knight by L-J Baker. Loyalty and honor clash with love and ambition in a medieval world of magic when female knight Riannon meets Lady Eleanor. (978-1-933110-75-2)

Dark Dreamer by Jennifer Fulton. Best-selling horror author Rowe Devlin falls under the spell of psychic Phoebe Temple. A Dark Vista romance. (978-1-933110-74-5)

Come and Get Me by Julie Cannon. Elliott Foster isn't used to pursuing women, but alluring attorney Lauren Collier makes her change her mind. (978-1-933110-73-8)

Blind Curves by Diane and Jacob Anderson-Minshall. Private eye Yoshi Yakamota comes to the aid of her ex-lover Velvet Erickson in the first Blind Eye mystery. (978-1-933110-72-1)

Dynasty of Rogues by Jane Fletcher. It's hate at first sight for Ranger Riki Sadiq and her new patrol corporal, Tanya Coppelli—except for their undeniable attraction. (978-1-933110-71-4)

Running With the Wind by Nell Stark. Sailing instructor Corrie Marsten has signed off on love until she meets Quinn Davies—one woman she can't ignore. (978-1-933110-70-7)

More Than Paradise by Jennifer Fulton. Two women battle danger, risk all, and find in each other an unexpected ally and an unforgettable love. (978-1-933110-69-1)

Flight Risk by Kim Baldwin. For Blayne Keller, being in the wrong place at the wrong time just might turn out to be the best thing that ever happened to her. (978-1-933110-68-4)

Rebel's Quest: Supreme Constellations Book Two by Gun Brooke. On a world torn by war, two women discover a love that defies all boundaries. (978-1-933110-67-7)

Punk and Zen by JD Glass. Angst, sex, love, rock. Trace, Candace, Francesca…Samantha. Losing control—and finding the truth within. BSB Victory Editions. (1-933110-66-X)

When Dreams Tremble by Radclyffe. Two women whose lives turned out far differently than they'd once imagined discover that sometimes the shape of the future can only be found in the past. (1-933110-64-3)

Stellium in Scorpio by Andrews & Austin. The passionate reunion of two powerful women on the glitzy Las Vegas Strip, where everything is an illusion and love is a gamble. (1-933110-65-1)

The Devil Unleashed by Ali Vali. As the heat of violence rises, so does the passion. A Casey Clan crime saga. (1-933110-61-9)

Burning Dreams by Susan Smith. The chronicle of the challenges faced by a young drag king and an older woman who share a love "outside the bounds." (1-933110-62-7)

Fresh Tracks by Georgia Beers. Seven women, seven days. A lot can happen when old friends, lovers, and a new girl in town get together in the mountains. (1-933110-63-5)

The Empress and the Acolyte by Jane Fletcher. Jemeryl and Tevi fight to protect the very fabric of their world…time. Lyremouth Chronicles Book Three. (1-933110-60-0)

First Instinct by JLee Meyer. When high-stakes security fraud leads to murder, one woman flees for her life while another risks her heart to protect her. (1-933110-59-7)

Unexpected Ties by Gina L. Dartt. With death before dessert, Kate Shannon and Nikki Harris are swept up in another tale of danger and romance. (1-933110-56-2)

Storms of Change by Radclyffe. In the continuing saga of the Provincetown Tales, duty and love are at odds as Reese and Tory face their greatest challenge. (1-933110-57-0)

Erotic Interludes 4: Extreme Passions, ed. by Radclyffe and Stacia Seaman. Thirty of today's hottest erotica writers set the pages aflame with love, lust, and steamy liaisons. (1-933110-58-9)

Broken Wings by L-J Baker. When Rye Woods, a fairy, meets the beautiful dryad Flora Withe, her libido, as squashed and hidden as her wings, reawakens along with her heart. (1-933110-55-4)

Sleep of Reason by Rose Beecham. Nothing is as it seems when Detective Jude Devine finds herself caught up in a small-town soap opera. And her rocky relationship with forensic pathologist Dr. Mercy Westmoreland just got a lot harder. (1-933110-53-8)

Passion's Bright Fury by Radclyffe. When a trauma surgeon and a filmmaker become reluctant allies on the battleground between life and death, passion strikes without warning. (1-933110-54-6)